THE AMERICAN WHO WATCHED BRITISH MYSTERIES

BOOK ONE

THE AMERICAN WHO WATCHED BRITISH MYSTERIES

ARTHUR — JOHN

Ainsley Publishing

Text Copyright 2025 by A.J. Rathbun
Cover art & design by Jon Sholly

All rights reserved. No part of this book may be used or reproduced in any manner whatsoever without the written permission of the author.

ISBN: 979-8-9926415-0-9

Library of Congress Control Number: 2025903237

FOR NATALIE FULLER, ON HER BIRTHDAY

1

Before walking up to the house and starting his interview with the man who found the body, Detective Marlowe stopped for a moment. He felt you could tell at least a little about a person by the place they lived. Not always, but often. Here, he saw a single-family, cottage-style house with, he guessed, an upper floor and basement. White with gray trim, and a bright yellow front door. So bright, it seemed to glow. Curious, that door. Two large windows, one on either side of the door, one small Japanese maple, and a second even smaller tree he couldn't identify that appeared to be dying and awash with bright pink flowers at the same time.

The yard itself was clean, but scruffy, like many yards in this north-of-downtown neighborhood where some homeowners took it as a point of "we don't live in the suburbs" pride to let lawns be wilder, less curated, less fussed over. It was in sharp contrast to its northerly neighbor, whose immaculately manicured lawn and impossibly straight-topped bushes must have been measured and trimmed with a straightedge.

Pulling his gaze back to the house at hand, he improvised a quick mental picture: middle-aged couple, no more than one kid, and an older one at that—no toys or evidence of child's play were in the yard, and he only saw one car, a black Honda Fit. Probably working in some part of the city's high-tech industry, vocal about their interest in local restaurants and organic produce, leaning toward pre-worn jean-and-button-down outfits, perhaps even with Crocs or sneakers. A couple who when not working tried their hands at painting or ceramics or other unprofessional hobbyist art and crafting (that door!), and more to account, people less likely to have a police record and more likely to be nervous around the police than an actual criminal.

Walking up the steps and sidewalk to the porch, another fact popped into his mind: dog. Of course they have a dog, which is how the body was found in the first place. As he hit the porch, he could hear a fairly high-pitched yapping coming from inside. Bingo, he thought, laughing to himself as the dog-song "Bingo" kicked off in the record player near the back of his mind. "Once a farmer had a dog and Bingo was his name-oh, B-I-N-G-O," trailing off as he went to ring the rusty doorbell.

Before he pressed it, the blindingly yellow door opened. The man behind it both fit and didn't fit the picture Marlowe had created in his imagination. Older for one, closer to sixty than forty. Balding, with glasses featuring nearly clear frames, only a hint of gold in them playing around corners, and wearing brown shorts—strange, in a way, as the weather was clocking in currently at fifty-five and cloudy with intermittent rain—black-and-white checked socks and an oversized red-and-brown striped sweater unraveling on one sleeve. He held the dog by its pink flowery collar, talking to it and Marlowe at the same time, before Marlowe even had a chance to show his badge.

"Hello," he said, the words bursting out like water from a cracked dam. "Ainsley, calm it down. You must be the police. Ainsley, quit it. Calm. Are you a detective? Ainsley, not everyone wants to play with you. Sorry, she is really friendly, overly friendly, though she might lick you. Ainsley, sit."

Marlowe hadn't said a word or moved from the porch. "B-I-N-G-O" still trailed musically in the back of his mind, for a moment switching off-key to "A-I-N-S-L-E-Y" as the man talked.

"Sorry. Ainsley, sit. Sit." And then, surprisingly as the dog's tail was metronoming at scherzo speed, it sat. "Sorry," he said again. "She gets excited with people. Obviously, I suppose. If she's a bother, I can put her in a bedroom, but she'll whine. Totally okay if you want."

"Let's see how it goes," Marlowe replied, sticking out one hand slowly so she could smell it. He tended to like dogs, while not currently having one of his own, and the city was a dog city, so he was used to dogs being part of cases. But he'd never seen one quite like this. About sixty pounds, a unique light-brown with darker-brown streaks pattern accented by a flash of white that ran up one side of her neck and chest, matching her white paws. The patterning style seemed nearer a big cat, like a lynx, than any dog he'd seen. She sniffed his outstretched hand, then started licking it. The man continued to hold her collar; a positive, because she was shaking with what Marlowe hoped was excitement and not aggression.

"Detective Marlowe, City PD." The man extricated one hand from the collar as Marlowe spoke, reaching out to shake hands.

"John Arthur. And this is Ainsley. You probably got that. So, you're police? And named Marlowe?" He talked rapidly, perhaps nervously. *Probably*, Marlowe thought, *just dog-owner nervous*.

"I've come to talk to you about this morning. Hopefully won't take long." The dog continued to lick his hand. Did he forget to wash his hands after his croissant and coffee breakfast? The licking didn't seem to be letting up, until John pulled her back.

"Come on, Ains, the detective's hands are probably clean enough."

Marlowe finally made it through the door, shutting it behind him. A stairway with chipped off-white walls in need of fresh paint rose directly in front of him, but he followed John and Ainsley into the living room on the left. He might make a full loop of the house later, but now wanted to focus on initial questions.

There were two couches, and as John pulled the dog to the smaller black and white one against the larger front window, Marlowe took the other, a low-slung royal blue number under a five-foot by four-foot print of Dante's *The Divine Comedy*, each book on the print one pillar made from tiny words. The room had a couple of lamps, an orange metal cabinet, a white table near another window topped with plants in need of watering, an abstract-y painting of a green bottle and a red square, but was dominated by two massive bookshelves on the far wall overflowing with books: old books, tall books, short books, cookbooks, classics, history, and others whose titles he couldn't see. Each shelf bursting with books, as well as pictures of dogs and people, glassware, old cameras, a rolling pin, a bust of Shakespeare, and other curiosities he couldn't define on first glance.

The bookshelves were separated by a lean, faded canary-yellow cabinet, door open, full of DVDs and a player, with square openings on the sides covered with wire netting. After a second, the phrase *pie safe* clicked in Marlowe's mind. There were also books in the fireplace—hopefully not to be burned—a stack of books on the floor, more books on bracketed wall shelves, a mini Charles Dickens figure sitting on one stack, and a book on his couch—*The Last Detective*. Oh, no, he thought, *not a mystery fan. Please not a mystery fan.*

John broke into his train of thought. "I'm thinking you have some questions? And to be clear, it's Detective Marlowe, correct?" He held the dog, who was stretching and straining toward Marlowe.

"You can probably let her go. I like dogs."

"She'll want to get up on the couch with you. And probably want to lick your face, or at least smell it closely. Then she'll relax."

"Well, let's get it over with."

John released his hold, and Ainsley bound over as he called out, "Ainsley, calm down." She jumped onto Marlowe's couch, raising her sizeable head right up to his, sniffing, and then gave him a lick on one ear. "Ainsley, stop," John said loudly. The dog looked at him, ignored him, licked Marlow's ear again, then lay down, half on his leg. He began to pet her, as John kept talking.

"So, Marlowe? Really?"

"Yes. Like Chandler's private eye. Like Bogart and Mitchum." He felt he might as well get it over with. The references happened every other case.

"Like the detective in *Shakespeare and Hathaway?*"

"Wait." This was new for Marlowe. "Shakespeare had a detective?"

"Not the playwright, the British TV show. It takes place in Stratford-upon-Avon, where Shakespeare was born, and is about two private detectives named Shakespeare and Hathaway. It's hilarious. The mysteries are solid, too. And the scenery around Stratford is a treat. Each episode is named after a Shakespeare line, like 'Toil and Trouble' or 'Beware the Ides of March,' and there is a police detective they sometimes work with named Marlowe. See, Frank, Frank Hathaway that is, used to be—"

"Wait." Marlowe held up his hand palm out like a traffic cop stopping a car. He felt the interview getting off track as John ramped up into a ramble.

John stopped mid-sentence, mouth open, then started again. "Did you just give me a palm stop? Amazing. Just like a real detective."

"I am a detective," Marlowe said, drawing each word out slowly to try and stop John from interrupting. "Now, Mr. Arthur, do you live here alone?"

"Yes. My wife passed away two years ago. Well, not completely alone. I have Ainsley here."

"But no kids or other person?"

"That's right, just me. Are you married?"

Marlowe wasn't getting drawn off track again. "How long have you lived in this neighborhood?"

"Hold on." John nearly jumped off the couch. "Did you just question-question me?"

"What?" Marlowe asked, so confused that he forgot about his resolution to focus. He was starting to think this was going to be a longer interview than expected.

"You know, the question-question. Classic police move. A favorite of both Inspector Tom Barnaby and Inspector John Barnaby. I'll bet it's taught at police college, right?" He talked at a fast pace, standing up as he spoke, dropping his voice a notch down as if to sound professorial. "When interviewing a witness or suspect, or shall we say a 'person of interest,' and they ask you a question, never answer the question directly. Instead, ask them another question. Even if it's a simple question, you never want to be the one answering questions. Instead, always keep the interviewee on the defensive, answering the questions and not asking them. This is how you'll get the best answers, so do it from the beginning." He returned to his normal tone. "A speech like that is probably trotted out the first day at detective school, right?"

"Wait," Marlowe said again, this time louder and with both palms out.

Ainsley glanced up, while John just smiled, sitting back down, slightly clenching his teeth together as if to hold in the words that wanted to come out.

"We're getting off track. You answer the questions. I ask them. Try to keep the answers simple."

Barely able to contain himself, John said, "Okay, Inspector, okay, but—"

Marlowe's hand went up before he could go on. "Detective. Not Inspector." A rare moment of silence later, Marlowe tried another tactic. "You read a lot of books featuring detectives that share names with either famous people or each other?"

"Haha, yes, I do read a lot. More now even since Marlene died. Some mysteries, a lot of old pocket books and pulps, but some modern authors, too. And the classics, Dickens and Trollope especially. I was just finishing—"

Marlowe's hand popped up again, along with Ainsley's head, as he said, "Wait," a third time.

"Right, sorry. Though, if I may, real quick."

Marlowe doubted the veracity of the phrase. He'd seen wild horses who stayed on track better than John Arthur.

"The shared-named inspectors aren't from a book. There was a series of books starring Inspector Barnaby, but oddly, I've never read them.

I was talking about the *Midsomer Murders* TV show. It's been on for ages, a British mystery show. You've never seen it?" Marlowe shook his head. "The main character retired after Season 13, Inspector Tom Barnaby, who was played by John Nettles. Then a *second* Inspector Barnaby, John, came on the scene, played by Neil Dudgeon. The cousin in the series, I think, of the first Inspector Barnaby. Fantastic, right? Never happen on an American show, but *Midsomer* kept on keeping on. The best part? Neil Dudgeon had played one of the murder suspects in an earlier episode called 'The Garden of Death,' playing like a flirty gardener, then he became the inspector. Pretty great, right?"

Marlowe realized his mouth was open wide enough to catch flies. What was going on? He'd meant to raise his hand yet again about halfway through John's speech, but got caught up in it. It was like watching a slightly out-of-control car you thought might jump a curb and hit a telephone pole, but then miraculously doesn't. "How about we skip the mystery books and shows, and you very succinctly tell me what happened this morning."

"Oh, sure. Sorry. Being here alone with Ainsley a lot of the time, I find myself talking through thoughts out loud to her, and to myself I suppose. Now it's nearly natural. Maybe more in-depth than another person would want?"

"It's okay. Walk me through how you found the body."

John stretched his arms in front of him for a moment, then reached over to take a drink of water from a quart canning jar. The momentary silence felt lovely, and Marlowe used the respite to grab a notebook and pen from his pocket.

"Oh, a notebook," John exclaimed. "'This is the most important piece of equipment you will ever own.'"

"Um, maybe?" Once more, Marlowe was more confused than he'd like to be in an interview.

"Sorry, *Hot Fuzz* quote. Seemed appropriate."

"Another show?"

"No, this time a movie."

Marlowe didn't even reply, raising his pen to the now open notebook.

"Right, what happened. Succinct. We, Ainsley and I, tend to walk the same routes most days. Like a lot of dogs, maybe all dogs, she likes routines." Ainsley's head popped up, but when he kept talking, she cuddled back into Marlowe's leg on the couch. "On Saturdays, we walk up 23rd Avenue to 85th, then over to 19th. Then we walk down 19th, across 80th, and down to 77th. Then we walk over 77th back west until we hit 23rd, then up and home. When we hit 77th and start walking back, usually we walk on the south side, which takes us to the Loyal Community Center right after we pass 20th. Hmm, I believe that's the full name? I'm not exactly sure. We usually call it the Center."

"Doesn't matter, keep going," Marlowe replied.

"There are fields for baseball and soccer to the south, but we walk by the big main brick building on the north. On that side, the sidewalk goes past a lawn and trees area, then abruptly stops due to parking spots. Or, it doesn't *completely* stop, but takes a sharp turn and curves down a stairs. To keep walking on it, you have to go through this shady, darker stretch alongside the building. There's a fifteen-foot garden type area of plants between sidewalk and building even with it being shady, but you feel under the eaves of the building, if that makes sense. Today, like most Saturdays, we walked down the stairs and sloping sidewalk into that area and that's where we found the body. It always seemed to me that we'd find a body there someday."

"Hold up," Marlowe broke in. "Seemed you'd find a body in this specific place someday?" He began to wonder if maybe, just maybe, John's talkative nature was pointing to him being more than accidentally involved. It wouldn't be the first time a suspect had talked themselves into an admission of guilt.

"Not seriously. Though I did used to joke about it with my wife. Seems a poor joke now." Getting no reply, John continued. "It's just that area is set down from the street and darker, as I mentioned. There's the building on one side, very tall. It contains a basketball gym inside, so gym height, and a four-foot brick wall on the other side, next to which are two massive industrial trash receptacles between it and the street. It's about a twenty-foot stretch of sidewalk blocked off from view. Ideal place to play hide-and-seek, a place not to be seen. That's one part of it. Add to that, the plants between sidewalk and building. Massive ferns, hostas, and philodendrons, with huge leaves draping over a lot of the ground, and high oak trees near entrance and exit. It feels shady, literally, as well as in the I'm-up-to-no-good-if-hanging-around-here-at-night way.

"I've walked Ainsley there hundreds of times, and past dogs even more. Nearly every time, I've thought to myself, if I was watching a person on a British mystery TV show walk their dog through an area like this—shady, overgrown, hidden but near houses—I would totally expect them to find a body. I never *actually* expected to find a body. But today we did."

TV mysteries again. As John stopped to take another drink of water—it seemed even for John that was a lot of talking—Marlowe admitted to himself that before the TV mystery business, John made pretty sound sense. That stretch of depressed sidewalk around the building was ripe for some kind of criminal activity. He didn't want to mention that to John, though.

Putting down his glass on a green felt coaster next to one of the drooping plants, John looked up. "I didn't even ask if you'd like something to drink. Maybe some tea? Is that too much of another British police moment? I could make you some. No biscuits, sadly. British biscuits, sweet kind you have with tea, you know? Though no American biscuits, either. I could get you some water, too, or coffee?"

Marlowe shook his head. "I'm fine. Let's continue."

"Okay, but let me know. From the amount police drink on TV and in books, I'm guessing all this is thirsty work. But back to the body finding."

Marlowe had decided when he walked in that John wasn't a tech worker, rather maybe a professor. He wasn't sure. There was something so odd about the man.

"Ainsley and I were on our walk and had gone down the slope into that stretch of shady sidewalk. She is always on my left at this point in the walk because the heftier bushes and the ground there is full, I'm guessing, of fantastic smells. We hit that lower level, and she started acting up, pulling harder on her leash toward a giant fern of some kind, leaves as wide as small tables arching up in big curves over the ground. At first, I concentrated on pulling her back. Then I saw a foot and the end of a leg poking out. I thought a mannequin or a set up for some *Candid Camera* or practical joking video or something, but that grayly pale skin color against the green leaf and the brown ground. Too real."

"Not something you see every day."

"Exactly. I pulled Ainsley past and saw a whole body under the leaves, only wearing underwear, the head hidden by the plant, and then dragged Ains out of the area even though she kept pulling. I stopped at the end of the building where the sidewalk opens up again onto lawn and looked slowly every direction."

"Why?"

"My first thought was *murder*, and I wanted to be sure the murderer wasn't still nearby."

"Why murder? And murderer?"

"'Sir, a woman has been murdered in your house. Therefore, it follows there must be a murderer.'"

"What?" Marlowe wondered if this guy was losing it; he'd dropped the last line in a horrible British accent.

"Sorry, *Midsomer Murders* quote."

"This is serious, Mr. Arthur. Let's stop with the TV."

"Sorry again. I don't mean to be flippant. I know it's serious. I'm just, well, nervous."

"Understandable. Back to—"

"Of course. I thought murder at first because the spot *did* always seem like where a body might be found in a mystery. Sorry. But also because while it could have been like a drunk passed out I suppose, getting rid of nearly every stitch of clothing before passing out feels fairly extreme. Doable, but extreme. Same with someone sleeping rough and outside. If it was a medical emergency, like a jogger having a heart attack, as we have lots of joggers, same point."

"Good sense. What next?"

"I caught my breath and realized my mind might be working overtime, then clenched up Ainsley's leash tighter and, after checking no one else was around, walked back down, edging closer to the body. I called out, but nothing—no movement, nothing. It was frightening, and for a second, I had no idea what to do." John paused, taking a big drink of water.

Marlowe sat quietly, hoping he'd go on and keep on his story this time.

"I called out twice and realized they weren't moving. Then I called 911."

"We know you called at 7:36 a.m. How long between seeing the body and calling?"

"Hmmm." John leaned back. "We left the house around ten past seven. Probably twenty minutes before we hit the Center. Four or five minutes between discovery and the 911 call, I'd guess. It felt longer and shorter, if that makes sense. Probably fifteen to twenty minutes until the first police car showed, then a few more before the ambulance and more police."

Marlowe nodded. Police staff shortages and the related response times were not new to him.

"While no one was in the Center or grounds when we arrived, being early for a Saturday, as we waited, we shooed off a couple other dog walkers. One goofy Labrador, very bouncy and wanting to play, and one fox terrier mix, very barky and definitely *not* wanting to play. Waving my arms wildly to keep them from traveling that lower sidewalk, I'm not sure if they thought Ainsley was dangerous and needed to be separated, if I was having a breakdown, or if we both were extra-territorial over our patch of park. But we kept everyone away from the scene of the crime to avoid contamination before the SOCOs arrived. Wait. That'd be CSI here in the US."

That was nearly TV talk. Marlowe shook his head but didn't say anything.

"There were two walkers as well—an older couple, even older than I—and a party of three joggers went by in the street, three women. We could hear kids' voices wafting over the building from the fields—soccer and baseball getting started. Luckily, no kids came by. I believe that was it. I gave Ainsley treats and waited. I looked around but didn't touch anything, I know that's a problem, and tried to keep Ainsley from touching things."

"This is very helpful, Mr. Arthur."

This time John raised his hand up. "Please, John is fine."

"John. Very helpful. See anything else?"

"Not much. Squirrel"—Ainsley raised her head—"or two"—then lowered it. "No other people. Not too much trash, either. That area, the whole center, feels like the people who work there and the people who live near it work diligently to keep it clean. But it is well used, even that shady bit. Kids play hide-and-seek, tag, sharks and minnows. Kids, dogs, and adults are always traipsing around, hanging out. Not sure I've seen a smoker back there, but I did see some butts. A kid's sock curled under one bush, Kleenexes, gum wrappers, random trash, and a facemask. Not litter-filled, but small stuff. Lots of dog hair, maybe children's hair even, clinging to the odd bush or tree branch or leaf." He leaned back again, gazing at the ceiling as he remembered.

"That's very observant." Marlowe knew nine times out of ten a suspect, witness, or 911 caller's recollections like this weren't helpful, but that tenth time could make it worthwhile. "Anything else?"

"Two things. I'm sure your team picked them up, or picked up on them. Well, two things I saw, and one thing I thought about," John said.

Marlowe raised his impressive eyebrows a touch in reply.

"The first thing, probably nothing, but there was a shoelace near the, um, near the foot of the body. It looked white, not too dirty to me. I didn't get too, too close, don't worry."

Marlowe hadn't heard about a found shoelace. He guessed the CSI folks found it, but was curious. "Why is that strange? Kids playing, lost shoes."

"Sure, good points, Detective. Though lots of kids' shoes don't even have shoelaces these days, for one. Still could happen, but to me if the whole lace comes out, seems like a parent would notice. But yeah, could be from a kid. Strange it was so near the body, however, because of the second thing I saw, which was two smallish grooves in the dirt, slight but visible. Maybe grooves is wrong. They weren't that deep. Ridges? I thought maybe they were there because the body had been dragged partially to where it lay under the bush."

"So . . ."

"The shoelace was on top of one of those slight drag marks. Why wouldn't it have been dragged too?" John stared up at the ceiling while talking, Marlowe watching his face. Was John thinking, remembering, or about to drop another TV reference?

"When I noticed it," John went on, "I felt maybe it was from the clothes the body had at one time been wearing. As if they had been killed there and then had their clothes removed, but when removing them, the murderer dropped the shoelace. That seemed a fair reconstruction of a possible crime. But why drag the body at all? To hide it under the bush to avoid it being found? Okay, but if walking close enough to see it as Ainsley and I did, which anyone walking this way would have, it wouldn't make a difference. The way that sidewalk is lower, combined with the tall Center on one side, the trees on the east and west, and the trash receptacles on the other, anywhere in there has nearly the same visibility."

For a moment, neither said anything. Marlowe jotted a few notes, thinking, *are these the roundabout confessions of a killer or just a guy with too much time on his hands watching too many mysteries?* After a minute, he said, "Interesting points, John. It was very civic of you to call when you did. The police and the rest of the calvary arrived. Next?"

"First, a squad car arrived, with two police constables in uniform," John replied in a rush. "Once they saw the body, it got very busy, very quickly. One of those first uniformed constables, the largest of the two— African American man, I'd say six feet two, at least two twenty, broad shoulders, bushy mustache, brown eyes, friendly manner—said his name was Sergeant Troy."

Marlowe, hand up again, said, "That's probably enough detail on the officers. They aren't currently suspects."

"Sergeant Troy asked me what had happened, and I told him what I've told you, skipping the last two things. I hadn't thought about them much then. He kept me close as more police cars arrived, then an ambulance, then he backed me off as they set up a perimeter. Soon the park became crowded with police, people in white suits, bystanders on the outskirts. I didn't see you there?"

"How long did you stay?"

John's eyes lit up. "You just question-questioned again. Amazing. I stuck around until a, I believe, a Jamie Nelson . . . ?"

"Probably. Then?"

"So, Sergeant Nelson? Or Detective Nelson? He was in uniform and seemed sergeant-y to me, no offense to him. He asked me more questions about the morning, took my details. Then another officer arrived, plain clothes, a Detective Morven."

Marlowe nodded in what he hoped was a *keep going* manner. It worked, as John went on.

"She took me aside and had me walk through the morning again, pushing for more specifics. Sergeant Nelson came along for a moment before she sent him off. Guessing they both work with you?" He glanced up, receiving another nod. "Makes sense. There's usually a team. Hard to tell in that short meeting what character types those two are. Like the learning-but-a-little-bumbling type, a Detective Sergeant Troy type following along the *Midsomer* tracks. Or a want-to-make-their-own-way-and-a-little-annoying type, like DS Scott. Or a hard-working, slightly joking, DS Jones type. Or a competent, might be ready to run a team DS Winter type."

Marlowe almost stopped him twice during the last monologue, but he admitted to himself that detective sergeant stuff from the show John was talking about had started to draw him in. Those types he sketched hit the nail on the head as far as the more junior detectives and wannabe detectives on the police force, too. He shook his head and petted Ainsley while taking another gaze around the room, noticing a half-chewed stuffed duck on the floor, enjoying the momentary quiet.

John perched slightly forward like a bird on the edge of the couch, as if either about to start talking or to take flight. Sun suddenly flowed in through the window like water, sparking off John's glasses. Outside, a nearby neighbor mowed a lawn. The day moved on.

John started to speak, "I can——" as Marlowe's phone rang.

Glancing down at the screen, he saw it was Detective Morven. "Gotta take this. Sorry, Mr——John." It felt odd to call a witness or suspect by his first name. Standing up, he walked past the front door into the adjoining room, which had a full wall of shelves packed with what looked like bottles of spirits and liqueurs. Was John a heavy drinker? He shook the thought off and answered the phone.

2

Marlowe was back at his desk at police headquarters. There was a north station he could have worked out of for this case, but he always felt more comfortable at his own desk. It was plain wood in a room with twenty-five other nearly identical desks. He didn't have anything very personal on it except a collection of coffee mugs that needed cleaning and an Italian wooden bowl his wife had given him before they'd divorced and she'd moved to Miami, Florida, of all places. Made of olive wood, he kept pens and paperclips in the bowl, but sometimes when no one else was in the room, he'd lean close to it, inhaling deeply. Sometimes he did it absentmindedly when people were in the room. It still smelled to him of olives and vineyards and Italy, where they'd honeymooned years ago.

Today, feet propped up on his desk, he tilted back in his chair, eyes nearly closed, as if about to fade into a nap. Noticing Detective Morven walking up assuredly to where his desk and hers sat, a thought slipped into Marlow's mind—here comes the competent, might be ready to run the team DS—before he shook it off, motioning to the younger detective to sit in the second chair that always seemed to find its way to his desk. They'd worked together for a handful years now, and while Marlowe was her senior by fifteen years, he didn't consider her a junior member of the team.

She was from New York, Queens to be precise, and had a bustling Puerto Rican family still there she talked about often. Her long black hair was braided and wrapped around her head like a crown above her round face—annoyingly clear skin the color of a latte—attentive brown eyes, and wide smile showing teeth white as snow atop a mountain. Her body had been honed by Muay Thai, which she competed in regularly, winning many local matches. It was only a matter of time before she did run her own team. Morven was driven.

She unbuttoned a stylish-for-a-city-cop deep blue suit coat and sat down, placing two cups of coffee on the desk. No one, Morven knew, showed up for a Marlowe chat the morning of a murder without coffee. The man's abiding love for even the station's ridiculously bad coffee was as well-known as his thick eyebrows, which often appeared to have a life of their own. Morven could barely drink the stuff. They lived in a metropolis with some of the world's best coffee, for gosh sakes. They could get any kind of latte or cappuccino known within five minutes and could even easily order *Café Bustelo* ground coffee to make at the station, but she didn't want to appear snobbish.

"Here we are," Marlowe said, reaching for the proffered coffee. "Go over the victim again."

Morven was well used to the older detective's meticulous going over of details and fairly taciturn manner. She also knew that when he looked asleep at his desk, he was invariably awake.

"The victim's name was Lucy Dixon. Caucasian female. Forty-four. Brown hair with blond streaks, blue eyes. Five feet, six inches tall. Hundred sixty pounds. Resided at 2010 77th Avenue Northwest. Directly across the street from where she was found. You probably remembered that."

Marlowe gave a brief nod mid-sip. Morven continued.

"She lived there with her son, Rory, who is seventeen, and her husband, Toby, forty-seven. Second husband, that is."

Another nod.

"More details on both are coming in. And the name of her first husband. But briefly…" Morven couldn't help smiling, knowing Marlowe's penchant for keeping conversations brief. "I met the current husband for a moment. He's a software engineer, she was a lawyer. He's tall, taller than me by six inches at least—so six two, maybe six three—thin, lanky I'd call him, brown hair, a classic craft-beer-and-jeans man. Drives a gray Ford truck and probably knows his specialty tools as well as his software code. He's going to come in and formally ID the body. I didn't see the kid yet."

"Got it. Now, the crime."

Morven continued, hitting the details specifically and rapidly. "Here's what we have so far, realizing it's early in the process. The murder, if we're calling it murder, and I think we are." She paused. Marlowe gave a nod, she went on. "The murder took place at or very near to where the body was found. It most likely occurred between 2:30 a.m. and 4:30 a.m., remembering that's a very rough guess as the pathologists say." She put air quotes around 'very rough guess.' "They naturally wouldn't pin down definitively yet what caused her death but, when buttered up with a few choice compliments, gave an opinion it could have been strangulation in some way, shape, or form. The CSI swarm was still there when I left. I haven't heard any more from them since. I'll follow up. Probably days though," she said with the tiniest bit of regret. Waiting for details from CSI and the coroner always took too long.

"Anything else concrete?" Marlowe asked, taking another giant sip.

"Not really. Uniform is going door-to-door around the neighborhood talking to people, seeing if anyone saw or heard anything. Sergeant Nelson is marshalling that effort. It was pretty late at night for that type of neighborhood, one without bars or a weekend party or drug scene. It felt like a sleepy-after-ten spot from my time on the scene. If I had to posit a theory, it would be that she wandered into the wrong place at the exact wrong time, when the wrong someone was passing through the area late at night looking for trouble, or looking to hand out trouble. She happened into the receiving end of it. A tragedy, but one that happens." Morven paused, reaching for her coffee mug. She took the tiniest of drinks, tried not to grimace, put it down.

Marlowe stared into space. "Maybe," Marlowe said. Another sip of coffee later, he changed direction. "What did you think of Mr. Arthur?"

"The man who discovered the body? Five ten, one seventy-five, round yellow glasses, sixty-ish, walking an overly affectionate tan and white dog? That one?"

"Brindle, not tan," Marlowe replied with a slight grin. "But yes. Suspect?"

"Suspect? Didn't occur to me. I wouldn't believe so, not on first meeting. Solely one of those old guys with a dog and not much to do, likes to talk a lot. Strange perhaps, or really strange? He said a few fairly random things. He did have a good grasp of the scene. I didn't talk to him as much as I could have. I knew you'd want to get to him fresh."

"Random things?"

He mentioned *evil* at the end of our interview, which felt odd and maybe suspicious, but it was strange the way he said it. Hold on, let me look at my notes to get the exact quote." She reached into her inside suit pocket pulling out one of the small police notebooks they both always had handy. "While he stared into the distance, Mr. Arthur said, 'It's an evil thing. The Community Center is bricks and mortar. If there's evil, it's in somebody's heart.' Then he said with a small smile, 'Marple. But in snow, and we're in spring.' Then he asked if he could go, as his dog was restless. How did you get on?"

Leaning back again now that he'd finished the coffee, Marlowe hummed. "Hmmm. I am not sure how I got on. Friendly enough. Precise at times, then going off on tangents about British TV. British mysteries. Good observations. Thought it was murder, and his thoughts made sense. I thought for a moment he might be involved. Trying to throw me off the scent with TV talk. Nice dog. Hard to understand. I might need to talk to him more. We might. Suspect? Hmmm. I left right after you called. Before I left, he told me something strange as I was giving him my card.

Told him to call if he had more information, and he said, 'I will. It seems like this will be a hard case for you, Detective Inspector. It's not like when you see a homicidal maniac running around with a pitchfork.' We'll need to talk to him again."

Morven, after a moment to see if Marlowe's speech had ended, followed it with another question. "What was his house like?"

"Books. Many. A pie safe full of DVDs. Lots of booze. A drinker? Your call came before I could check the whole house." His desk phone rang. Picking it up, he answered, "Marlowe here," then gave a few short "okays" surrounded by pauses, before saying, "I'll come down," and hanging up.

"Interesting," he told Morven. "Mr. John Arthur is here at the station wanting to talk to us. I'll get him. Meet in interview room five. You get behind the glass."

Interview room five was one of the bigger, though still institutionally basic, rooms for talking to suspects and witnesses in the station. Plain plastic-topped table in the middle, a couple of metal chairs, one wall blank, one a two-way mirror to a second room, in which Detective Morven sat surrounded by recording devices and electronics. As the door to room five opened, John walked in, followed by Marlowe. Marlowe had left his sports jacket at his desk, brown suspenders with miniscule red checks visible vertically across wrinkled white shirt. The room's bright fluorescents sparkled like stars off Marlowe's bald head.

"Need water or coffee?" Marlowe asked before they sat down.

"No, I'm good, thanks," John replied, glancing around the room, stopping before the two-way mirrored wall. "Wait. This is a two-way, right? Is someone back there? Detective Morven maybe? Your boss? I don't see a recorder on the table though. Shouldn't there be one with an ear-shattering whining sound before we start talking?"

Marlowe sat, motioning John to do the same. "Sit, please."

John sat, but kept talking while staring at various spots in the room. "How can you do good cop, bad cop if it's just you? I can't believe I'm in a two-way room. I hope whoever is there is focused intently through the window. Are you going to Miranda me?"

"You came in," Marlowe replied, slowly shaking his head, remembering how John could go on. "Amiable conversation. This room was free. What's on your mind?"

"Sorry. I've never been in a police station before. Since I was a kid, at least, in Kansas, when I got pulled in for a curfew violation, if you can believe it. 'You do not have to say anything, but it may harm your defense if you do not mention when questioned something which you later rely on in court.' For curfew."

Marlowe started to raise his hand, but John went on before he could.

"I heard after you left my house who the murder victim was. Lucy Dixon. I couldn't believe it."

"You knew the victim?"

"Yes," said John, "I knew her. Knew seems such an awful a word here. So deficient. But I knew her. Not too well. I had been at parties she'd been at, had drinks with her and her husband, had seen them around the neighborhood. An old friend of mine who lives across from the Center, Jimmy Haydock, is friends with them. They have parties together, along with a few people who live adjacent. My wife and I used to go, occasionally. I've been to one or two by myself since she died. That's how I heard, he let me know. They had a party last night at his house. I wasn't at that one."

"And you wanted to come down . . ."

"To let you know I knew her. I didn't want you to think I was holding facts back when we talked earlier. But, well, also I thought . . ." He hesitated.

Marlowe's bushy eyebrows raised a quarter inch, like lazy caterpillars, and John continued.

"I thought when hearing it was her, then thinking about the crime scene, that it would be helpful if I sketched out a map. I'm awful at sketching, my wife was the artist in the family, but I gave it a shot and felt I should bring it down. That it might help to have the lay of the land, or lay of the neighborhood."

"Why?"

"A neighborhood, when the people are friendly and interact, like the one Lucy Dixon lived within, is like a classic village, even in a big city's middle. I follow the Marple line of thought. You know, 'There is a great deal of wickedness in village life.' Which translates into one of the people in this 'village' being responsible. A map of the people involved should help the investigation." Folding his hands, he sat back in the chair.

"A village? The Marple line of thought?" Again, John induced confusion.

"Miss Marple lives in a small, middle-of-last-century English village, St. Mary Mead. She's one of Agatha Christie's main sleuths and, while seemingly a quaint older lady, solves murders by relying on knowledge she's gathered and gossiped about while living in the village, plus her own incredible observations. She says, 'Human nature is much the same everywhere, and of course, one has opportunities of observing it at closer quarters in a village.' The books were made into a TV series. A couple of TV series, with different actors playing Miss Marple, including—"

Marlowe's hand was up. "That's fiction. This is real."

"It could still be helpful. You can learn a lot from watching TV and reading. Not that I'd tell you how to do your job, but here, take a look." John reached into his pocket, brought out a piece of white typing paper onto which had been sketched in pencil a rough map, with a key to one side.

Not being one to turn down any information that might be useful in a case, no matter how out of left field, Marlowe gave a nod. John spread the paper on the table between them. Even if John could be like a puppy off the leash, dashing from one scent to another, it might be helpful.

"This is a map of the houses directly around the Center, where those folks who I believe were at Jimmy's last night, the regulars, live and surrounding streets. The village, to follow the Marple scenario. If the murderer isn't random, and I don't believe it is, and following along the logic of nearly every small-town British mystery I've seen, and I've seen a lot, the murder lives in one of these houses. Want to go through them?"

"Very briefly." Marlowe dragged the words out slower and slower, as if they were breaks trying to reduce a car's speed before the car wreck. Letting a witness—Suspect? Random member of the public?—into an investigation like this, especially so early in the investigation, wasn't normal police procedure by a Kentucky Derby stretch. But something about this lover of British TV intrigued Marlowe. Having an early look at the people who might be suspects or witnesses, or filling in more background about the victim, couldn't be bad.

"Briefly. Let's start with Jimmy Haydock, who like I said is an old friend of mine, going back all the way to college, though he went to University and I went to State University. But we had mutual friends, liked the same bands, and both of us were, let's say, interested in the bartending arts. When my wife and I moved here thirty-five years ago, he came to visit, loved it, and eventually moved out here with his wife, Joanna, and daughter, Geraldine. He's a pediatrician, loves kids, a swell cook, likes a well-made drink and hosting. He's about five nine, big brown beard, T-Rex tattoo on his right arm."

He stopped as Marlowe's hand began rising. "Not briefly enough?" John asked.

"For now," Marlowe replied, "stick to names, ages, occupation if you know, and where their house sits in relation to the Community Center."

"Can do. Jimmy. 7701 20th Avenue NW. Pediatrician. Fifty-seven. Married to Joanna, fifty-eight. Freelance graphic designer. One child, a daughter, Geraldine, eighteen. Student. Their house sits on the corner of 20th and 77th, across from the east lawn and back corner of the Center. Their front door opens onto 20th, so they don't face the center, if that makes sense. Their backyard faces an alley and that yard is where the party was, as it was a nice night."

Marlowe rewarded John with a tight nod and slight smile.

"Next." John made an effort to keep things going quickly. "Neville Cassell. A friendly person. A little restrained, nearly military in manner. Between us, he was never in the Navy or any other branch."

Marlowe's expression cooled again.

"Briefly. Sixties. Editor at a tech company, Royales. Florence Cassell is his wife, late fifties, early sixties. Botanist for the City. They live at 1914 77th, kitty-cornered from the Center. Then there is Joyce Howard, who lives with her wife, Sarah Howard, at 2104 77th NW. I'd say both are early forties. Joyce owns the Bloombox flower shop. Sarah is a professor of biology at the University. They have a daughter, Betty, thirteen. House faces the west edge of the Center, and partially, the Center's park and playground." While talking, John pointed out houses on the map. "Make sense?"

Marlowe gave another tiny nod.

"Hopefully brief enough." John smiled when he said it. "Jumping over to the Center's other side, diagonal from the Haydocks' and across 77th from the Cassells, 7554 20th Avenue. Suri Cane. Spelled c-a-n-e like the walking stick, but sounds like Khan, like Genghis. Suri was a marketing manager at a software company before being elected to city council in the last election. Her husband is Steven. PR manager, freelance. Both early forties. They have two kids, eight and eleven or thereabouts. Prem and Padma? That seems right. The newest in this village of houses, they face the back of the Center and the west lawn. That's the main party group, unless I'm forgetting someone."

Marlowe hadn't taken a note, staring at the map while John talked. He knew Morven would record the conversation and take notes, and he wanted to concentrate both on the layout and the man going through the names. John had covered nearly every house on the immediate north and west side of the Community Center, the houses making an L around the sunken sidewalk where Lucy Dixon's body had been found. All but one house.

Marlowe pointed at the map. "You didn't mention this house."

"That one. That is Tim, seventy-five or seventy-six. Last name Fink? Finch? Finch sounds right. Lives alone. He's not part of the above group.

Doesn't go to the parties or interact with those others, unless to complain about people parking in front of his house, which is at 2108 77th NW facing the playground. He's not friendly. Creepy. Well, that's my opinion. I didn't mention him because he didn't seem part of the village."

"Don't villages always have an outsider, someone on the edge of town?" Marlowe somewhat surprised himself with the question.

"I guess you're right. They do. I should have mentioned him. He's so unfriendly I blanked. Definitely put him on the list. What else can I tell you about everyone?" John's eagerness to delve into a murder investigation wasn't normal, but you couldn't fault his willingness.

"That's good for today. An ordinary enough bunch of people?"

"'We're all very ordinary in the City's north side.'" John's voice went up a notch, slipping into a slight English accent. "But ordinary people can sometimes do the most astonishing things."

"Another quote?" Marlowe said, the slimmest grin on his face for a moment, like a brief splash of sunshine through clouds.

"Yes, Detective. Miss Marple again."

Back at his deck, Marlowe decided John would have stayed longer and talked more, hours and hours, but he'd kindly escorted him from the interview room after the last quote. They'd run into Morven, both detectives sharing a look half eye rolling and half 'that was interesting' behind the older man's back as they walked him out of the station. John continued to chatter as he left the building, even as the big glass doors swung shut. "Don't hesitate to call, or even stop by, anytime you want to talk more about the case. We didn't talk about Lucy, the victim, I mean. Hard to believe. But come by, we can talk more. I have a few thoughts—"

Marlowe leaned down to smell the olive-wood bowl, which gave him a dreamy refreshing vison of vineyards and Umbrian sunsets, then placed his feet up on his desk. The map, chicken-scratch drawing though it was, wasn't bad to have, maybe even helpful, he admitted. Having the neighbors now somewhat arranged in his mind helped him begin to form a picture of the circumstances, the victim, and who might have been around during her last hours alive. He could have gotten more, more than he'd want probably, from their uninvited guest, but that had been enough John Arthur for one day. They'd set up interviews with the neighbors, corralling deep details about each, as the investigation kicked itself into higher gear.

He caught Morven's eye as she walked into the cavernous room they shared with many other officers, and with a sideways shake of his head like a fly-bothered horse, motioned her over. She walked briskly through the space, knocking a pen off a table but picking it up in stride and depositing it on Marlowe's desk as she arrived, not a stitch of her suit out of place. "I brought you a new pen." Morven laughed.

"Thanks," Marlowe said sarcastically, a trace smile appearing. If he tried rapidly traipsing his bison-esque form through the room crowded with desks and chairs, he'd be bruised and two or three desks along the route would be newly positioned or in need of repairs. "This pen is exactly what I needed—to point to houses on the map Mr. Arthur made. Sit, sit." He motioned Morven into the other chair with the pen. "How's your mother?"

"Mami is recovering," Morven said, pulling out the chair and sitting between their desks. The second-youngest of eight, her one surviving parent was older than people expected the mother of someone her age to be, and Marlowe knew she worried about her, about being so distant. She'd slipped and broken her arm recently during a New York spring storm, and Morven had stopped to call and check in after the interview with John Arthur had ended.

"Glad to hear it. Miss Marple? Know her?" His smile expanded slowly.

"Hah." Morven shook her head. "No, I don't. I have *heard* of her. Agatha Christie character. Grandmother age with a knack for solving crimes. Funny that Mr. Arthur brought her up. He seems obsessive, if that's the right word?"

"Not a bad choice," Marlowe admitted. "Obsessive." He tapped pen on desk. "That map. The idea of the village and someone in it committing the crime. What's your take? As opposed to random act of violence."

"I don't know. I still would lean toward the victim being in the wrong place at the wrong time, running into the wrong person after she'd been at this gathering with the neighbors. Not to speak ill of the victim, but perhaps having too much to drink, or an argument with her husband, and she wanders off. Then some person with bad intent happened to be driving through the neighborhood, or was there browsing for trouble, maybe even to break into parked cars or the Community Center. They saw the victim, a woman alone late at night, and decided to act. Or she saw them in the act. That's a probable scenario. Lots of small crime in sleepier neighborhoods. She probably came across one being committed and interfered, or stumbled into a criminal who saw her and decided to go from small crime to a bigger one, spur of the moment."

"Fair enough." Marlowe nodded, his head moving up and down lazily. "Let's put the wagon wheels in motion. Listings of criminals busted in that neighborhood or near. Theft, sex offenders. Background, etcetera. Draw on assistance as needed." He paused. "However, we'll get background started on everyone on this map too. We'll want to talk to them, learn the victim, and the night of the crime. Tomorrow, first thing, victim's family. Make a schedule of when we can talk to the others. Check?"

"Check." Both pulled their small notebooks out, jotting down notes and checklists as they spoke, Marlowe leaning back in his chair, feet back on his desk, Morven stretching her legs out in the space between the desks

"Forensics, CSI, technical details, probably a few days?"

"Yes." Morven shook her head. "We can spend our time wishing we could get that information faster, but they won't be rushed."

"True," Marlowe replied. "One more thing."

"What?" Morven looked up from her pad, slightly confused, as they'd covered everything she could think of.

Marlowe sighed, as if a little embarrassed at asking. "Any chance you'd grab us another cup of coffee? Please. But watch those desks. Wouldn't want to spill a drop."

Later that evening, once Marlowe and Morven decided they'd hit the point when working more wouldn't accomplish much, might actually make the next day less productive, she'd gone to the gym and he'd wandered westward from the station, down a slope toward Settler's Square. An older part of the City, not that it was easy to tell that today. Touristy, effervescent with restaurants, shops and bars, and very crowded with the City's homeless, as well as a criminal element. He didn't love it, but he did love Gary's.

Marlowe's favorite bar in the City, Gary's maintained a singularity in Settler's Square—it wasn't a sports bar. Gary's had a single small-screen TV that showed the local football and baseball teams, the Osprey and the Seafarers, as well as old movies and TV shows. It wasn't a dive, but a white glove treatment would have turned up a fair finding of dust. Under previous names like The Old Port and, for reasons he'd never figured out, The Dolphin, a bar had occupied the space for at least fifty years. It wasn't very hip and didn't pretend to be a speakeasy or faux historic throwback; neither did it have neon signs saying 'BEER HERE' or bathrooms with sinks that passed as art pieces.

It was, simply, Gary's. Fairly long and lean, with wooden booths along one wall, a handful of wooden-topped tables, and a fifteen-foot, L-shaped oak bar with a big mirror behind it, sparkling glass shelves of booze, red vinyl barstools, and handy purse and bag hooks. The walls were brick and bare outside of a few framed pics of black-and-white European liquor ads: Campari, Fernet Branca, Chartreuse, Strega, Underberg. They served well-made drinks at what might have seemed a high price in Manhattan, Kansas, but whose average cost was three bucks less than any nearby joint. Surrounded by $150-dollars-a-head restaurants, beer halls whose walls consisted of SUV-sized televisions, chain fake-Irish pubs, and meat-markets where the staff was required to wear less fabric than one of Marlowe's suspenders, Gary's was an anomaly and an oasis.

Walking in, Marlowe grabbed his favorite stool at the short end of the bar's L-shape, to the left of the door near the front window, tossing his long and thready sandy-brown sports coat on the stool before sitting. The bartender was at the other end of the bar, pouring a few drafts of locally made True Confessions Pilsner for two middle-aged men in shirts and ties watching the Seafarers blow another ninth inning. Marlowe caught his eye.

The bartender was the bar's owner, Gary, and another reason Marlow liked the spot. Gary'd been 'behind the stick' as he called it for fifteen years, buying the bar eight years in. He wore his regular uniform of black jeans and a clean white shirt buttoned all the way up. Lean like a greyhound, probably only five five, he had shoulder-length brown hair and a wisp of a goatee whose streaks of gray reflected his fifty-odd years of age, as did the reading glasses donned when propped up with a book, usually history, behind the bar during slow periods. He reminded Marlowe of what St. Francis might look like as a bartender, even with the hint of an accent giving away the fact he was English by birth. Marlowe had been a regular for years and knew Gary well. Knew he'd moved to the states, as he called the country, when a young lad breaching legal drinking age, but that he'd moved behind the bar when an even younger lad, pouring draught real ale at his parents' pub, The King's Hounds, in Faversham, Kent, in the UK as soon as he could stretch up to reach the hand pumps.

Gary gave Marlowe a small salute, saying, "Kit. Alright?" He called Marlowe "Kit" after the playwright and Shakespeare contemporary Christopher "Kit" Marlowe, a historical personage Marlowe hadn't known the first time he'd done it, which since they'd both had a few at the time caused no end of confusion. But even so, it stuck. It was a nickname Marlowe would only allow Gary to use because it was always the right path to humor your bartender. Especially when they were a friend.

"Alright," Marlowe replied. "You?"

"Can't complain my friend, can't complain. And if I did, would it matter?" Gary gazed at the bar's corrugated ceiling, philosophically. "Perhaps, but probably not. How are things with the police, the fuzz, the Old Bill? But wait. What kind of an innkeeper am I? The first question should have been what drink tonight? Saturdays, they play havoc with my head."

"Just Saturdays?" Marlowe replied.

"Cheeky sod." Gary lightly smacked his hand on the bar. "More comments like that and it'll be no drink for you, copper."

"How about a Negroni?"

"Coming right up. Any particulars on the ingredients?"

"Bartender's choice is good."

"My favorite words." Gary spun around, started pulling bottles off the well-stocked bar shelves.

Marlowe had fallen for the Italian Negroni way back when introduced to it on his first visit to the country, loving the ideal balance between gin, sweet vermouth, and Campari—bitter and sweet and herbal mingling. When he'd first ordered one back home after that long-past Italian trip, the bartender he'd ordered from had no idea what he was talking about. He'd had to walk him through the drink construction step by step. Now, Gary had told him that there's a whole Negroni week bars around the country take part in. The world, it had gotten smaller.

Before his musing got any further down the global gully, Gary set the drink in front of him with a minor flourish. "Ta-da. One country-trotting Negroni, made with Italian Campari, Spanish vermouth, and British gin. And an orange twist from Florida, I surmise. And local water in the form of ice. Cheers."

"Cheers back." Marlowe sipped deeply as Gary stepped away to refill drinks for a couple who had walked up. The bar was busy, but not so much yet as to be crowded, or loud. One of the bars he walked by on his way, The Time Machine, had 80s hits blasting at a level he thought might burn ears into ciders, while here, the Stones' "I Just Want to See His Face" provided background accompaniment not the main event. As he drank, Marlowe traveled the day's events in his mind, trying to file away and sort and arrange the important facts known already. But he got stuck thinking about Mr. Arthur, or John, his television theories and quotes, and was still thinking of the man five minutes later when Gary ambled back over to Marlowe's far end of the bar.

"Need another already?" Gary asked with a slight bow and a point at Marlowe's nearly empty glass. "Tough day?"

Marlowe knocked back the last sip. "Confusing. Yes, please."

Gary made the drink, grabbing bottles off shelves, while Marlowe tipped his glass up again, hoping one more invisible sip remained. But only ice bumped coldly against teeth. He sighed, putting glass back on the bar.

"Round two," Gary said, setting a fresh Negroni before Marlowe. "That should definitely cure the sighing. And perhaps unlock the day's confusion."

"Indeed," said Marlowe. "Actually. Have a moment?"

Gary gave the room the once-over, didn't see anyone in urgent need of a drink. "Happy to help. But you once said bars and bobby business didn't mix."

"That's it." Marlowe's voice raised. "Bobbies. British slang for police." Gary's confusion was evident. "Not that exactly," Marlowe explained, "but British mysteries, television ones. They've come up in what I'm working on, through someone I was talking to today."

"Person of interest?"

"Hmm, not quite that far. I should keep it vague. Policing. This person kept bringing up *Midsomer Murders* when we met, quoting it. Heard of that show?"

Gary leaned back laughing. "It's an institution in England. Legendary Sunday watching. You have your Sunday roast, then watch *Midsomer Murders*. Classic. Starring the also legendary John Nettles, ace actor who made it big in an 80s show called Bergerac, a favorite of my father's. Set on the lovely island of Jersey near the French coast. Nettles was the lead there, definitely the cop who goes by his own rules archetype. Then he switched, becoming a more measured, friendly though firm, police detective inspector solving hordes of murders in quaint English villages in *Midsomer* county. Which isn't real."

Nodding while sipping, Marlowe motioned with one hand for him to continue.

"Nettles was replaced by another actor, Neil somebody, and many thought it would be the end of the show, and for some, the world. But *Midsomer* keeps on, people keep watching, and people keep getting murdered. It has this ability to be murderous and somehow lighthearted at the same time, while showing off the village life my countrymen and women are enamored with. An outstanding array of murder implements too. I haven't seen it in donkey's years, but if memory serves, the ways of committing murder include everything from jellied eels to flying tires to pitchforks to giant stacks of newspaper to a giant wheel of cheese. Sad, that waste of cheese."

"Sounds creative. If I was funnier, I'm sure there's a joke there. Though it is murder."

"Murders in each direction, but people still won't skip the local pubs. That's a point in the show's favor. Sounds like you have an obsessive fan."

"Possibly." Marlowe raised both hands in a don't ask me manner. "He also talked about villages and Miss Marple? Any insights?"

"Marple? Agatha Christie detective. Older woman who runs rings around you lot. My favorite Marples are the classic Margaret Rutherford ones from the 60s. *Murder at the Gallop*, *Murder Ahoy*, a couple more. She was a bit batty. Solved the crimes but didn't get so serious about it. Some thought too over-the-top, but good fun. More modern TV series based on the books and stories. Two different actors played her in that, one thinner and wilier, one less thin and more of a thinker. Interesting connecting that up to *Midsomer*. Village life, I suppose. Frustrated wannabe police or private dick? Maybe just a bloke watching too much British TV?"

"Could be, could be. You're getting busy." A party of five had crowded up to the bar.

"Duty calls," Gary said. Turning, he welcomed the new arrivals. "Hello, folks, good evening. What might you be having tonight?"

Marlowe nursed his drink, relaxing while green and gold visions of English villages trotted through his mind. *Heck, he thought, I've never even been to England, and I'm daydreaming of villages.*

Once Gary poured the newcomers' drinks, he came back, continuing the earlier conversation as if in mid-sentence. "No more English murders tonight. The Seafarers have just been put out of *their* misery, which means no more baseball tonight either, which means I am switching the TV to old fashioned American murder via the legal shenanigans of one Perry Mason. A show that boasts one of my favorite quotes: 'If you have to wait, there's nothing like a bar. After a few drinks, it becomes a fairyland. People are so kind and considerate.'"

"That's good. You wrote it on a bar napkin for me once."

"Most likely I did, at that." He began fiddling with electronics under the counter, and a closed-captioned episode of Perry Mason started on the bar's small TV. "One thing I forgot to mention," he said mischievously. "In *Midsomer Murders*, there's never only one murder per episode. Oh no. Our village greens have more red blood on them. Usually three murders. Sometimes four. Never less than two. Just thought you might want to be prepared."

3

The day after the body was found, Marlowe and Morven drove to the victim's house. Morven was behind the wheel as they traveled north from downtown, maneuvering through the traffic at a speed nearly slower than a weekend 10K runner. Bright sunshine reflected sharply off every building and car they passed. Marlowe wasn't opposed to driving, especially in his own car, which needed more work than he could keep up with, but after staying late at Gary's, he felt foggy, not completely woken up. Plus, reliable Morven driving meant he could roll his window down, watch the city as it scrolled past, and go over the case while drinking coffee. *Not a bad way to start the morning.*

As he was finishing the thought, Morven spoke. "Before we start, what besides the sketch details do we know? We know family members, and spouses even more, are by the percentages going to often become number one suspects. I still believe persons unknown is a solid option, but last night when sparring at the gym, I started shifting toward the husband as a possible." She maneuvered coolly around a ripe-orange hued Ford Fiesta that had cut them off, causing Marlowe to grip the bottom seat cushion tightly as she continued un-fluttered. "I did some research and one study said almost one percent of each 100,000 couples end in male spouse on female spouse murder. Not sure how reliable that source was, but it did have me rethinking. Maybe Toby Dixon should be at the top or near the top of the suspect list?"

Marlowe stretched his hand out of the window, catching the breeze. "Could be, Morven. Worth a gander. But in case he's not the murderer and just a person who has lost their loved one, not too hard, too early on this visit. Facts first."

Morven nodded. "Of course. Standard approach."

"Anything new from the scientists?"

"Forensics?" Morven swung the car left off 15 Avenue NW, one of the buzzy main arteries north from downtown, onto 77th, moving past a dueling car repair shop duo ("Lowest Priced Oil Change" vs. "Even Lower Priced Oil Change"), a café, a hamburger joint called Twinkys famous for over-the-top toppings like fried mozzarella sticks and mac-and-cheese, and into a tree-lined side street full of single-family houses with tree-dotted lawns.

"Forensics. C – S – I." Marlowe spaced out every letter. "Or even a report from Doc Scientist. Forensic pathologist Doctor Jones Peterson, I mean."

"Doc Scientist. That's like a cartoon super villain." Laughing, Morven neatly avoided a geyser-blue Subaru Outback pulling out of a driveway without looking, one of many SUVs they were passing.

Marlowe leaned back his head, rolling his eyes and grinning. "Doc Scientist, indeed. Anything?"

"Nothing when I last checked right before we left the station. I hope for preliminary findings soon. I asked for a rush, but there's a rush and then a rush rush? I'll check before we go in. Perhaps we'll get some useful information before the interview. Vic's house coming up on the right." Instead of parking in front of the house on the quiet street where there was already a marked police cruiser, she flipped a U-turn into one of the diagonal Community Center spaces. "Parking here in case we get to review anything before going up. And in case we need to revisit the SOC. And I suppose in case we want to get out quick." Beneath a giant maple growing on the edge of the Community Center's parking, the tree's shade took them out of sun and into shadow.

"That's a full barrel of cases," Marlowe replied laconically. "SOC?"

"Scene of crime." Marlowe's lack of acronyming was as well-known as his love of coffee, but sometimes Morven couldn't resist.

"Easy, it's morning. Check to see if we've got any reports from Doc Scientist. Then let's go over what we know before we go inside."

Morven pulled her phone out of her pocket, hitting the on button and entering her passcode in two fluid motions, the actions gracefully done before Marlowe finished speaking. Two screen-staring seconds later, she reported, "Received an email from Doctor Peterson. Preliminary findings on Lucy Dixon are available and attached. Something about 'knowledge is the wing wherewith we fly to heaven,' but basically for now he's saying that none of this is information he would swear to in court, yet, or that we should take as 'indelible gospel.' His words. But he knows it's a rush. Opening attachment, reading. Ready?"

Tilting his head back and closing his eyes, hands folded over his stomach, Marlowe replied, "Hit me."

"Victim is female, mid-forties, five-foot-six, 158 pounds. Brown hair, green eyes. Nails painted red. Ears pierced. No tattoos. Rarity these days. Tattoos are everywhere."

"Let's stick to case facts for now, Encyclopedia Brown."

"Was that a joke?" Morven acted incredulous. "A Marlow joke so early in the morning? Taking a note in my phone to commemorate the occasion. Back to the report. No visible scars pointing to traumatic external injury in her past. There is significant bruising around neck. Also small marks visible encircling neck. They seem to have been caused by a cord or small textured rope. Doc Peterson says, quote, 'My preliminary opinion on cause of death would be asphyxia due to external pressure on the neck from some type of ligature, or ligature strangulation. The damage to her throat points to this, but we need to have full postmortem results, which we should have in the next few days. Two more notes from this preliminary examination: it does not look like she was raped, and she has had at least one child. She did not arrive here with any jewelry outside of a wedding ring and an engagement ring. Expect an in-depth and finalized report where truth is truth.' That's it from Doc Scientist."

"Hmm, strangulation. Up close and personal. A question for you: did Mr. Arthur mention a shoelace he saw at the crime scene when waiting for the police?"

"No, not to me."

"Told me he saw one near the body. I'm sure CSI is on it." Marlowe opened the door. "To the husband." Stepping out of the car, he reached back in to grab a sandy-and-burnt-toast checkered, slightly worn XL sports coat he'd flopped over the back of his seat. He shrugged it over his suspenders, rumpled white collared shirt, and tan slacks. He'd skipped a tie, as usual.

Morven buttoned her suitcoat as she walked purposefully around the car. It was a bright sky-blue shade that shimmered as she moved. Brooks Brothers, slim fit, over a crisp white shirt, with shoes a slightly darker shade of blue—dawn sky to the suit's high afternoon. The day was surprisingly clear, so clear the sun reflected sharply off Marlowe's bald head as they passed out of the shade from the trees and into the street.

"Should have worn a cap," he muttered to himself as the tiniest smile appeared on Morven's face.

As they approached the patrol car, a large African-American officer got out of it, saying in a deep sonorous voice, "Detectives."

"Officer Troy," the two responded simultaneously, then looked at each other as he laughed. Marlowe continued. "Thanks for being here. Anyone left or arrived recently?"

Troy flipped open his notebook. "I arrived two hours ago. According to the previous detail, no one stopped in during the eight previous hours, and no one from the family inside had or has left. I haven't seen anyone, outside of the victim's husband, Mr. Toby Dixon, who came onto the front porch approximately forty-five minutes ago. He stared in the direction of the Community Center for a few minutes, then noticed me and the car. He approached, asked if I would be here long and then, before giving me a chance to reply, changed the question to ask if I needed anything. I said no, he returned inside. That is it."

"Thanks. We're heading in." Marlowe shook Troy's hand as he spoke.

The detectives walked the curving sidewalk to the Dixon house, past a well-manicured front lawn of healthy grass dotted with three three-foot tall metal planters boasting an impressive array of Lacinto kale and red-leaf lettuces, orange daisies, and the beginning of what would mostly likely turn into a fruitful tomato crop. The nearly all-white, bungalow style house featured well-maintained gray trim around windows and doors, and two stately Greek Doric columns built in to the wall paralleling the door, giving it a vaguely colonial nod.

Morven trotted up the three gray front steps and knocked on the door, with Marlowe a step behind. The door opened, framing a tall man who said, "Hey. Guessing you're cops?"

"Detectives Marlowe and Morven," Marlow replied. "Sorry to bother you, Mr. Dixon, during what I'm sure is a trying time. We were hoping to ask you a few questions."

"Questions. Sure. Come inside." Toby Dixon stepped back into a dining room with a long wooden table on top of dark wood floors, but motioned the detectives the opposite way. "We can sit in the living room."

They walked into the room, which also had wood floors polished to a hard sheen. A luxuriously cushioned silver chenille rolled arm sofa sat up against the front picture widow, which itself was framed in draping white and gold baroque curtains. A fireplace painted white with columns on either side, matching those outside the front door, with a massive gilt-edged mirror over it, a few black hard-backed chairs, and a Persian-style rug furnished the room. It would have given a full romance-novel vibe if not for the small shelving unit to the right of the couch loaded with pictures of, Marlowe guessed, the son playing baseball at different ages.

"Here okay?" he asked, pointing at the couch, worried about lowering his heft onto such a period piece.

"Sure, wherever." Toby sat unsteady on one of the black chairs, stretching long legs out in front of him, staring at the wall. He was, as Marlowe's grandfather would have said, a long drink of water. Six four, long limbed, wearing an unadorned black T-shirt and faded jeans, with slightly red lined, mild brown eyes beneath tightly cut black hair peeking out under a Makita baseball cap. Stubble dotted his sharply defined chin, which drooped as he talked like a plant needing water. An open bottle of a local IPA, The Hanging Captain, was in one hand, and even from across the room, Marlowe could tell it wasn't the first for him that day.

Setting the bottle beside the chair, Toby seemed to become aware of the detectives again. "Sorry. Either of you need anything? Drink?"

"All good, thank you. Hopefully this won't take long. Rory here?"

"In the yard out back. Do we need him?"

"Not yet. Maybe later. For now, this is fine." Marlowe carefully leaned back onto the couch. As if planned, at the same time Morven leaned forward, smoothly pulling her notebook out of a suitcoat pocket, along with a small pencil. The couch creaked but held.

"These are routine questions, Mr. Dixon, as we begin tracking various lines of inquiry," Morven said professionally, sounding like she could be the line coach for a police drama. "Let's start with last night. Walk us through what you and your wife and Rory did, giving us specific times if you can remember, and if anyone else was involved with what you are doing. Everything you can recall can help us form a picture of the evening, which will help as we continue investigating."

"Oh, okay." Toby replied slowly, as if speaking through one of the city's thick morning marine mists. "Last night seems like years ago. Typical Friday night, I suppose. We went to the Haydocks at around six thirty for a barbecue and some drinks. They're like the block entertainers, and we and a few other neighbors go there just to hang out, usually eating as Jimmy Haydock is a genuinely awesome cook and makes great drinks. Fridays and Saturday nights we often go there. Or we did. Last night, we stayed until I'd say ten thirty, then came back." He took a lasting pull at his beer, as if he contained a great thirst.

"Good start, Mr. Dixon, very helpful." Marlowe glanced up from his notebook and chimed in while Toby was drinking. "A few follow ups to what you've said. Can you tell us what you did in the daytime before the party, in broad strokes. And be more specific about the 'we.' Who specifically was at the party during the same time you were? Anyone leave and, if so, what time and for how long?"

"It wasn't a party really, not a big deal," Toby replied after another drink. "Just neighbors getting together. In the day, Lucy and I were at work. Rory was at school, then baseball practice. Lucy and I met there to watch practice. He's on what they call a select team, in an elite league, for years and years. Plays third base, but if he goes on to play college or, who knows, pro ball, he might shift into the outfield." Toby's energy hit a different level talking about Rory, as if he'd forgotten the murder. "His fielding is top notch, but might make sense to move positions; his arm is a plus. And his hitting really sets him apart—he's got average and power tools, and speed on the bases. His mother really pushes him and it shows. Or, pushed him."

Another big swig, then he starting again, slowly.

"Last night, Rory left after like about an hour and a half. Had some flank steak from the grill, few veggies, chips, a soda, then he came home as he was tired. Or wanted to watch TV or highlights on his phone. You know. Lucy and I stayed. A few beers for me, white wine and G&Ts for her. Eating, drinking, talking. It's a fun crowd, always. Ten thirty, we walked back here and had, um, I believe I had another beer, or a drink, then I went to bed. That's the last thing I remember—coming back here and asking about another drink and feeling sleepy. I can't recall exactly who was still there when we left. That's it."

"You didn't ever hear Lucy come to bed?" Marlowe leaned back up, both he and Morven perched for a moment on the delicate couch edge like crows on a windy wire.

"No, ah, between us, Detective, I was out. I'd had a couple, and I sleep like a log. I didn't hear her come in, but I'm sure she did."

"Why?"

"Her purse was in the bedroom. And her hat, an orange baseball cap she wore. So she came to bed. Not sure why she'd leave again, or how whoever . . ." he trailed off.

"This morning?"

Another swig. "I was woken by police banging on my door. They told me about Lucy. I couldn't— I mean, I still can't believe it. Last night feels years ago. Decades."

"This is very helpful." Morven's measured voice rang oddly off of Toby's wavering depressed demeanor, like a clapper on a broken bell. "Last night, as specific as you remember, can you let us know who was at the Haydocks? What time they arrived and left?"

"I can try, I guess. Like I said, we got there around six thirty. Neville and Florence Cassell were already there. About, oh, say a half hour later, Joyce and Sarah, our neighbors, came with their daughter, Betty. Around a half hour after that, Suri and Steve stopped by. Cane is their last name. They brought their kids, younger than Rory."

"Anyone leave while you were still there?"

"Like I said." Toby's tone slid into surly. "Rory left about an hour-and-a-half after we arrived. We left around ten thirty, and by then, only the Cassells were still there. Joyce, Sarah, and Bets left a drink before us, so say about nine forty-five. The Canes left about an earlier. That help?"

Marlowe, feeling Toby's mood change, wondered how long the interview could continue. "Very helpful," he said in a low, calm tone. "A few more, then we will be out of your hair." Toby nodded, finishing off the bottle with one last steady drink. "Did anything odd or strange happen that evening? Did you see anyone you didn't recognize?"

"Nah, it was a normal night. Good fun. Food and drinks. Lucy had a great time, like she always does. Did. I spent most of my time kicking up drinks with Jimmy and Neville, man-ing it near the grill. The ladies sat and snacked and talked it up. Kids were inside and outside, back-and-forth, with Gere, the Haydocks' daughter, playing with the younger kids.

Didn't see anyone at the Center on the way home. Some kids in the playground earlier. Nothing or no one weird. You think some stranger coming through killed Lucy? You got suspects?"

"Let's switch streams for a moment, if that's okay?" Morven caught Marlowe's nod and continued, hoping to get a few more details. Toby was slurring a little.

"Sure, one sec. Gonna grab 'nother beer. Need one?"

Both detectives shook their heads in the negative. Toby left, coming back in a minute with a shoe box tied tight shut with string in one hand, an unopened beer and a freshly opened beer in the other. He took a drink as he sat unsteadily, setting the box and unopened beer beside the chair.

"Mr. Dixon, thank you for the help. Now, we'd like a little more background as we try to put a picture together. To do that, I want to ask about you and Lucy, ensure that our details are correct. You were her second husband?"

"What the heck does that— Wait, do you think her jerk first husband, Johnny Creek, was involved? He's way back in Florida. She hasn't talked to him in, well, since Rory turned one—so sixteen years. He's involved?"

"We're just getting our facts straight currently. Lucy was divorced then sixteen years ago. And you married when?"

"We married eleven years ago, when Rory was six. I adopted him you know? He's more my son than anyone's. Outside of Luc. Lucy. Damn it." He took another drink, his hand brushing the box as he sat down. "Oh yeah, detectives?"

"Yes, Mr. Dixon?" Morven asked.

"Wanted you to take these." He opened the box, which was full of envelopes. "Bank stuff I think. Lucy had her own account. Plus ours. She worked hard. Found this. Maybe it'd help if there's some work thing involved or someone stole her card or something. Want to help you to catch the bastard who did this, however I can. My Lucy. She was something."

Stepping gingerly off the couch, Morven took the box from his outstretched hand. "Thank you. At this stage, everything is helpful."

Marlowe decided to wrap it up. "One last question, Mr. Dixon. Can you think of anyone who would have wanted to harm Lucy?"

"What? Someone we know? No way. Life of the party, my Lucy. Friends with everyone. Perfect." He slumped down in his chair.

Marlowe and got up. "Thank you, Mr. Dixon. We will want to talk more later. And with Rory too. We can let ourselves out."

"What did you think?" Marlowe asked as they walked back to the car.

"Our number one suspect? I'm not as sure where he fits now."

Marlowe's eyebrows raised questioningly.

"He did seem genuinely in love with his wife, genuinely grieved at her death. He didn't seem to be using anger as a shield. Instead, completely confused by it, which felt honest. Or he's a very good actor."

"No one drinks that much IPA without being seriously depressed."

Morven's laugh echoed. As they reached the car, a high-pitched bark cut in. Turning, Marlowe saw John Arthur's dog, Ainsley, running down the sidewalk that cut through the Community Center playground and park, pulling John behind her like a kite in the wind. In a second, the pair was at his side, Ainsley jumping up to lick Marlowe's outstretched hand.

"Ainsley, no, down. She is very friendly," John said between deep breaths. "Wait, *mon ami* Marlowe."

Morven dropped the box into the car, then walked back to Marlowe and John, whereupon Ainsley switched her attention to Morven's hand.

"And *mon ami* Detective Morven. Ah, mes amis, it is good to see you. Ainsley, sit. Detective Morven may not want to be licked."

Marlowe looked toward Morven for help. "Mon ami? French?"

"Yes, French," she replied.

"No, no, I am not a little Frenchman, I am a little Belgian," John said with mock seriousness. Both detectives' faces showed a blank, Ainsley jumping back and forth between the two. "Sorry, detectives, feeling Poirot-ish this morning."

Again, Marlowe looked at Morven, raised eyebrows doing the questioning once more.

Before Morven could speak, John said, "Poirot? Detective Marlowe, you *have* to know Poirot? Agatha Christie's Belgian detective. Egg-shaped head. Tight-fitting spats. Immaculately dressed adherent of method and order, always method and order. Played for years on TV by the wonderful David Suchet, though also by others. Peter Ustinov was fun, but Suchet had the manner down pat, and the shape. He—"

Morven dammed the river of Poirot-ing, "He's a fictional detective with an oversized, memorable mustache."

Marlowe slowly nodded. Holding up one palm to keep John in check, he asked Morven, "And you know this how?"

"There were a couple of movies starring his character recently. I saw one. Not bad. A little fanciful. He didn't have an egg-shaped head, however."

John jumped in. "Right, the recent movies featured a skinnier, more action-esque Poirot. Slightly less manicured moustaches. Thicker, like yours Detective Marlowe. But still Belgian and still method and order, *mon amis*. Much like you detectives, I am sure."

"More coffee and paperwork." Marlowe's low-key delivery caused a moment of silence before both John and Morven grinned. "Sunday walk take you here, too?" Marlowe asked. Ainsley had stopped licking hands and was now sitting, staring intently at a squirrel high-wiring across a jungle gym in the playground area. Marlowe, watching Ainsley, also now stared at the squirrel.

"Not usually, Detective, now that you mention it. Usually, our Sunday morning walk is in the opposite direction. I have to admit curiosity after yesterday plus wanting to see the scene once more after our talk has us back this way. I hope that doesn't sound morbid. Or wait. Does it give you 'criminal always returns to the scene of the crime' vibes? I hope that isn't happening either."

Marlowe motioned to the car's hood. "Have time to sit for a moment or need to keep walking?"

"We can sit. Ainsley come." The dog had been inching off toward the playground, but when John walked around the front of the car, she followed, sitting down herself as the three sat on the car hood. Only her panting could be heard for a moment before Marlowe spoke.

"Okay if we ask a few questions here, informal like?"

John nodded. Morven slipped her notebook out.

"Nice. Thanks. We were talking to the victim's spouse. You knew the victim, correct."

"Yes," John replied. "Not closely, but I'd been to a couple of gatherings she was at, had a few drinks with her and her husband. Are you looking for my impressions? Trying to understand the murderer by understanding the victim, getting into the psychology? That'd be very Poirot."

"Bingo," Marlowe said. "What was she like?"

"I can give *le psychology* a whirl. Lucy Dixon. Usually larger than life, and the life of the party. A very loud, boisterous laugh might be her main memorable trait. One you could hear, it seemed, for blocks, and one unleashed at any joke, especially at ones a touch, hmm, is bawdy still a word people use?"

Marlowe and Morven gave short nods in tandem, the former motioning for John to continue with his hand, a gesture which caused Ainsley to get up and lick his palm.

"Good, bawdy's a good word. I always found under the brassiness, talking to her before the evening got too cozy to midnight and the drinks too high-proof, that she was very astute, very smart, and had the ability to pick up every subtext out of a conversation. She was interested in people, with a way of appearing the center of a conversation until later you realized she hadn't talked that much, instead managing to get others to talk to her. For example, once when we two were talking, she asked me, 'What's the worst thing you ever did?' She probably knew more about her neighbors than anyone. Getting people to bare their souls while having fun.

That's hard to balance. She liked to have fun, she was flirty. No, that's not exactly right. More gently racy, suggestive, but jokingly. Hard to believe someone with that much vitality is gone."

"And physically?"

"Attractive enough, flowing black hair against pale, clear skin. Leaning—leaned—toward dressing maybe a few years younger than she was. Not bad, I don't want to speak bad of her, and not in the way of the phrase 'mutton-dressed-as-lamb,' which seems a put-down. She was curvy and wasn't afraid to dress to accent it, like a renaissance heroine in a way. One who knew who she was, how she looked, and was comfortable with it. You know?"

The detectives answered by way of a few more nods.

"Well, Lucy had a sort of knowing way about her, combined with a slightly sexual attitude, which could be off-putting. But like I said, she seemed to be a good time to hang around with, have a drink with."

"Know any background?"

"Not much. Toby is her second husband. Rory, her son, plays baseball. Talented, I've heard. They've lived in the Community Center village for I'd say eight years, but I gathered they'd been in the city three more. She made reference to living in Florida before here, as well as various spots in the Midwest. She had been a trial lawyer but left to become VP of legal affairs for a swimsuit company, Catsuits. She talked about her 'lawyering days' and 'lawyering connections.'"

"The others, the ones attending the neighborhood, or village, parties." Marlowe's hands swept as if to include their surroundings. "She get along with everyone?"

"Everyone liked Lucy. Most of the time. I mean, no one likes everyone *100 percent* of the time. I noticed a few of what could have been dust-ups or out-of-the-norm interactions with her and others. I was at a party at Jimmy's once. Midnight-ish, dark, I was heading in for the bathroom and noticed her and Neville Cassell. Did you talk to him yet?"

Marlowe's head tilt and Morven's negative head shake answered his question.

"Tall and handsome. I caught him and Lucy mid-clench under the side eaves of the house. They were fairly tipsy; she'd been patting his leg a lot, touching him. Probably nothing, though nothing is often something. At the next party I was at, they seemed over-obviously cool in relation to each other. And Lucy was rarely cool toward anyone. Something there? I don't want to gossip."

"No gossip. Just observations. Orderly and methodically," Marlowe said but didn't look up, so John went on.

"I did hear her and Joyce Howard, who lives next to door to Lucy, arguing heatedly once when I was walking past with Ains. On the Howards' porch, right there." He gestured across the street. "I didn't get exactly what was said. Maybe the words 'money' and 'past?' I heard angry tones and saw some nearly striking gestures. It was midafternoon, and their hands were moving like riled-up birds. Not sure what that was about, but it's hard to be always angry with neighbors; you see them so often. My guess is Lucy got Joyce talking, heard something personal and then brought it up. She liked to stir the pot."

"Indeed? Anything else?"

"No, that's it. Hold on. Suri Cane. She was one rare person I don't think liked Lucy. I only saw them together once, on the street. The Canes are new to the village, but I sensed a dislike in their body language. Suri's a city council member, and Lucy's here-and-there suggestive manner, as well as a tendency to run conversations, might not have gelled with the councilor, who leans center-ish. No harsh words, but harsh looks. Helpful in putting your picture together, detectives?"

"Very. Thank you."

"If I remember more, I'll call. Or stop by the house. Ainsley is happy to receive visitors, and I'm happy to dredge my memory for more information. 'Our weapon is our knowledge, but it may be a knowledge we do not know we possess.'"

"One more question. What did you answer?"

John's curious expression led Marlowe to follow up with, "When she asked you what the worst thing you'd ever done was."

"Oh, that. I refused to answer the question."

"What did she say? Was she upset?"

"She laughed and said, 'Lucky you.'"

4

Marlowe and Morven drove a short way from the Community Center back to lemon-yellow painted Lynley's Café so Marlow could top up his coffee and grab a croissant, and Morven could indulge in a berry smoothie. Between smoothie sips, she checked email. Marlowe stretched his legs out from the wicker chairs they'd picked, drank coffee, and thought. For ten minutes, neither talked. Finally, Marlowe spoke up.

"Any news? Background reports? Scientists?"

"Nothing yet, I'm sorry to report. It *is* Sunday, which will back up reporting, and pleasant outside too." Morven gazed out of the café's big front windows as she spoke, her eyes reflecting her desire to be in the sun.

"Day of rest for some, not for us. Inchworm's progress this morning, but miles to go before we sleep as they say."

"Who says? Belgians?" Morven smiled. "French? British actors playing Belgians and French?"

Marlowe stood up, brushing crumbs from his shirt. "Americans. Who are on to the next doorstep."

Marlowe motioned Morven to park kitty-cornered from the Community Center, saying, "Let's start by seeing if the Cassells are in."

The Cassells' house was a chocolate-brown with white accents two-story cottage, highlighted by an expansive front porch with a red hanging swing and neat craftsman railing. Sunlight trickled down like water through a beautiful tall red alder onto a front yard lush with wildflowers and small plants around the worn sidewalk heading to the porch.

Morven's knock was rapid, purposeful.

A man opened the door nearly as quick, as if he'd been watching them arrive. "Hello. Sorry, we don't buy—" He caught site of their upraised badges after starting his canned speech for doorstep solicitations. "Police?"

"Correct. I am Detective Morven and this is Detective Marlowe. Are you Neville Cassell?"

"Yes, yes, I'm Neville."

"Can we come in? We're investigating last night's incident, talking to people in the neighborhood."

"Indeed. Come in." He ran his hand through wavy pepper-and-salt hair. Just over six feet tall, he wore a loose white button-down shirt tucked in tight to tan cords. His trim build, tall stance and walk appeared ex-military, combined with a high, intelligent forehead and mutely masculine features—not too harsh. Outdoorsy, like a college history professor who took his class into the field, one every sophomore had a crush on for a month. Maybe it was residual John Arthur in his brain, but Marlowe could see this man as an actor.

The front door opened directly onto the living room, where a slightly rumpled, low-hung, sage-green, mid-century modern couch was along one wall, alongside a brown recliner. They passed a bookshelf going in, full with military histories and the occasional modern novel, alongside a big basket filled with shoes: bike shoes, running shoes, three types of muddy work boots, shoes in disrepair torn and lacking laces, shiny shoes only appearing to have been worn once. The walls were dotted with four-by-three-foot, black-and-white photographs of nature scenes—an acorn in extreme close-up, a beach empty of all but a picnic table bench, an oak tree shot from below.

"Please, please, take the couch, I'll grab another chair." Neville, who had a habit of repeating words they soon found out, walked into what appeared to be the kitchen, grabbed two green metal chairs and said into another room they couldn't see, "Florence, could you come in here?" Walking back into the living room, he sat. "I've called my wife, too, which is hopefully okay?"

"We can wait for her," Marlowe replied. "Nice photos. Photographer?"

"Yes, I took those. Not my day job, but I do like photography. I'm an editor, technical documents mostly." He noticed Morven writing in her notebook. "Is that important?"

"We like our facts straight, Mr. Cassell. Taking notes is an important part of police procedure."

"I see. Here's Florence. She's a botanist for the city, doing a project on trees."

His wife had walked in, and the detectives stood up, introducing themselves. She was tall as him, slightly slenderer, with well-defined arm muscles visible in the sleeveless, fog-gray sundress she wore. Her bob-cut hair, gray streaked with black, flowed around her face as she slightly bowed when shaking hands. Marlowe wasn't surprised by the strength in the shake, but by her hands, which were heavily callused. Her slightly drawn-out face may not have been traditionally attractive, but sun-swept green eyes and a perfectly shaped chin provided a striking countenance.

"Trees?" Marlowe asked.

Neville sat upright in his chair as if attached to a steel bar, but Florence perched easily, her feet in two unadorned black flats crossed at the ankles in front.

"Trees indeed," she replied, eyes twinkling. "I found long ago that I tend to like trees, and other plants, more than humans in the main. Luckily, I found a job with the city watching over, or checking on, trees in our parks. Supervising replanting, replacing if needed, making a case for keeping them and why when developers get too anxious. I could tell you my favorite trees in each park, but my guess is you two aren't here on a Sunday to chat about deciduous and coniferous. You're here about last night."

"Correct," Morven confirmed. "And we don't want to take up any more of your time than necessary. We are establishing timelines for everyone in the neighborhood, so if you could please talk us through what you were doing last night. Be as specific as possible on times and places."

"That we can, we can do." Neville glanced at his half-dollar-sized watch as if to check the time. "We were here in the morning, having breakfast, doing chores, and reading. At one, we went to Davison's Hardware to purchase a new electric drill. We bought a Makita Lithium Ion cordless drill, returning home approximately 14:15 p.m. I took a nap until 15:45 p.m., while Florence made brownies. The rest of the afternoon, we read, had tea, and did chores. At 17:45 p.m., we walked to the Haydocks, where they were hosting a barbecue for neighborhood friends. I was there until 22:30 p.m. It takes approximately seventy-five seconds to walk there or back. Returning, we brushed our teeth and went to bed."

Marlowe and Morven were like deer who had walked into very precise, bright headlights. The latter replied after a minute's silence.

"That is very accurate Mr. Cassell, thank you." Neville gave a sharp twist of the chin as a response. "Do you have a general idea of who was at the Haydocks, when they arrived, and when they left?"

"I do." Another watch check. "We arrived first, at 17:46 pm. The Dixons arrived next, at 18:32 pm. The Howards arrived at 18:45 p.m., and then at 19:15 p.m., the Canes arrived. Rory Dixon left at 19:45 p.m. The Canes left at 20:45 p.m. The Howards left at 21:45 p.m., and then Toby and Lucy Dixon left at 22:30 pm."

"We know, if that helps," Florence said when he was through.

"Know?" asked Marlowe.

"We know it was Lucy who was found in the park around the Community Center. The neighborhood here is fairly connected and word travels fast."

"Like in a village?"

"I was thinking like wind in a grove of trees," she said wistfully. "I thought it might save you time to know we know, as well as everyone else there last night knowing. Now you can ask more pointed questions."

"Thanks, that is helpful." Marlowe caught her slight sarcasm, but wasn't sure if it was toward them or the situation.

"Can you tell us what happened at the Haydock house last night? It will help us continue to paint our picture of Mrs. Dixon's last evening." Morven's words hung in the air for a moment before Neville nervously began.

"I can. We gather at the Haydocks regularly; Jimmy is the ultimate host. Last night, last night I had five lagers from Widows and Orphans, a brewery about twenty blocks south of here, not even a five-minute ride. I spent part of the night talking, talking to Jimmy and Toby, then Steven later, at the grill, then part of the night talking to Florence and the Howards while eating. Jimmy made flank steak, spicey sausages, a bunch of grilled peppers, onions, eggplant and zucchini, some garlic dipping sauce, and a cucumber salad." He was very exact. "Florence had wine, white wine I believe?" She nodded. "And spent most of her time talking to Joanna at first, then the Howards and the Canes at the picnic table. Everyone appeared to have a fine time. Fine time, lots of laughing, eating, drinking."

"What did you talk about? Anything out of the ordinary said?"

"No, normal things. Kids, TV shows, jobs, bike rides, vacations in the past or upcoming. Normal things."

Marlowe noticed Neville hadn't even mentioned Lucy. "What about Mrs. Dixon?"

Florence replied before Neville. "She spent time as she usually did, butterflying between groups, drinking gin and tonics and wine, starting and stopping conversation."

"Arguments?"

"No. Well, maybe one? She was in a corner with Suri, and Suri didn't look pleased, like Suri usually looks. Only lasted fifteen minutes or so. Lucy could start and stop an argument with a snap."

Marlowe's eyebrows raised as if they were small woodland creatures. "Explain that please."

"I feel honesty is best, so can say that I didn't always enjoy Lucy's, let's say, conversationally aggressive manner. She could be blunt, and prying, and overly flirty, all within a five-minute period."

"You didn't like her?"

"I didn't dislike her, if that makes sense."

"For now. What about you, Mr. Cassell?"

"What? Me? Lucy? I don't know. She was fine. I didn't know her well. Well, I didn't talk to her that much if I'm going to be tested on it. She could be a lot of fun." He shifted to glance at his wife, who was looking out the window, then continued. "She could be a lot of fun, but was somewhat loud, somewhat boisterous, compared to others. Is that enough?"

Marlowe ignored his question. "Earlier, Mr. Cassell, you said you were there until ten thirty. Florence, did you leave then too?"

"No, I stayed to have a last drink with Joanna and James. I wasn't tired."

"Did either of you see anyone you didn't recognize there, or at the Community Center on your way home?"

"I didn't. I'm sure it was a stranger. A stranger. We get lots coming through these streets, being close to 15th and only fifteen to twenty minutes, depending on traffic, from downtown." Neville's posture hadn't changed, still sitting at a hard ninety-degree angle.

"I didn't either," said Florence.

"Thank you both." Morven started to put her notebook into her suit pocket, before reopening it and asking, "Before we leave, can you think of anyone who would want to harm Mrs. Dixon? Or who might have had a grudge?"

"No," said Neville in an oddly clipped tone. Florence shook her head.

"Thank you again. We may have more questions later. Here is my card if you think of anything else."

They'd almost reached the car when Neville walked vigorously out of the house toward them. "Excuse me, detectives, detectives!" He had a business card in his hand. "Felt like I should give you one of my cards, too, in case you needed to reach me." His voice boomed until he reached the two, when he lowered volume dramatically. "Also, I—if you have, if there is time—I have one more item I wanted to bring to your attention." Even rattled, he had a touch of the military bearing.

Nearly in the driver's seat, Morven stepped back out, taking out her notebook. "We have time, Mr. Cassell. What is it that you would like to add?"

"I, I, I…" Neville shook.

Marlowe said, "Take it slow. Take a breath." Leaning his bulk back against the car, he tried to radiate a James Dean type calm to help the conversation along. It didn't seem to be working.

"Take it slow. Take it slow. This is embarrassing, but I felt I should tell you in case you heard anything from anyone"—Neville jumped like a skipping record—"anyone around here, that . . ." Deep breath. "Lucy and I had an, I guess, an affair. Or affair-like thing. One, probably two or three, people may have known or guessed, and I didn't want it to come out later."

"Smart, telling us now. We appreciate it. Still going on?"

"No, it ended two months and three weeks ago. It wasn't a full affair. Or I mean, it was some moments. She'd said she wanted to take up riding, bike riding, full-time, and I'm an enthusiast. I have three road bikes, two mountain bikes, and I offered to ride with her, help her build up her endurance. We became close, then closer after a couple of rides—riding to breweries, having a beer or two, then riding back. She is—was—a very affectionate person, very lively, and I can be sheltered. She had a way about her of making you feel important and making a moment feel passionate." The last word caused his cheeks to grow red. "We first got together after one too many bourbon nightcaps at Jimmy's when everyone else had gone home. No sex, mind you, then. But not too many days later we went on a ride, had a few beers at Widows and Orphans, she suggested a hotel, and it began."

"How long did it last?"

"Three months and two weeks."

"Very precise. Who ended it?"

"Who ended it? She did, though it was mutual too. I asked her to go on a ride, which at that point was code for ending in a hotel, and she said no, she was busy. Next time I saw her, she was friendly, but I could sense that the *affair*"—the word came out angrily—"was ended."

"Upset?"

"A little, little bit angry. *Not* a little bit angry too. It had felt like I was acting out in a way I hadn't, but never felt like we were going to run away together or anything like you'd see on TV or at the movies. Passionate, but not a grand passion. I was never going to leave Florence."

"Does Florence know?"

"Yes, she does. We talked it over. She forgave me. She is very good."

"You still saw the Dixons? Without trouble?"

"At the Haydocks. We saw them at the Haydocks. It would be awkward not to go, and she, Lucy, never appeared bothered. She was as always."

Overhead, a crow swooped in, perched on a streetlight, cawed twice, then flew off.

Neville said, "Now you know. Do you need more from me? DNA or fingerprints? I didn't do it."

"That can be it today," Marlowe replied. "An officer will be by later today or tomorrow to request DNA and fingerprints from all the neighbors. Completely on a voluntary basis. At this stage."

Neville nodded, then walked away.

"What do you think?" Morven asked as soon as they sat down in the car. "Mr. Arthur was right about the affair, and Cassell's wound tightly. She ended the affair without being pained about it. He's angry. On the suspect list, at least."

"Early days, Morven, but agreed. Back to the café, top up. Then let's tackle the Haydocks."

Arriving at the Haydock house, the only response to their knocking was a furious series of high-pitched yaps. It could have been a single very excited dog or five dogs. Marlowe suggested they try the Howards. They'd parked again across from the Community Center playground, near to their house.

Walking up the sidewalk toward a radiant royal-blue bungalow with rose-gold shutters on two big casement windows, Marlowe, gazing abstractedly at the sky, nearly ran into a kid's bicycle covering half the sidewalk, causing him to trip slightly in avoidance. Morven gently shifted into the grass for a step. When he recovered, the trip had him facing the house to the west, where he noticed a telescope peeking right at him out of the corner of a window before the blinds rapidly shut. A tall fence with no visible gaps in the wooden slats stood sturdily between houses.

"Someone knows we're here," Marlowe noted.

The front door opened as Morven was beginning to knock, which made it seem as if she might hit the forehead of one of the two women standing in the doorway, before she altered the direction of her hand, making the movement appear all but natural.

"Hello, Mrs. and Mrs. Howard? Detectives Morven and Marlowe. We're investigating the incident that happened at the Community Center recently and would like to ask you a few questions if possible."

"Definitely," said the woman Morven had nearly rapped. "Come inside."

The two women backed up into a large front room. A ten-foot-long wooden dining room table dominated one side, at which was sitting a teenage girl with straight blond hair surrounded by a mini-mountain of colored pencils, markers, and loose-leaf paper. To the other side appeared to be the living room: two pewter-colored suede couches, one L-shaped and one chaise, a mounted mid-sized TV, a few bookcases, an antique clock on the wall stuck at 2:35, and a five-foot multi-level cat scratching post, where a cat the same color as the couches slept. There were five or six vases bursting with a rainbow riot of flowers – roses, hydrangea, daisies, carnations, baby's breath—some tied with colorful cords, ribbons, and twine, some flowing freely unencumbered, as well as two massive rubber tree plants and a few ceramic planters swelling with succulents.

"Let's go into the living room," one of the women said. Making a half bow in the direction of the dining room, she added, "This is our daughter, Betty. She's working on art. Seriously at it, right Betty?" The girl didn't budge.

The two women moved to the chaise, renouncing the L-shaped couch to the detectives. The woman talking as they came in continued. "I'm Joyce, if you didn't know already, and this is Sarah." The second woman gave a wave.

Marlowe guessed they were near in age, early forties, but in appearance were very different. Joyce was in what he thought was an actual cashmere cardigan, saddle brown, over a turtleneck of the same color, with pressed slacks a shade lighter. Her just-past-the-shoulders auburn hair didn't have a strand out of place. It, plus ruby-polished full lips and long lashes over brown eyes within an oval face, gave an overall European model appearance. Sarah, on the other hand, sported a baggy bright-red T-shirt with block-lettered *The Truth Will Out* on it in florescent yellow and well-worn Levi's. She had a round, friendly smile with slightly buck teeth, skin that had spent time happily outside, and what could only be called a mop of white curls.

"What can we help you with, detectives?"

"As mentioned," Morven said, "we're looking into last night's incident. Could we start with what you three were doing yesterday?"

"Got it," Joyce said. "I was working at our flower shop, Bloombox, during the day. Sarah, you and Bets were home, right?"

"Yeah, all day, housebound mostly. I was grading papers—I'm a biology professor at the U—and Bets was doing Bets things after school. We did go to Crabbe's bakery mid-flight, grabbed two brownies after Bets cleaned her room."

Marlowe was nearly overwhelmed by the room's floral perfume, but came out of the haze to say, "And that night?"

Sarah spoke first. "We went to the Haydocks for a block-together."

Joyce followed up. "Specifically, I came home from the shop around five thirty, showered, changed, and we headed over… six thirty?"

Sarah wove in without a beat. "All three of us were there from six thirty until nine thirty, nine forty-five. I know we were back by ten because that's Bets's usual Saturday night bedtime, right Bets?"

Only silence came from the other side of the room.

She went on before Marlowe or Marlowe could speak. "While there, we chatted with the neighbors, ate—"

"I ate far too much," Joyce interrupted. "Jimmy is a grand griller. Sarah does like haggling with him about vegetables on occasion. Biologists. We brought chips because we both tend toward kitchen fails. And wine. We do love wine. Since it's summer, we brought two whites, both from central Italy—a Vernaccia di San Gimignano and an Orvieto Classico."

"Joyce loves Italian wine. Definite an Italian wine snob, in the best way."

Marlowe nodded, shaking off the floral fog. "I like Italian wines myself. To get back to last night, did anything odd happen? Did you see anyone you didn't know?"

Both took a moment, before starting at the same time.

"No, we—"

"Nothing, I—"

They laughed, and Sarah said, "I'll go first. It was a low-key evening, as per usual. Chatting, eating, drinking, laughing. I didn't notice any strangers coming or going. Bets, how did you like last night?"

Bets finally raised her head. "Last night was fun! Geraldine is so goals. She let us hang out in her room. She's cool." Head down.

"Geraldine is the Haydocks' child. She is very cool with the younger kids," said Joyce. "I didn't see strangers. The night felt lovely. Hard to believe given what happened to Lucy. It feels different now."

It seems the Cassells were correct: everyone in the neighborhood group knew. Marlowe wondered how tightly knit the group must be. Mr. Arthur popped into his head, and the detective Poirot. He liked to get into the psychology. Or order and method? Both? Whichever, the psychology of this group of people was becoming interesting to Marlowe, along with Lucy's, how she related to the others in the group.

He said, "Glad that you brought up Lucy. We're investigating her death, as you know, and need to ask you how you felt about her."

Nobody said anything for a few seconds, then Joyce answered, smoothly saying, "Lucy was a member of the block squad, all the Dixons were. She liked a drink, a good laugh, conversing. She could be flirty, wasn't scared of mixing it up, and was a very high-key information getter when drinking. She bought flowers from me a few times, came by the shop. I liked her. We weren't best friends, but I liked her."

"I feel the same," said Sarah.

"No trouble with her and any of the . . . block squad?" Morven asked.

"No. Well, I'm not one to gossip. I mean I do, but I shouldn't say."

"Everything is between us unless it becomes directly involved with the case. If so, at such time as it becomes relevant, we will let you know."

"All right, then. She and Neville may have had a hookup. Saw them together at a bar looking extra cozy."

"That's true," Sarah echoed. "And she and Suri—have you met Suri, Councilor Suri Cane? She and Lucy were dusting up a smidge last night. Probably nothing. Lucy wasn't afraid of mixing it up a bit."

"You two never had a problem with her?"

"Nope," Sarah replied to Marlowe while looking at a hand-sized yellow rose tinged with red that was half blocking his view. "She could try too hard to get your life story when the night was late and the liquor deep in your cells. Like wanting to know secrets, or body count, embarrassing moments. That could grate on people's nerves. Sometimes secrets are secrets. Not to speak ill of her. Wait," she added, before anyone could reply. "One more thing. Last night, late, coming home, there was one person we saw. Not a stranger. The creep was out."

"The creep?" Morven asked.

"Tim Finch. Not a neighbor, even though he lives next door. The creep we call him. He was out weeding his yard, if you can believe it, when we walked home. He's not our favorite. We've had some issues."

"Issues?"

"Caught him too many times peering through his telescope at Bets and us. Also, he yelled at Joyce for parking in front of his house. Shoots song birds—"

"Perching on our fence, which we put up to try to screen him out. That's the creep." Joyce had swept up Sarah's trailing sentence as if it was her own. "If we're creep talking, Lucy did have an issue with him. It got salty from my point of view. We were talking about him to her, the telescoping, and then she caught him pointing his telescope at her across our lawn a couple of times. Used her lawyering to, like, get a restraining order, or at least had the police stop by. Called the ASPCA, too, on the bird side. They did not get along."

"Good to know. Anything else?"

"That's it," the women replied in tandem.

"Thanks very much to you both." Morven reached out while standing. "Here are our cards. Please call if you remember anything else, any details you think might be relevant to the case."

Walking out, Marlowe added, "We might be back in touch."

"Of course. We're happy to help." It was impossible to tell who the reply came from as the door shut behind them.

On the way to the car, Morven heard a repetitive clipping noise. When passing the westside fence, she saw Tim Finch outside trimming box bushes in front of his brick A-frame with the help of a level, a T-square, and tiny clippers. He was wearing tight designer jeans that would have appeared silly on a person twenty years younger than his seventy-five years, over slightly bow-legged legs, a neon-orange T-shirt with a sailboat on it, and old black boat shoes. Morven walked toward him, Marlowe following in her wake once he noticed the direction change.

"Hello, Mr. Finch," Morven said as heartily as she could muster after the conversation with the Howards regarding the man. "I'm Detective Morven, this is Detective Marlowe. Could we have a word?"

Tim kept clipping for ten seconds as the detectives stood awkwardly. Finally, he spit, shaking his white mop of hair that seemed to shaggily mimic a tired '60s Beatles cut, and said one word: "Cops."

"We are police officers." Marlowe stepped closer. "And we *would* like to ask you a few questions, sir, about your movements last night. Could you put the clippers down, please? And could we ask you some questions? It might be easier inside."

"Got a warrant?"

"No, but I am not sure we need a warrant. Can you think of a reason why we might need one?"

"If you're going to badger me, hound me in my own home, you need a warrant; that's the laws." Tim snarled. "I know my rights, even in this darn city. I remember when cops used to help the folk who lived here and not just pander to the newcomers. Today, the cops are as bad as the others." He bent down and clipped a leaf a quarter-inch taller than the rest.

"Mr. Finch, we have a few brief questions we would like to ask you about the incident that happened across the street from your house." Morven kept her eyes on the clippers while talking, just in case. "There is no intention to badger you, or hound you. If you would like us to wait until you called counsel, if you believe that is needed because of reasons we don't yet know, then you are allowed to do so."

"Counsel. You mean lawyers. Worse than cops. Ask your questions."

"Would you like to go inside?" Morven again took a step toward the house.

"Here's fine. I got nothing to hide, even from the fools living around me."

"As mentioned, we're investigating last night's incident. Did you see anything out of the ordinary last night?"

"Nope."

"Can you go over your movements?"

"I was here at my home. Every moment. Alone."

"What were you doing?"

"Is that your business? Isn't what I do at home a freedom still?"

Morven let that question lie. "Were you inside or out here in the front yard?"

"Inside."

Marlowe decided to push. "We had a report you were outside at approximately ten thirty."

"One of those gossipy bitc— You know what they are? Be no use to tell you, I suppose. Cops. Yeah, I was outside. Weeds grow at night, too, you know. Okay with you if a man takes care of his yard? Or is that against your laws too?"

"You don't get along with your neighbors?"

"I'm easy to get along with. But that lot?" He motioned in an easterly direction. "I got no time. Not like any of them have lived here long. My parents owned this house. They're newcomers. I don't cause any trouble, no matter what you've been told."

"What about with the Dixons?"

"The dead woman? Thought you'd catch me out, but I know she's dead. We weren't friends, but I didn't kill her. She had some notions about me and tried to get lawyer on me cause I like to look at the stars sometimes and don't like pests and varmints destroying my yard. I take pride in my yard, unlike some. I watch over the neighborhood, make sure no crimes are committed. Someone has to. I see lots happening. Lots. Hey, you cops might like to know about things I've seen. How much you pay for information?"

Neither Marlowe or Morven rose to the question.

"Nothing, huh. Figures. Cheap cops. But those folks, the Dixons and the others. I leave them alone, and they leave me alone. Détente. Ever hear of it? That all, detectives?" The last word said with another spit.

"For now." Marlowe was well sick of Tim already and stopped the interview.

5

When the knock on his door came, John Arthur was rewatching the first episode in Season 7 of the British mystery series *Death in Paradise*, "Murder from Above," where a bride-to-be falls to her death from a hotel balcony. He'd seen it before but felt watching a fictional murder take place on a palm-treed island paradise, reggae playing in the background, sandy beaches and local rum on all sides, might transport him away from the murder closer to home. Plus, earlier he'd been watching *New Tricks*, the British show with retired cops coming back in a special squad to solve cold cases, and in it the actor Denis Lawson had just replaced James Bolam. Denis Lawson was also in this episode of *Death in Paradise*, providing a continuity of British mystery murder universes John appreciated. It felt cozy.

Ainsley had been napping next to him, curled up nearly in a ball, one usually floppy ear up as if radar to hear any treat he might happen to drop while watching. Strangely, she hadn't heard footsteps before the knock. Neither had he. *Both getting old*, he thought for a moment, as she started barking and jumping in circles. He paused the show, getting up. Hopefully not early twentysomethings soliciting funds for saving the world. He was big on giving but wasn't big on giving at the door. But with the events of the last few days, he wasn't sure he could turn down any positive cause.

With a quick, "Sit, Ainsley," who completely ignored him, jumping instead on and off the couch closest the door, he opened the door to see his old friends, the Haydocks.

"Hello, come in. Now I see why Ainsley was so excited." The dog loved humans, but especially loved Jimmy Haydock. Probably because he was always ready for playtime, plus, as he cooked a lot of meat, his hands were delightful for licking, an activity she began the minute they walked inside.

The Haydocks walked into the living room, Joanna first, Jimmy stopping to give John a quick hug before entering a room they knew well, sitting on the larger of the two couches with Ainsley behind, licking hands the whole time. Though near in age to John—only a handful of years younger—both Jimmy and Joanna appeared closer to ten years younger. Jimmy had a rich, full, brown beard and had a huskily healthy shape, moving like a retired golfer who'd just hit a hole-in-one. He typically wore comfortable jeans and jolly pleated Guayabera shirts, of which he had many; today's was white with a hint of red threading. With a regular twinkle in his eyes, if the beard were white and he were thirty pounds heavier, he could have been mistaken for a vacationing Santa Claus.

Joanna was slightly shorter, with ginger-colored hair traipsing past the shoulders. She wore a neat emerald T-shirt, flowing dark-blue skirt, and wood-bottom sandals with a green band that matched the T-shirt. Unlike Jimmy's steady walk, she had a slight limp from a car accident, her right leg dragging, mostly imperceptible to the majority of people, though John noticed it, especially in times of stress. While Jimmy's face was round as the top of a top hat, hers was longer, thinner. Where his grin was habitual, her resting look was more inwardly artistic, as if always thinking of a different color she might paint the room or how a quick redesign of the furniture could help the flow. Today, though, both their countenances matched: solemn, sad, tired.

They sat in silence for a second, Ainsley's panting the only noise, before Jimmy said, "God, can you believe it? Awful crappy news about Lucy. What the hell?"

"I know, it's crazy," John replied. "Absolutely crazy. Impossible."

"Did you really find her?"

"Yes, Ainsley and I, at the Center. I didn't know it was her until after, just saw part of the body and definitely didn't get close enough to see her face. I saw the Nevilles later when walking, they told me. But yes, we found her and called the police. First 911 call I've made in a long time."

"That sucks. I mean, it all sucks. Sorry. Just so hard to believe, even after hearing the sirens, seeing the police and ambulance, the people in white suits. She was just at our house last night, you know?"

Joanna echoed the thought. "It seems impossible that we were having a glass of wine last night, talking about the differences between the two kinds of kale—Lacinto kale and curly kale. She was growing the former and put it in a salad she brought. I mean, it was silly and mundane, and now she's dead."

She started to cry, and John jumped up and grabbed a box of Kleenex from on top of the coffee table, handing it to her. "Hey, here you go. It seems so stuffy in here, so sun-flushed outside. Counterintuitive that it would be such a nice day. You'd expect rain or clouds, and instead, it's like we're on Saint Marie— Sorry, that's the island from the show *Death in Paradise*. Completely inappropriate, but I was just watching it." Both his visitors knew John's love of British mysteries, were used to his asides, and shrugged it off. "Should we move into the backyard? Plus, then maybe Ainsley will stop licking you."

"She's fine," Jimmy replied, rubbing Ainsley behind the ears with both hands, sending her into spasms of happy twitching. "But going out back would be great."

Ainsley led the way out the back door, across a small porch and down the back steps, bounding from the fourth step to the ground and sprinting into the fully fenced-in yard. She stopped at the small patch of grass to relieve herself, before jumping the sidewalk onto the immense curving wooden deck that dominated the back half of the backyard. And she did all of it before the humans even reached the rickety, slatted wicker couch painted a peeling sky blue and two newer, woven wicker outdoor chairs. That was the only furniture in the yard, though there was plenty of random décor, including antlers spraypainted black and pink—one set hanging on the fence and another from a bush—plants in need of TLC, a giant pinecone in a planter with toy soldiers climbing it, license plates (Kansas, Texas, Kentucky, and Washington) made into a vertically stacked mobile hanging on the back gate, bird appetizer plates attached to the fence, and an old croquet set painted red. Eclectic or messy, depending on the visitor.

John motioned the other two into the chairs, and was about to carefully sit onto the couch when he stopped. "Wait, sorry, I'm losing it. I know it's been a long, long, day. Do you need anything? Drink?"

Jimmy smiled. "Definitely. Please."

"Whiskey for you, right?"

"Yep. Wait. Maybe not today." Jimmy paused for a moment, then continued. "How about bubbly? Highball-y? Gin sounds good. Gin Fizz? It is sunny and nearly summer."

"Sure, that seems a fine choice. Joanna, guessing that's not for you. I could open some wine? Cider?"

"Oh, I'm not sure I could drink anything. I maybe had too many last night, then today's been . . ." She brought her hands up to her face as the sentence faded.

"Sparkling water? Coffee?"

"Sparkling water. Lots of ice, please."

While making the drinks, he could hear Ainsley sprinting around the yard and the occasional 'smack' of a rubber ball hitting fence and knew Jimmy was tossing one of the plastic yard balls to the dog. But once he was back at the seating area, drinks on a tray, she was sprawled out on the deck's edge.

"Ainsley, 100 mph one second, napping the next. I'm always jealous." Handing the drinks around, he said, "Here's to Lucy." They toasted silently and sat sipping, listening to the *shook, shook, shook* sound of a Steller's jay perched on top of the telephone pole in the alley adjacent to the back fence.

"Damn," Jimmy finally said. "Hard to believe. The whole neighborhood crew was hanging out at the house last night. She was the life of the party. Always fun, Lucy, always ready for a good drink. Maybe a few too many here and there, but it happens to everyone now and again. Loved the eats, too. Ready to try anything. Who in the world would do that?" The silence descended like a closed door for several minutes, each lost in their thoughts, before he spoke again. "Guessing you talked to the police?"

John took a sip of his drink, then answered. "A number of times. First, the officers who showed up at the scene of the crime; uniformed officers, very basic information. They held me at the Center quite a while. Ainsley was not impressed with their lack of petting. I've seen enough to know I should stick around. After the ambulance and more uniforms showed up, and as the CSI team and white suits were showing, I talked to a Sergeant Nelson, nice guy, young, then a Detective Morven, slightly older female, more serious. If you think of them in *Midsomer*—" He stopped when realizing Jimmy was giving him wry grin, peeking out from the gloomier looks. "Sidetracked into PBS Masterpiece Mystery land for a moment. I talked to Detective Morven— she okay'd us to leave—and then later an older detective, Marlowe, came by the house."

"Marlowe?" Jimmy was amazed.

"I know. Detective Marlowe. I felt a little silly, but my first thought was the Detective Marlowe from *Shakespeare and Hathaway*, this British mystery show taking place in Stratford-upon-Avon."

"You didn't think Philip Marlowe?"

"I'm ashamed. At the big bar in the sky, Raymond Chandler just spit up his bourbon."

"The ghost of Humphrey Bogart is haunting you tonight," Jimmy answered in a passable among friends 1940s tough-guy accent. "'Your story didn't sound quite right.'"

"'Oh, that's too bad. You got a better one?'" John's gangster accent was shameful.

"'Maybe I can find one.'"

"You two." Joanna smiled for the first time, the tissues still close at hand.

"Forgive me," John said. "I skipped Philip Marlowe, and also skipped Shakespeare pal playwright Christopher Marlowe, who may have died mysteriously in a bar fight or because of a second career in espionage. Such a real-life mysterious character he should have popped up in my mind. Instead, I went right to a secondary character in a British afternoon mystery series. Embarrassing. He thought I was mad."

"You might be."

"Bang! Marlowe, Philip that is, would be proud of that wisecrack."

"What's he like? The real Detective Marlowe."

"Bigger fellow, balder even than I." He ran his hands through the tufts of dwindling hair over his ears as if reminding himself some hair remained. "With a memorable bushy mustache. Much like when you trim your beard but leave the 'stache. Half cowboy, half Statham gone to seed feel, like he could knock people about but didn't care enough to stretch his suspenders. He stayed at the house awhile. I didn't know it was Lucy at that point."

"You had the full police experience, man."

"That's not even the complete police story. Later, when I learned who had died, who I had found, I decided heading to headquarters was needed. There, I talked to both detectives again, mostly more Marlowe."

"Why'd you do that?"

"Too many TV mysteries?"

Both Jimmy and Joanna looked confused.

"Knowing the victim and not telling, that's a recipe for putting yourself on top of the suspect list. Happens all the time."

"Happens in TV," Jimmy replied.

"That's me in a nutshell—too many TV mysteries. I thought it was the right thing to do, so went down to talk to them, tell them I know—or knew—Lucy and mention the neighbors who knew her, the park layout, that kind of thing."

"Why? It had to be some random maniac, right? I mean, some criminal, wrong place, wrong time thing. They can't think it's one of us?"

"My guess is they're keeping all lines of inquiry open, as they say. I just felt I should help them out."

"Consulting detective. Your dream comes true."

"Hah, no Holmes here. I can't tell what you had for breakfast by crumbs on the coat sleeve. But you had a bagel with cream cheese?"

"I had a bacon sandwich."

"I would have sworn those were bagel crumbs." As John spoke, Jimmy checked his shirt and pants, both spotless.

"Even the station visit wasn't my last police interrogation."

"There's more? You must be top of the Most Wanted list at the post office."

"Most wanted dog walkers, maybe. I saw them again this morning when walking Ainsley. She's taken with Marlowe. He probably had bacon for breakfast too." One ear from the sleeping dog rose as if by magic when bacon was said a second time. "They had been interviewing Toby. Asked me a few more questions about Lucy, the folks at the party. I got too Poirot-y, told them they'd need the psychology to solve the case."

"Consulting detective. Just like I said."

"'I am the detective unique, unsurpassed, the greatest that ever lived'. Not me, *mon amis*. I'll leave it to the little Belgian, or the police."

"You did say the detective had a big mustache. That's a start. Incredible facial hair equals success."

"As you should know. That's my police proceduring. I'm guessing you've talked to them?"

"Not detectives. Maybe we're missing them being here. I'm sure they'll stop by to get the details of last night. We might have been the last people to see her, if you can believe that."

"Outside of the killer, of course."

"Right you are, Watson. Or Holmes."

"More like Mrs. Hudson."

"You're not making enough tea. We have seen a few uniformed officers. Came by pretty early this morning, asked for our details, said there had been an incident, that kind of stuff. Very basic. Had some coffee."

"You offered them coffee?"

"They seemed to be working hard and happy to have it."

"French Press?"

"Yep."

"Probably the best coffee they've had. Policing does seem thirsty work."

"As is talking about this. What are the chances of another drink?"

"How do you like your gin, sir?"

"In a glass. Marlowe, *Philip* Marlowe, style."

John walked off to get more drinks.

Following the Tim Finch fiasco, as Marlowe poetically thought about it, and as it was early Sunday evening, Marlowe decided interviewing was finished for the day. Back in the office, activity around the case continued. No more reports had come in, but an incident board had been made and placed strategically in front of Marlowe's desk, with photos of the victims as well as some of the neighbors and what other information they had already. Much of the work had been done by uniformed Sergeant Jamie Nelson, who was tacking a picture of Lucy Dixon's body onto the board when the detectives walked in.

"Sergeant Nelson, thank you. Fine work." Marlowe half bowed his direction before sitting at his desk, taking his normal position, feet up, olive-wood bowl in one hand, peering at the board. Nelson also gazed at the board, as did Morven, in a bit of silent admiration.

Still in uniform, his buttons and shoes polished to a fine sheen, locally born Nelson was an eager—sometimes overeager—younger officer who had helped the two detectives in the past, and who was determined to become a detective himself. He had tight blond curls, and a runner's body that pointed to an infatuation with physical fitness and sports of all kinds.

"You bet, Detective. How'd the locals perform for your two?"

"Tip of the iceberg, filling some gaps. Thanks also for helping with the door-to-door."

Nelson brushed an imaginary speck of dust off his sleeve, saying, "Any tell you the whole truth and nothing but the truth?" The untrustworthiness of witnesses and potential suspects was a running joke.

"Not a one," Marlowe said, holding up one finger, then pointing with it toward the board of pictures and Post-its. "Or if they did, they didn't mean to."

"What's the latest theory?"

Marlowe shrugged like a lazy walrus. "What do you think?"

Nelson took off as it he'd heard a starter's pistol. "There are many possible theories in a crime like this," he said, Marlowe and Morven giving him the same look parents give children hoping to be praised. "Many. First: random stranger. Criminal passing through sees victim late at night and no one around. Crime of happenstance. Second: crime of passion, spouse-related. Did you know that 20 percent of marriages or partnerships of the intimate kind involve assaults at some time?"

Both nodded.

"You do." Nelson's smile was wide as a two-by-four. "So, spouse, Toby Dixon, could be a suspect. "Third," he continued quickly. "Crime of passion, not spouse-related."

Marlowe held up a hand, causing Nelson to pause. "We found during interviews that one of the victim's neighbors, Neville Cassell, had been in an intimate relationship with victim."

"Really?" said Nelson. "That's interesting. Good lead." A picture of Neville already graced on the board, but he moved it up higher, along with his wife.

"He admitted it to us, and the wife knows." Morven cocked her head at the board and pictures. "As do other neighbors. Neville says their relationship is over, but he was very nervous. About this or in general or both. Also, the Howards weren't, as they said, best friends with her, and neighbor Tim Finch, who is very unpleasant and wears very poorly chosen jeans, had a run-in with her too. As perhaps did City Council Member Suri Cane."

"Ooh, a city council member involved, tricky. Talk to her?"

"Not yet," said Morven.

"That gives me a fourth possible motive," Nelson enthusiastically said. "Revenge."

Marlowe smelled his olive-wood bowl, transported for a moment. Morven was so used to this behavior, she didn't even find it strange. Nelson didn't want to call out anything about the detectives as strange, so stayed silent until Marlowe set the bowl down.

"Detective Marlowe," Nelson cut off Marlowe's lingering dreams of Umbrian olive tree groves as if he were a chainsaw once the bowl was down. "Why didn't you two talk to Councilor Cane?"

"What? Oh, the councilor. Never bug a politician on Sunday night, as my grandfather used to say. Learn that Nelson, you'll go far." He rubbed his head. "Nice catch-up. We learned about British mysteries too, Sergeant. That can wait for Monday. Let's call it for tonight. Or, let's get notes in to the computer, then call it. Monday's a full day. Manic it shall be, as the Bangles taught us. Before your times. Morven, first thing Monday, do you mind building out our picture more fully? Background on victim, family, neighbors, Mr. Arthur. Finances, what we can find."

"Sure. Including the box of bank statements Toby Dixon was kind enough to give us."

"Nearly forgot that, thanks. Criminal history. Personal history. Political history. History. Sergeant, can you aid Morven?"

"Yes, happy to." He gave a short fist pump before realizing the others were watching, which caused him to try and act as if he were scratching his chin. Morven and Marlowe glanced at each other as if to say, *You can't fault his energy.*

"Excellent. Pull in other officers. You'll need them. This is priority one: more information rapidly. Also phone your friends the scientists in white suits, putting a rush on. My Monday agenda, before you tell colleagues I'm cuddling under blankets, is to corral the council member for questions, plus her husband, then ask questions of the party hosts, the Haydocks. We're all down but nine. Let's change the lane next week."

He hitched his body out of the chair, sniffed the air. "Coffee brewing?"

Ambling out of the station, Marlowe headed for a moment in the direction of his car, but then like a steamship made a slow turn away from the parking lot and in the direction of Gary's. He tried to not to make a habit of hitting his favorite bar two days in a row. Some days he couldn't resist. He tried also not to make a habit of watching *Gunsmoke* reruns until midnight, but he found himself many late nights drawn back to Marshall Dillon, Festus, Kitty (who he harbored an impossible crush on), and Dodge City. As he walked, he tried to leave the Lucy Dixon case at the office, tried shedding it like clothes at the end of the day as he passed the blocklong construction site—site being a generous description as it'd been an empty lot for years—separating the station from the beginning edges of Settler's Square. But he couldn't get it out of his head.

He felt he was already missing something in the case, not yet two days old. The first forty-eight hours were important, and they'd covered the bases, talked to people, saw the scene, started the wheels rolling down the tracks. They weren't moving rapidly enough, he knew. People, suspects, witnesses, friends of the victim, acquaintances of the victim, rolled through his head like a flipbook. Who was lying wasn't the question. Intentional, suspicious, embarrassed—people had reasons for not telling every detail of their lives. He knew that was the case here, and he knew it took time to get the facts that might unlock the truth. They needed more facts, and the CSI team, all the teams, would supply what they could. Maybe that'd be enough. Maybe the pieces would fall into place easily as a three-year-old's puzzle of an apple. Maybe.

A thought popped up: *One of Mr. Arthur's fictional British detectives would be farther along.* Heck, probably already solved it, and have a better accent while doing it, whether British, French, or Belgium. His sea-splattered northwest drawl wouldn't register a second callback for TV. Mr. Arthur, John, was curious; the British mystery buff, living alone with his dog, books, and Dante's *Divine Comedy* in Italian. The shoelace he'd brought up, finding the body, showing up a second time at the scene. In the case but out of it. Bringing up 'the psychology' and holding up TV detectives as if they could provide illumination into a real murder case. And, Marlowe had to admit to himself, John was astute in a way that had been helpful, had started him wondering more about the tangential people involved, the neighborhood community. Or village.

It was a clear night, matching the clear day of early summer, but the stars were suddenly overwhelmed by neon and streetlights, headlights and bar signs. He'd walked the six blocks to Gary's without noticing a single specific person or thing passed along the way. Not the finest in observational skills for a police officer. Another habit he'd tried to break, but failed at.

His luck held in one way, however, as his favorite barstool was empty. The bar only held two handfuls of customers: a party of four in one corner playing UNO, the rainbow of cards visible from a distance; two couples enjoying the tail ends of what he hoped for them were lazy Sundays; and two other solitary barstool holders, one watching a muted game on the television—The Seafarers surprisingly up five to two—the other reading the local rag's Sunday edition. Gary took his eyes off the game to walk over as Marlowe tossed his coat on the stool and sat.

"Kit, as I live and breathe." Gary held a bar towel in one hand and absently polished the bar. "Two nights in a row. Alright? Special occasion? Holiday? Birthday?"

"Alright. Long day."

"The opposite of a holiday. Leave your troubles at the door then, and let the day pass into the past, as my father opined."

"Smart man, your dad. Hard to do, somedays."

"Let me assist by asking my favorite question: what will you have to drink?"

"Questions. Feels I've been asking them for hours, and you turn the tables. Good question."

"Negroni?"

"I was feeling Negroni'd this morning, and Monday's going to come with the dawn."

"Stay in the family with an Americano?"

"That's it. Hitting the nail right on the booze bottle."

"Family members, the Negroni and Americano, more than just mates. Have I told you the story of the Negroni?"

Many times, Marlowe thought, but said, "Perhaps not this week. Remind me."

Gary grabbed a gin and a sweet vermouth, putting the drink together while talking. "It is a grand legend, though there may be doubters, more facts unearthed in the modern age. But a good story makes a good drink taste better, and so I choose to believe. The tale takes us to *bella Italia*, long a home of good drinks and good stories. Picture, Kit, if you'd be so kind, the kind of ball you see sketched well in Trollope novels: nobles in finery, ladies in skirts wide as a Mini Cooper, handheld fans hiding flirtatious glances, string quartet in the corner of a room the width and breadth of a basketball court.

"Our hero, Count Camillo Negroni, who I'm sure boasted bushy late-1800s style whiskers, the bees-knees of the ballroom, gives a performance this night. One long remembered among Italian nobility of the female persuasion, taking many a lass through her paces, dancing the Volta, the Galliard, and other pretty steps deep into a summer's evening. A hard worker at the high kicks, our Camillo, and not one to skip a second helping at the punch bowl… or a third, even a fourth, and then some, to where he barely recalls the carriage ride home. Right knees up.

"Next morning, sure as you like, his head's pounding, he's knackered, so where's he go? Smart lad, Camillo goes to his local bar, Café Casoni, in Florence. In consultation with bartender Forsco Scarselli, who like every legendary bartender is ready for customer consult at any moment, Camillo has his Americano fortified with *gin*, leaving soda out, realizing to combat the last's night revelries he'd need stronger medicine. For you, we're taking a backward path between our two Italian beauties. Soda in, no gin." He set the finished drink down.

"Quite a night."

Gary gave him a sideways look while wiping the bar.

"A night where so much happened it caused him to change his drink."

"That's a party to remember."

"True story?" Marlowe asked as he'd asked in the past, taking a sip.

"True enough for this bar." Gary's standard reply. "Truth is objective, as Plato told us. More in a bar than anywhere. Definitely more in a bar than a courtroom. Cheers, Kit." He walked over to refill the paper reader's beer.

Marlowe sipped the tall herbal-and-bitter bubbly drink, watching the game until Gary finished and came back. "You've a mug like someone swiped your wallet, copper. Is DCI Barnaby's American brother bothering you still?"

"That's the *Midsomer* detective, if memory serves. Not bothered today with Barnabys. Today, not an English detective at all, but a French—no, not French—a Belgian detective named—"

"Hercule Poirot," Gary finished the sentence.

"How'd you guess?"

"'The little gray cells.'" His reply came in a higher-pitched, badly imitated French accent.

"The whatits?"

"'The little gray cells,'" he repeated, with an even worse accent.

"Gray cells?"

"'One cannot hurry the little gray cells, my friend.' Poirot continually talks about himself and his brain, the little gray cells, allowing him to be such a brilliant detective, the world's greatest. Top-notch TV for many years. Amazing sets, period pieces, '40s cars, deco apartments. Starred David Suchet in a fat suit and patent shoes that pinched his feet. Poirot's entered your case?"

"It seems."

"It is I, Hercule Poirot! Fond our Poirot, from what I remember, of talking about himself in the third person and about his brilliant ways and observations. And of reminding people that he is not French,"

"Belgian."

"Righto."

"The little gray cells of the world's smartest person. Seems like a superpower. My super little gray cells."

"A mystery solving superhero. Probably need a different name. The Incredible Poirot?"

"The Amazing Poirot?"

"The Mighty Poirot?"

"The Fantastic Poirot?"

"Poirot-man?"

"Super-Poirot?"

"Super-Poirot." Gary raised his arms. "And his mighty moustaches. In his immaculate costume without a speck of grime or dust from the street. I believe the hard-boiled shamuses favored last century by many here in the US were in some part a response to Poirot and his fastidiousness. They'd have wanted to punch him. Your second namesake, for example."

"Which one?" Marlowe held his empty glass up. "And another, fine sir, if possible?"

"Cheers, Kit." He began drink-making. "Philip Marlowe. Gumshoe. PI. Trench coat. 'Everything the well-dressed private detective ought to be,' as Chandler said. But Poirot wasn't just popular, he was and is a phenomenon. So much, even Agatha Christie herself got sick of him. Called him an 'egocentric little creep' I read. Killed him off in a book. But he stuck around."

"She Reichenbach Falls'd him?"

"You *do* know your British mysteries."

"I've read Holmes. Required in the police academy."

Gary wasn't sure if that was a joke or not. Marlowe had quite a poker face, which he held for a minute before breaking into a smile.

"Not exactly Reichenbach'd." Gary set down the new drink. "She wrote a book where he died but held on to it for thirty years before publishing it when she herself was ailing. Dead to her, you might say, but alive for fans."

"At least my drink is alive again."

"More alive than Poirot. Though his mustaches probably live on."

"Mustaches are forever."

"Like a good story. But not like The Seafarer's lead, it appears." He turned back to the TV, where the score was tied five to five. "I'll need a drink myself if this continues."

6

The next morning found Marlowe solo at Lynley's Café, Morven and Nelson station-bound to dig into background information about the victim, neighbors, and anyone on the criminal registry who might be in the area and fit the crime. He felt more than a little self-conscious about being happy he wasn't in front of a screen and they were. It was another beautifully sunshiny June day, temperatures coasting slightly above average. Sitting on one of the café's comfy cushioned orange couches near the wide front windows, watching morning traffic wake up on 15th Ave NW, Marlowe sipped a *grande* café Americano. *Ended the night with an Americano and starting the morning with one. Not bad.*

He'd made it out of Gary's before the clock even hollered at eleven, but stayed up once home watching an episode of *Gunsmoke* where tipsy towny Louie Pheeters stumbles onto viewing a murder where one line of a love triangle killed another, but then isn't sure if he dreamt it or not until running into the murderer in the Long Branch saloon. Framed, jailed, and nearly hanged, Louie is in bad shape until Marshall Dillon tracks and shoots the real killer, catching a bullet himself. *Hazardous, Dodge City. Hazardous to view a crime, especially a murder, and not say a peep about it, though saying something about it can be trouble, too.* He couldn't believe not one neighbor saw anything around Lucy's murder. It was late, sure, but something must have stood out—some unfamiliar passing or stopped car, some small violent act presaging a later one. The idea of telling the police might feel dangerous, or maybe they didn't trust the police. Maybe the neighbor bond was too thick, or maybe they wanted to use the information themselves. *Early days*, he reminded himself.

He still had potential witnesses to meet, the Haydocks and the Canes. The former, the party hosts, might be a better bet, but the Canes topped his morning list. Before leaving his house, he'd called Suri Cane's office to book a meeting, as showing up unannounced for a city council member would engender the same chill as if driving with windows down alongside the Pacific in December. After a hold, he'd received word that catching her at home would be best, sometime between eight and nine. As it was now seven fifty-five, he pulled himself up off the deep couch and headed toward the Community Center, but not before adjusting his tie—a rarity, but, city council member—colored an identical sandy brown to the lighter notes in his sports coat, both a shade lighter than his slacks.

The Canes' house was the biggest in the blocks surrounding the corner of the Community Center. A two-story Colonial painted a rich cobalt with white trim, a front porch big enough to seat eight, with six-foot white steps leading to it through a green, treeless front yard. Overall, a stately effect that had Marlowe double-checking his shirt was well tucked. While massive, the porch was completely clean of the detritus you often see— shoes, chairs, kids' toys, planters—outside of a traditional blue door mat blandly saying in white, *Welcome*.

He rang the bell and heard the echo before a man opened the door with his hand out ready for shaking. "You must be the detective," he said in a cultured voice. "I'm Steven Cane, spelled C-A-N-E but pronounced Khan. My parents, who moved here from Mumbai, felt Khan wasn't proper American, so changed the spelling but kept the pronunciation." A handsome fifty-five leaning a smidge on the heavyset, Steven had thick black hair slightly widow's peaked above deep-brown friendly eyes that locked onto Marlowe's, and the strong jaw of a '40s matinee idol.

His golden, lightweight crewneck sweater, jeans, and lush red slippers matched the man's quiet, confident, manner.

"Please, come in." He'd held Marlowe's hand a moment, slightly pulling him inside.

"Thank you, Mr. Cane."

"Shall we sit at the dining room table?"

The entry hall drove back straight from the door, with parallel doors on either side, a staircase past them going up on the left, and what appeared to be a very clean kitchen at the hall's end. As he spoke, Steven opened the door to his left with a motion sweeping Marlowe into a large, wooden-floored formal dining room where a well-polished, ten-seater traditional cherrywood table with tall-backed chairs dominated.

"My wife will be in in a moment. Sit wherever. Here, at the head of the table. Do you need anything? Tea? Coffee?"

"No, thank you, Mr. Cane. I don't want to be a bother. I would like to ask you and your wife a few questions about the incident two nights ago."

"Yes, of course. A tragedy. Lucy was a bountiful woman, very full of life. Hard to believe she is no longer with us. Our thoughts are with her family, Toby and Rory. We have not lived in the neighborhood long, but it is a very communal community. Let me see where my wife is, as I know your time is precious."

"No problem."

"Do you need to speak to the children? This is their first week of summer, and I am sorry to say they're not jumping into it actively, instead taking the opportunity to sleep in. They are very saddened by the event."

"Not at the moment, unless they have something specific they saw or wanted to tell us."

"Not that I can recall. Let me go and get Suri." He left by a different door than they'd arrived, leaving Marlowe alone staring at the centerpiece, a floral arrangement magnificent and flowing free with yellow roses, lilies, lavender, and three volleyball-sized sunflowers. Dramatic, considering the room had no other décor outside of a framed black-and-white map of the city on the wall across from him.

Five minutes later, with Marlowe beginning to wonder if he was forgotten, Steven returned followed by Suri, who took the lead after Steven slid slightly to the side, reaching out her hand to a now-standing Marlowe. She shook his hand heartily, saying briskly, "Detective, thank you for coming out. Sorry to keep you waiting; a call with the mayor." She gave him a conspiratorial head tilt, as if they both dealt with mayoral calls regularly.

"Fine, no problem," Marlowe replied while soaking in her dominating presence. Even at a petite five feet two, Suri's challenging air radiated from high cheekbones, thin mouth, and light-blue eyes. Her hair was pulled back in a businesslike bun, and she wore a designer sheath dress matching the lilacs in color, with short cap sleeves and slight pleats at the center, as well as a string of small pearls.

"I am a big fan of our police, have been since I began my first campaign."

"Yes, thank you for—"

Suri kept going. "I know you've had attrition in the ranks, losing 25 percent of the force in the last few years, and I know this has put a drain on morale and made your important jobs of protecting the city much harder. Some council members believe we should reduce the force, and some of my political opponents believed the same. But I think while reform *is* necessary in the force, as in the government at large, as in business, with change and growth essential, we need to keep people safe first and foremost. That's why I know your job is so important. The safety of our neighborhoods and of the people who live within them is a crucial part of my platform."

"Thanks, I—"

"Which is another reason why I am so saddened at the death of our neighbor and community member Lucy, Detective."

"Another reason?"

"The first being that we knew her, our children know her child, our friends are her friends. But please, sit, relax. Let me know how we can help with your investigation. I don't have a lot of time, but we will do whatever we can."

They sat, Marlowe at the head of the table, the Canes directly on either side of him, as if they were getting ready to interview him, leading him to a wordiness he'd have liked to avoid. "To start, I'd like to ask you some questions about Saturday and Saturday night. We've talked to most who were at the gathering and have a general idea of timetables, when people arrived and left, but we want to be sure our timetables are correct as we investigate Lucy's last hours. Your family arrived at seven and left at eight-thirty, correct?"

Suri replied first. "Very diligent of you, Detective. We know the police are hard workers, and we support the work you do."

Steven quickly followed, saying, "The times you mentioned are correct, yes, at least approximately as we didn't check the clocks before we left or returned."

"It's not a long time to spend at a party."

"We would have loved to stay even longer," Steven wistfully said. "The Haydocks are consummate hosts. Knowing I am a vegetarian, James grills me the finest tofu, as well as a garden of vegetables, and makes a G&T worthy of the queen."

"A city council member's work doesn't operate on normal nine-to-five hours, Detective, as much as I wish it did." Despite saying this, Suri's enthusiasm belied that wish. "Sometimes I—we—have to make sacrifices for the good of the city, even when it equals not being able to spend as much time with friends."

"That day, what were you up to?"

"Up to? I was on calls and reading reports all day in my office. Very busy. Steven?"

"I took the kids to their soccer matches, made lunch, did house maintenance, checked in with a client—I still do freelance PR work, though much of my time is spent helping Suri—made a pie to take to the Haydocks. Does that help?"

"Immensely. What kind of pie?" It was hours to lunch.

Steven laughed joyfully. "It was blackberry and apple. Perhaps a strange pairing at first glance, but it appeared to work as every slice was eaten. Thank you for asking."

"Now, Detective, I am very sorry, but I'll have to leave momentarily. Council business. Hopefully this was helpful?"

"Very, Mrs. Cane. Council Member Cane, I mean. Two more, quickly. First, did you like Lucy Dixon?"

"Like?" Suri's confusion floated out like a cloud as she repeated the word. "Like? Strange question."

"Forming a picture of the victim."

"Like?" she repeated. "Lucy Dixon. A nice person, very much a part of her community, good mother, good lawyer I believe, too. We even thought of bringing her aboard to help with the next campaign, if schedules allowed, as she was very energetic, very willing to talk to people." Steven nodded along. "A great loss. Tragic that this crime should happen in our city. We must continue to work together to stop it. But surely it has to be a wandering criminal. You can't believe it was someone at the party?"

"We are following all lines of inquiry." Sometimes you had to revert to police-speak.

"Very good of you. Sadly, I must go." She stood up. Steven followed first, then Marlowe, saying as he stood, "One more question. We've been told that you and Lucy had an argument Saturday night. Can you tell me what it was about?"

"What!" Her anger escaped from her politician façade as if out of a cage. "Who said that? People should not be talking about me like that. This should not happen!"

"Suri," Steven cautioned.

"Well." She smoothed her dress. "It was nothing, of course. Lucy carried strong beliefs and liked a vigorous debate, as do I. Without debate and a free flow of ideas, our democracy isn't as strong. She had an issue with a series of proposed intersection islands I'm trying to get installed. She thought they would cause traffic problems, while I believe they'll make our streets safer."

"That got heated?"

"Oh no, Detective, not heated. Just, let's say, energetic. Good discussion. I didn't feel any of the other guests were interested, so we went to the side of the house to continue our debate."

"You left right after this debate?"

"Yes. As you well know, duty calls. Called. Speaking of, I really must be going. Thank you for all you do and don't hesitate if we can help more. Reach out to my assistant at the office, or even to Steven, as needed." She opened the door to the hall, and Marlowe knew the interview was at an end.

At the station, Morven and Nelson perched in front of computers, Nelson at Marlowe's desk, Morven next to him at her own. They'd been there since seven thirty tapping away or on the phone coordinating background research, checking forensics, and tracking known criminals in the area, taking a break only for coffee and bagels. It was nearly noon. A bustle of officers moved around, behind, and sometimes in front of them, but they barely shifted, as if in a sitting and staring competition.

Finally, Nelson broke, vaulting out of his chair and to the ground, starting rapid-fire push-ups even though he'd subbed out his uniform today for a white dress shirt, gray tie with minuscule white lines, and gray suit pants—matching jacket hung neatly on Marlowe's extra chair. He counted until he hit twenty-five.

Morven angled away from her screen when he hit fifteen, stared directly at him at twenty, and at twenty-five said, "What. In. The. World?"

Back in his chair, Nelson breathed out heavily. "Gotta keep the blood pumping. That sitting and staring started to cause brain shutdown. Did you know the average office worker spends 1,700 hours a year staring at their screen? That many hours, muscles atrophy if you don't keep moving."

"You don't say?"

"You laugh, but I'll jog out of here when you're too sore to leave."

"Is that a knock on the age of your elder detectives?"

"No, not a bit." Nelson flustered the words out.

"Kidding, Sergeant, kidding. Any questions so far going through things?"

"One. I know we're doing background on the list of attendees at the party where Lucy was last seen; makes sense. But this Mr. Arthur who's also on the checklist, I don't see listed as a party guest in the notes you've transcribed."

"Glad to hear you've read my notes."

"Of course."

"Mr. Arthur found the body while walking his dog."

"Okay, but why the background check? Possible suspect? Pulling the 'I found the body, so it can't be me' trick?"

She smiled. "I might not call it a trick, but astute reasoning. He was also friends with the victim, or acquaintances, and with the hosts and other guests. An odd man in some ways. Marlowe wanted to keep Arthur in the frame. I agree."

"Odd how?"

"Not sure if you caught any of this at the scene, but he keeps bringing up British TV mystery shows, quoting and referencing them. I think he's just a TV-obsessed man. TV can be like a drug."

"British mysteries?"

"Yes. Like Agatha Christie's Poirot and Marple."

"I've heard of them, I think, but haven't seen the shows. Do I need to watch them?" he asked worriedly.

"Not yet. We'll see if it comes to that." She sometimes couldn't help gently kidding Nelson.

Nelson gave a clap. "Just let me know. I'm up for anything to help the team."

"We appreciate it," she replied, turning back to her screen. She slowly turned back to Nelson when he continued.

"Do you or Detective Marlowe think this TV mystery obsession might have turned Mr. Arthur into like an avenging angel type? Sees something in the victim that makes him decide they deserve to die, and he, like his crime-solving heroes, is the one to dole out the punishment? Then talks relentlessly about these shows to throw us off the scent?"

"Feels overly dramatic, but keep it as a note, a theory. Between us for now." She looked over his shoulder out the window for a moment, considering. "Honestly, I believe part of his oddness is that he's very lonely. Reminds me somewhat of my uncle Antonio."

"British TV buff?"

"No. But he was also a widower. My mami's older brother. Lives in NYC. Saw him at holidays, weekends, all the time. Lovely uncle. Guitar player. His wife, Alicia, beautiful woman, made the best tostones—that's fried plantains—and delicious almojabanas—that's a kind of cheese bread. Sadly, she passed away from cancer. We didn't see Antonio for a while after the funeral. His mourning weighed too heavily upon him to carry it amongst people, Mami said. The first time he did show up again, to a family Easter gathering maybe a year later, I remember that he seemed sad, but also that he talked a lot. An odd dichotomy, which I asked Mami about. She said he'd been within the silence of his own home so much that, when back with other people, all the words he hadn't used during those long lonely months had to come out in a hurry, all at once. John Arthur feels that way to me."

Nelson thought for a moment, his fair forehead wrinkling. "That makes sense. Sorry to hear about your aunt."

"Thanks, Sergeant. It was a while ago. Hey, should we grab lunch? We deserve a break."

"That's an idea worthy of a TV detective. Race you?"

She seemed to mull it over, then laughed. "Nelson, you know there's no racing in police headquarters. It's in the manual."

Marlowe made a short stop at Lynley's for a coffee and flakey chocolate croissant. He was beginning to think of Lynley's as *his* café. Already, he'd become passing friendly with shaggy black-haired café owner Nate, who he suspected was or had been in one of the city's louder bands—quite an accomplishment, as one of the city's claims to fame was musical volume—before owning the casually cozy spot, due to his asking, "Repeat that for me, would ya?" after most orders. Taking his order to go, Marlowe pulled up in front of the Haydocks' home. The house, as Mr. Arthur had noted on his sketched map, a photocopy currently folded up in Marlowe's pocket, was on a corner—one side facing the Community Center, front door facing 20th Avenue.

In his car under the day's faultless blue sky, Marlowe felt in the very center of a complex hedge maze, with catching the murderer the exit. His thoughts rolled this way and that way through the hedges as he finished his coffee. *This house is where I should have started. If one of the party guests is our murderer, the rest of the houses, the people within at the party, radiate from here. This is the center, and everything, every person, is a path we have to go down before finally finding our way out. Which means I should have started here, not ended here.* Oh, well, he decided, putting the cup down, opening the door, and grabbing his sports coat. *You can't step in the same river twice, as Heraclitus said, and I suppose you can't start over when in a garden maze.*

The Haydocks' cute one-story, dove-colored cottage sported silvery accents and thin modern street numbers. To reach the front door, he walked past a short three-rail fence and through a yard curiously covered completely in clover giving it a fairytale feeling, reaffirmed by a full-figured dogwood tree to the south blooming white with blossoms, blocking off the Community Center once you went a few feet into the lawn. Bees flew and settled, flew and settled around lawn and tree, buzzing like an amplifier left on. James Haydock had been sitting on the cement front steps, but stood up as Marlowe passed the fence, walking toward him with hand outstretched to shake as he spoke.

"Howdy. I'm going to take a guess that you're Detective Marlowe."

"I am. Mr. James Haydock?"

"That's me, and please, call me Jimmy. Everyone does. James sounds formal to me, like a Sir or a saint."

Marlowe found himself calling the man Jimmy, even though he tended to stick with Mr. and Mrs. on a case. The twinkle in Jimmy's eye, the rosy cheeks, the blue guayabera and matching blue baseball cap, plus his easygoing motions and friendly, radiating charisma made the formality of titles feel wrong.

"Jimmy, then. Sorry to stop by unannounced. Glad I caught you."

"Don't worry about it, Detective. We missed you, was it yesterday? Feels like a week ago. Saw the card you left, meant to call, but forgot. Hard to keep track of things with all this"—he motioned to the Community Center—"tragedy going on. Heard about you from John Arthur. Glad we're here today. Decided to take off work."

"Do you have time for a few questions?"

"Nothing but, and happy to help in any way we can. Joanna, my wife, is inside. We sent Geraldine, our daughter, over to a friend's for lunch. I felt getting away from here might do her good, take her mind off Lucy. Goodness, I must have lost my manners in the hours. Please, come on in." He walked up the steps, opening the door for Marlowe.

"Thank you very much. I like the clover, by the way."

"Nice, isn't it? Easy to take care of too. A bear to dredge up the grass, a snap to plant the clover, and once it comes in, lovely stuff. Bees like it. I keep telling John to update his lawn to clover, but nothing doing yet. Too busy watching mysteries and playing with Ainsley."

They walked into one long room, an open-air kitchen in the middle between two living room extensions on either side, a bar separating the front room from the kitchen. It was not only quite a room, but the perfect setup for a party. Everyone likes hanging out in the kitchen, and this put the kitchen in the star turn, allowing those in the kitchen to feel a part of the action in the sitting areas. The furnishings, from marble countertops to stainless steel, double-wide fridge and gas stove, sparkled and shelves boasted an array of glassware. Walls painted white or a dove gray that matched the exterior were speckled with a few colorful paintings, and a front room bookcase held vases with flowers, a clock, and two identical sets of baby shoes in an open box frame alongside a low-slung, L-shaped white couch.

"Want to sit in here?" Jimmy asked. "Or since it's swell outside, we could sit in the back."

"The back is perfect." Marlowe wanted to get a good view into that yard.

"Great," Jimmy said, walking through the kitchen, Marlowe trailing. On the kitchen counter sat a big glass jar full of what looked like used lime halves and water, causing him to stop for a second look, which Jimmy noticed.

"My lime experiment. It's a way to use zested lime husks, reduce the waste. Soak the halves in cold water with sugar and citric and malic acid. End result's a solid Margarita mix."

The door to the yard was just past the kitchen on the left after a step into the back living room, whose two orange couches, TV, and matching short oak coffee tables were overshadowed by a massive bookcase filled with records surrounding a turntable.

"Impressive amount of vinyl," Marlowe admitted.

"Haha. Joanna's not so sure. I love it. Mostly '60s and '70s rock. Some '80s and '90s. I'm a collector but not driven to madness. Not much." He stalled opening the door. "Okay with dogs? John said you and Ainsley bonded. Asking cause we have two, who together weigh about as much as her. Friendly, but might bark at first."

"Dogs are dandy, thanks."

It was as if a foot-high yapping tornado circled his ankles on stepping outside, one a brown and yellow terrier, Yorkshire perhaps, one a pure white ball of fluff, maybe Bichon Frisé. Marlowe's small dog familiarity wasn't much better than his British television knowledge. He couldn't tell if they were chasing each other, untying his shoes, or about to scar his shins.

Jimmy came to the rescue. "Hey, Hodge, Bosewell. Hey pups, over here, down from the detective or he'll put you in doggie jail." The words combined with a few treats pulled from a pocket brought the dogs to heel next to a long green picnic table sitting on a deck attached to the house by stairs. Joanna sat at the table, rising as Marlowe descended stairs.

"C'mon down, Detective. This is my wife, Joanna."

Walking to meet Marlowe, he noticed her very faint dragging of the right foot.

"Hello, Detective, a pleasure to meet you. Sorry about the dogs, and sorry to meet you on such a sad occasion." Her red eyes appeared dry and drained out from crying.

"Nice to meet you, Mrs. Haydock. Sorry to bother."

"It's understandable," she said, sitting again. The deck, twelve feet in length, featured steps at one end that led to a lower level of the fully fenced-in yard, where another ten-seater wooden table sat, a water-faded emerald umbrella on a stand in the middle, flowering plants on two sides, and a gleaming blue-and-black grill the size of a two-seater car on the third. Tucked to the grill's right was a wooden door leading, via steps, Marlowe deduced from their elevated feel, to the alley.

"What can we help you with, Detective?" Jimmy asked.

"I have a few questions about Friday. First, was the party spur of the moment or planned?"

"Not a party in the massive sense, just neighbors hanging out like we do, no big occasion needed. This time, Jo'll correct me if wrong, we decided Thursday night that Friday night was free, so sent out a group text."

She nodded.

Marlowe followed up. "Same group usually shows on occasions like that?"

"Yep." Jimmy nodded. "Sometimes certain folks are gone or busy, and some show more often than others. The Canes don't make it as much, the Cassells always do, and the Dixons might be late if Rory's playing ball. Stuff like that. Very casual."

"Got it. Anything different last Friday?"

"Nope, just food, drinks, folks chatting. Time to relax, kick back, get distance from the work-a-day world, you know. Heck, the adults usually even leave cells at home. Kids mostly up in Gere's room, outside of Rory. She's good with younger kids. I like it when they hang with us too. They're fun, and sometimes, I teach them cooking and stuff."

"Did you notice anything, Mrs. Haydock?"

"No, it felt like any other night. I still can't believe it wasn't. You can't imagine it was someone who was here who did this awful thing, right?"

"We're following all lines of inquiry. I know the Dixons left around ten thirty, leaving you and the Cassells?"

"Rory left earlier." Jimmy tilted his head back, searching his memory. "Maybe seven thirty? Toby and Lucy stayed until ten fifteen, ten thirty. She came back fifteen minutes or so later."

"She did? Why?"

"Toby can drink for England, as John likes to say, on occasion, and it seems that night was one of them. He knocked back a bunch of beers, plus three or four fast whiskeys when we switched drinking lanes, as well as an Underberg or two. So, he was due south for bed, and Lucy wasn't. It happens, and they're just across the alley, so she must have poured him into bed and then came back for a nightcap. This reminds me—do you need a drink? You look like a whiskey man, am I right?"

"A little early, and the whole 'on-duty' line too."

"If it wasn't on-duty time, whiskey, beer, or another drink your top tipple?"

"I've been known to enjoy a whiskey and a beer, at different times. But my favorite drink, if pushed, is probably the Negroni, an Italian cocktail."

"I love a good Negroni. Sure it's too early? I could whip us up two."

Jimmy's jolliness was contagious, but Marlowe felt he should rein it in. "Not right now. But thanks. When Mrs. Dixon came back, was it just you two? What time?"

"Nah, the Cassells were still here having a nightcap or two. When

I went in to make her a drink, Neville did leave, citing tiredness. It was maybe eleven."

"Just Mrs. Cassell and Mrs. Dixon then? They get along?"

"Sure, we all got along. Lucy—hard to believe she's gone—she got along with everyone. She could be brassy at times, bawdy to be honest after a few drinks. Once, she tried like heck to get us to streak across the Center playground after a night of gin-and-tonics. Loads of fun. Loved talking to people. Tipsy talk, if that makes sense?"

"Not sure. Could you elaborate?"

"You know, when you've had a few you'll open up more than normal. Lucy loved that time of night, tipsy and late. My guess is she knew more secrets about everyone than anyone."

"Got it. Mrs. Haydock, if you don't mind me asking, what did you think of Lucy?"

"A good neighbor. We weren't best friends, but friends. Her tastes and mine didn't align in everything, but she, well, she fit in. And now she's gone."

"Sorry. Don't want to dredge it up, but we have to ask questions. Mrs. Dixon and Council Member Cane; we've been told they argued that night. Anything to that?"

"I was grilling, but did see them on the side of the house. A little heated maybe. Then Suri walked off, as if she had a call. She was the only one who never left her cell at home."

"Happen before between them?"

"Not that I'd seen. Jo?"

"No, no."

"Got it. Anything out of the ordinary, any strangers around that night?"

Both shook their heads, with Jimmy saying, "Not that I recall. We get a lot of people using the playfields for soccer and baseball, and families using the park in the daytime, but nothing suspicious."

"This house seems the epicenter of the neighborhood group. If not a stranger, can you think of anyone who might want to harm Mrs. Dixon?"

"No," Jimmy replied firmly. "Not a one. She could dig into people, but we're not a violent crowd."

Joanna nodded as Jimmy continued. "I did see her have an argument with the guy up the street, Tim Finch."

"Met him. Is he a problem for the group?"

"He is, if you'll excuse my French, an ass. Trying to rile people up, spying on people. But between him and Lucy, I'd take Lucy. She could be nails tough."

"Thanks. Very helpful. That's it for now. We may have more questions later."

"Whatever we can do, let us know. And come by outside of working hours some night. We'll have that Negroni."

7

Leaving the Haydocks, case ideas spinning in his head like dust in a dust devil, Marlowe took his car at a crawl past the Community Center, noticing Tim Finch out in his yard, clippers and level in hand, snipping. He glared at the car as Marlowe passed, the middle finger of the hand holding the clippers slipping up.

"Did he just flip me off?" Marlowe said out loud. "What the? No one is jerk enough to flip off a detective." Taken aback, he missed his right turn on 22nd. "I had to have imagined that. Maybe he is that much of a jerk? Not worth stopping for. Yet." He pulled right onto 23rd and when driving by John Arthur's house saw the man in the yard in front of a mower. John noticed the slow-moving car, then Marlowe in it, and gave a big wave. Marlowe pulled over, deciding even if going sideways into television mysteries, it'd be a friendly balance to the Tim Finch flip off.

"Hello, Detective Marlowe."

"Hello, John," Marlowe replied, stepping out of the car and walking toward the mystery buff. "How goes the grass mowing?"

"More attempted dandelion beheading, as the grass has gone to gray from green." He opened both palms in a ta-da type gesture. "But felt I should give it a go. How goes the case?"

"We're following multiple—"

"Lines of inquiry?"

"Indeed."

"I've always wanted to say that."

Marlowe nodded.

"I'm sure you're busy with the case and can't discuss it, but if you have time to sit, I'd be happy for a mowing break." John sat on one step, motioning to another.

Sitting slowly, Marlowe stretched out his legs. "I could use a break myself."

"What's the latest you *can* tell me?"

"Tim Finch flipped me off thirty seconds ago. That might be a clue."

"The charming Mr. Finch. He and I had an, well, call it an interaction once. I was walking Ainsley." He pointed to the window, behind which Ainsley perched on the couch, watching with 'hey, I should be out there' dog eyes. "He must have been trimming the bushes, his second favorite pastime, because as we walked past his house, he jumped up from behind them, saying, 'I saw your dog crapping in the park and you didn't pick it up.' A foolish assertion, because I never leave without multiple pick-up bags and was *carrying* a poop bag tied up and full. Finch isn't shy, I'll give him that. And out for a chance to make a buck, as he followed up by declaring, 'You know, that's a federal offense. You'll get a ticket if I call the cops. But we can forget the whole thing for, say, twenty bucks.' I laughed and walked on, feeling that was the best course of action. Never heard another word. That's our Mr. Finch."

"Not a good neighbor."

"There's one bad apple in every village. Though they tend to be the ones getting murdered."

"Life doesn't work out in hour-long episodes."

"Usually fifty minutes or one-and-a-half hour episodes for what I watch."

"Commercial time included."

"That might take them to an hour. There I go again, tangenting into TV talk." Marlowe shrugged as John went on. "I know you can't talk about it, but I'll admit, the murder has been rolling around and around in my head. Not that I'm getting anywhere. More like a hamster on a wheel then a mouse finding their way through a maze. And it's such a 'peculiarly mixed set of emotions.' That's a line from an old book, *The Cornish Coast Murder*, you'll be happy to know, not TV. That's how I feel. Horror and dismay at the tragedy, as it says, on one side—for Lucy and her family—but also full of curiosity and interest. Murder is awful, but the mystery side of it, the what and how and who, keeps overwhelming my conscience. Then I feel awful about not feeling awful. Not sure how you manage it, Detective."

"That's the hair in the butter, as my grandfather used to say."

"A new turn of phrase to me. Brilliant."

"His way of calling out a complex situation. He was a police officer too. Influenced my decision to become one. Not a detective, a beat cop. Worked hard, tough as nails, never gave up on a friend or family, that type. Reminded me of Sean Connery's Jim Malone in *The Untouchables*—tall, grizzled, balding, mustache, could wear a suit well. Probably me being romantic. He told me early on when I wanted to follow in his cop footsteps that I'd have to learn to look directly at the tragedies, look at all sides of them without ever looking past them. That's the map to justice, he'd say, which is where you want to end up once you've made the journey. Mixed metaphors did not scare my grandfather."

"Sounds a poet policeman."

"Cowboy poet. Did his best."

"Was your father a police officer as well? Family business?"

"My father? No. He died fairly young. My grandfather raised me, by and large."

"Sorry to hear it. About your father."

For a moment, overhead they could hear a crow perched on the roof picking at the rain gutter, beak on metal going *pop, pop, pop.*

"Thanks. The book you mentioned. Did the police officer with the dilemma solve the mystery?"

"I'm not finished with it, but I'll let you know. It wasn't police with that dilemma, but an English small-town vicar."

"Crime solving priest?"

"There are a few. I watched one earlier this morning, Father Brown. Watched on TV, that is."

"I sorta took that for granted. Go on, tell me more. You want to."

"*Father Brown* is one of my favorite British mystery shows. Based on a classic series of around fifty crime detection stories written by G.K. Chesterton, who wrote about theology, and a bio of Dickens too. They feature a Roman Catholic priest, Father Brown, who doubles as amateur detective in the intuitive bent. Less deductive than Sherlock Holmes, more student of human nature gleaned through being a parish priest. Best friends with a French reformed thief carrying the majestic name of Hercule Flambeau."

"Hercule, like your pal Poirot?"

"Which probably rankled both of the authors. Hercule, the Flambeau one, appears at least once a season in the TV show. Not reformed. Father Brown in the stories is short and stocky, while in the show he's played by the marvelous Mark Williams. You've heard of Harry Potter?"

"I don't reside with my horse in a secluded yurt on the Montana prairie, John. Yes, I've heard of Harry Potter. Boy wizard."

"Mark Williams is Harry's best pal Ron's dad in the movies, among many other roles. He's tall, not short. He plays Father Brown more compassionately than the books, saying things like, 'But every human being, beyond doubt, is worth more than the worst of their actions.' Insightful and knowledgeable from being behind the pulpit and in the confessional, but more caring. Cuddlier. A priest liking a pint with working class folks, like us. It's one of the occasions where I enjoy the TV show more than the written word. He does carry a big black umbrella in both books and show. And gets to the bottom of each episode's murder."

"One an episode?"

"Usually. And usually the crime takes place within or near the small fictitious Cotswalds village of Kembleford, where he's vicar of St. Mary's

Catholic Church."

"Dangerous village."

"Father Brown is there to ensure no murder is unsolved, as a few of the local coppers aren't the finest, and souls are saved. He's as vested in saving the souls of the wicked as sending them to the nick."

"Nick?"

"British word for jail."

"I need a translator."

"I'll check the slang. Promise. Or I'll try. The town it's filmed in, Blockley, is a pretty old English village, all stone and village green, centered around the Church of St. Peter and St. Paul, which is used for Father's Brown's church. It's a beautiful chapel with soaring belltower and an old cemetery dotted with moss-covered gravestones. My wife and I visited it years ago, on the Father Brown trail I suppose."

"You don't go halfway, do you?"

"Nope. Overly fixated? Maybe. There's a jolly supporting cast who help out and provide extra color, character, and humor, something British mysteries seem to excel in. There's the parish secretary, Mrs. McCarthy, inveterate gossip who swears she never gossips and makes award-winning strawberry scones and—"

Marlowe's hands had gone up to the whoa position.

"Too much?" John smiled.

"Without me converting to Catholicism. Or converting to British mystery-ism."

"Then so long to Kembleford and its denizens. Back to our own mystery and tragedy. You've been hard at work, I'll bet. Detective Morven, too, though conspicuous in her absence."

"Left her in the car."

"What?" John stood up to double-check. "She doesn't seem one to sit around."

"Very observant."

"Have you interviewed those at Jimmy's? Any insights? Viewings of strangers circling the Center?"

"We are—"

"Wait, don't say it."

"—pursuing various leads."

"There it is. Slight variation for effect. My *guess* is you've interviewed the neighborhood squad, as one of the Howards calls it. I'd wager a second guess you've been to the Haydocks' backyard, the pre-scene of the crime we might call it, where Lucy was last seen."

"I'll admit that. Nice people."

"Jimmy offer you a drink?"

"Two, I believe."

"He's a host at heart. A welcoming combination of bartender, chef, babysitter, joke teller, and maker of merriment. He'd have made a perfect pub owner as a British mystery regular."

"The TV creeps back."

"I'll stop. *This* time I promise."

"Jimmy did seem ideal as saloon keeper. Always been that way?"

"As long as I've known him, since university. He's welcoming as sunshine, mostly. Like all of us, not every day is full of flowers and unicorns, even for Jimmy."

"The Howards are full of flowers."

"Very true. Blooming, even. So you've been there. That's two for sure."

"You don't miss much."

"I'm no Poirot, but try to keep up. I have been thinking about the murder, even when trying not to. Trying to remember Lucy herself more, and the situation, the crime, less. But it's hard."

"It is at that. You have to acknowledge the corn, to yourself if no one else."

"Another grandfather colloquialism?"

"Yep. Meaning tell the truth. If you're thinking about the mystery, be honest. As long as you let me know if you have any leads."

"Naturally, Detective. No leads. Curious questions, but no leads.

The two I brought up way back in our first conversation have been joined by several more."

"Do tell."

"Sure," John said, standing up as if to present in court, pacing slightly in front of the steps as Marlowe and Ainsley watched, her through the window.

"One. The shoelace. I'm guessing you can't say if forensics found anything on that. Two. Grooves in dirt on top of which said shoelace was found. Why? Three. Jimmy told me Lucy came back to the party without Toby. Why? She feels very driven by desires. Is another drink enough of one? And what time did she leave? Four. What was Lucy and Suri's argument about? Five. Was Lucy and Neville's dalliance more serious? Why did it end? Did it end? Six. How did she get from Jimmy's to the Center? Why wouldn't she just walk through the alley home? I haven't heard of a secondary crime scene. Seven. Where were her clothes? And—we'll call this seven B—even if it was late, in our quiet neighborhood it's hard to believe no one saw anything" John sat back down. "Maybe you've already answered some of these?"

"Maybe you have?" Marlowe asked.

"A question-question. My favorite. No definite answers yet. Some can probably be knocked off too. Every time questions are listed in a book or mentioned in a show, half, or more than half, are red herrings."

"Herrings. That reminds me, the sun's over the yardarm. I'd better be off. Thanks for the chat. Much friendlier than the middle finger of Finch."

"Tim Finch. That reminds me, if you'll allow me one more Father Brown digression?"

Marlowe gave a rueful smile as the crow restarted his beak's gutter hammering.

"I'll keep it short. The episode I was watching is called 'The Passing Bells,' about a group of bell ringers, or campanologists. One is the muddily named Mervyn Glossop, who threatens other characters in a blackmail-y way. Turns out he's done a fair bit of spying. Father Brown says, 'Mr. Glossop was a keen collector of secrets. He made it clear that he knew certain things.' Then Glossop gets stabbed to death in the bell tower."

"Unfortunate. Not very musical."

"Untuned. Like in many shows, it's the bad apple skewered. I bring it up because Mr. Glossop reminded me of our Mr. Finch. Crabby, spying, collecting secrets. I haven't heard of blackmail, outside of his pathetic poop attempt, but wouldn't put it past him. Thoroughly unfriendly."

"Interesting parallel. Seems I should spend less time on police procedure, more time watching *Father Brown*. Or have you make a list of of pertinent British mysteries."

"Detective Marlowe, was that sarcasm?"

Standing, Marlowe shrugged and smiled. "It's been diverting, John, thanks."

"One more thing."

"Another episode?"

"No, I swear. Ainsley will never forgive me if she doesn't get to say hello."

"We wouldn't want that."

John opened the front door, slipping a leash on Ainsley before she bounded outside, tail wagging so rapidly it appeared to be a rotating helicopter blade that might life her airborne from the bottom up. Marlowe bent down to give her a scratch behind the ears with his right hand while she smelled and licked his left.

Marlowe made another stop at Lynley's for a coffee refresh and second croissant before pointing his car back at the station downtown. He didn't make it far, caught at the Corston bridge, one of three bridges over Lake Pearl and its ship canal connecting northerly neighborhoods and the main part of the city, which was up. Turning off his car, he stared at boats: single-family fishing boats chipped with faded ocean blue or sea green paint; a few industrial-sized, iron-hulled trawlers spotted with rust; one or two white, shiny pleasure boats.

"Nice day for it," he mused out loud to himself, staring at a yacht passing, then the starkly clear blue sky above. "But not forever," he added, noticing a bank of clouds forming ominously from the southwest over the sound that framed the city's downtown water side. "The clouds are coming. That sounds deep, Detective. And now you're talking to yourself. It's the case. Or Father Brown's in the backseat waiting for confession."

Marlowe munched croissant, confessing to himself. The case was troubling, as hard to see through so far as the thick foliage where Lucy Dixon's body was found. Stopping at John's wasn't the finest use of his time, but he found himself glad he did. The man's enthusiasm, mingled with a lack of the jadedness long-term police wore like a heavy woolen jacket, gave Marlowe a boost, a respite. Being honest with himself, he acknowledged that John possessed observational skills and insights different from his own and that of the team. Somewhat wacky, born out of watching many British mysteries, but there. Outside of circumstance, who knows, maybe John traveled a different path and became a detective. Marlowe wasn't sure he'd wish that on him. It wasn't easy work.

This case, for example, had kept him up long into the night after he turned his own TV show of choice off last night. *Maybe Morven and Nelson have turned up a local offender whose crime history fits the pattern of this crime*, he thought. The Xs and Os aligning like a game of tic-tac-toe with a toddler. He didn't believe it'd be that simple. He hoped it. However, too many strange questions tangled, as John pointed out, with a couple more of his own.

For one, everyone enjoyed Lucy's company, but no one came right out and called her a friend. She had a habit of rubbing people the wrong way and yet was the life of the party. How does that balance? How did Florence Cassell sit drinking wine with someone she knew had an affair with her husband? Why would Suri Cane let herself be drawn into such an argument at a party, something not very politic? Would old crank Tim Finch take advantage of the situation if he saw drunken Lucy stumbling home? But how to get her in the park? And why were her clothes neatly folded and placed behind a bush, where John didn't even see them.

Or did he? Was Marlowe being led down the proverbial garden path by John's stories and friendliness?

Just as he was about to smack the wheel in frustration at the questions circling his head like hungry buzzards, the bridge went down and traffic began slowly moving again. He shook his head as if chasing off persistent flies. *I'd better focus on driving, or I'll be part of an investigation, not running one.* He chuckled. Getting back to the office safely was job one. Then seeing what Morven and Nelson had accomplished with background checks, what the scientists had turned up. Facts, that's what's needed. Time to put the television sleuths in the rearview. Time for police work, the real kind.

The room was full of activity as Marlowe made his way back to his desk, detectives working many different cases. He exchanged nods and slight waves to numerous colleagues, winding his way toward Morven and Nelson. Glued to computer screens, they didn't notice as he watched.

"How's tricks?" he asked.

"What?" Nelson jumped as if he'd sat on a tack. "Detective Marlowe, you're back. Didn't see you. You'd be very effective trailing a perp."

Morven swiveled gracefully to face Marlowe. "Agreed," she said. "But this room is pretty busy." Three phones rang on various desks as if to underline her point.

"As are you two. Fruitful morning?"

"Yes and no," Morven replied. "Yes, in that we've been digging through what financial records we can find about the neighborhood residents most connected to the victim and have discovered a few interesting points. The bank information Toby provided has been interesting as well. We've had a lot of help from other officers trying to track down potential repeat offenders or other criminal cases or incidents that could seem related. Sadly, nothing's panned out on that front. A few that looked promising, but routine checks alibied every past offender in one way or another, so no luck there."

Marlowe nodded, staring at the board full of photos and case notes.

"Also," she continued, "we tracked down Johnny Creek, Lucy Dixon's first husband. Still located in Florida and has a locked-up alibi."

"Locked up?"

"Mr. Creek is wearing orange in a jail cell."

"Ah. Interesting."

"It is. I mean, his case is. Breaking and entering, residential house. A neighbor saw a light and knew the residents were out of the country. Called the police, who caught him on the lawn carrying the silver, among other items. Pretty straightforward, right? Not as much as it seems. All the doors and windows were locked, including the front door, which only locks from the outside. Mr. Creek didn't have any keys and none were found on the premises. When asked how he got in, he replied, 'By magic.'"

Marlowe's eyebrows raised marginally. "Magic?"

"That's what he says, even now while serving time."

"Magic. Hmm. Reminds me, any more from CSI or pathology?"

"Not a full CSI report yet. We reached out and were told we will be getting one in the next three-to-seven days. However, they did relay a few facts beyond the underlining timelines. One small update from pathology, too, and we should have their full report Tuesday or Wednesday."

"Got it. Break out the highlights for me."

"Happy to. First up is CSI. No full report from the scene yet. They did say, however, that the scene was very difficult to process due to the sheer quantity of DNA evidence combined with the amount of small refuse and potential trace remains. 'A DNA stew' was specifically said. Basically, where the body was found is a very well-used spot, both by children and adults, with the former especially leaving lots of traces. Close to the playground and Community Center, tons of game playing is my theory: hide-and-seek, tag, that kind of thing. Plus, it's utilized as a path for runners, walkers, dog walkers. If that wasn't enough, it appears teenagers aren't opposed to using it as a hook-up spot or a place to smoke."

"That makes sense. Thorny for facts, though."

"Definitely. They did share a few specifics around items we know are of interest. The shoestring discovered near the body, which we surmise was used to strangle the victim, had no DNA on it except the victim's. Helpful and not helpful."

"Agreed."

Somewhat shyly, Nelson offered up, "It points to premeditation on the part of our perp. They must have either cleaned the murder weapon after the fact or taken pains to avoid getting any DNA on it to begin with when perpetrating. That should help us develop our profile."

"Good point, Sergeant," Morven said, then continued her summation. "Secondly, her clothes. As we know, a stack of clothing we postulate was hers was found near the body, tucked under a large"—she looked at her notebook—"Hosta bush. A pair of black yoga pants, white tank top, bra, underwear, black flats. We now know, thanks to CSI, those were definitely her clothes, as her DNA was found on them. One other set was found in some saliva on the tank top strap. We've requested and received samples for DNA testing from the party guests and will be able to see if that second set of DNA is a match with any of them as soon as they finish running the tests."

"Good to know," Marlowe said, still staring up at the board kaleidoscoped with photos and notes. "One follow up: did we get a sample from Tim Finch?"

"The friendly Tim Finch?" Morven shook her head. "No, we have not. I can request an officer go by and request it from him ASAP."

"Let's do that. He'll complain. And probably decline. Request away anyway. More?"

"One more item. The small grooves in the dirt that led to the victim's body. We thought they were made by the victim being dragged, and they've now matched the dirt to dirt found on the victim's heel, so the probability of dragging is high. Those are the most important facts so far."

"Nice work, very nice. Anything pertinent on the overall finances? Nelson, want to take the reins?"

"I can. We've begun digging into the finances of the victim and victim's family, as well as pertinent neighbors—those at the Haydocks Saturday night and Tim Finch. The digging hasn't gone deep or completely into the historical substrata of every person, because as Detective Morven has reminded me, we can't get that information without a warrant, subpoena, or court order, and we'd need more specific probable cause to get one of those. And even then, it can be tough."

"You're learning fast," Marlowe said. "For now, what have we can found out?"

"Most it seems are in fine financial shape. Houses purchased in a normal manner, at jobs for reasonable amounts of time. Did you know that 46 percent of people miss a mortgage or rent payment?"

Both listeners shook their heads, Marlowe's eyes rolling a miniscule amount.

"It seems the Dixons have at least two savings accounts, one we surmise they share, and one that, rereading Mr. Dixon's interview notes, seemed to be the victim's. That's where the box of statements comes in. Oddly, she didn't seem to go digital, all paper statements. That's weird to me. Anyway, this account is where the financial fact we think is most important arises. First, there's over 75K in that account. Second, there have been two separate deposits of 5K within the last three months. That might be odd, might not." Nelson's excitement ramped up. "Here is what seems interesting. Those are the only deposits in this account over the last six months. Her salary from work must go into the other, shared account. We don't know of any freelance work. Where did this money come from?"

"In-ter-esting." Marlowe drew out each syllable.

"Payoff? Blackmail? Drugs?"

"Best not to surmise."

Morven spoke up. "That's the biggest callout. We'll keep digging. We've gone into recent police records. Not a lot. Tim Finch has a penchant for calling police over what he calls 'offenses:' people having a drink on front lawns, noise complaints, trash bins not in the right places, kids doing kid things. He should, in my humble opinion, be given a ticket for wasting police time. He was cautioned by police about his stalking, as the Howards mentioned. The others? Nothing has turned up so far, outside of a few parking tickets. We're digging."

"Dig, dig. I'm here to handle a shovel, too."

"Can you tell us about your morning?" Morven asked.

"Shall I start by telling you about getting flipped off by Tim Finch?" Frozen looks on their faces vaguely reminded him of a squirrel who'd just heard a dog approaching. After catching them up on his interviews, Finch drive-by, and conversation with John Arthur, they stared at the board, the office humming behind them, for a few minutes before Morven spoke.

"The argument between victim and Council Member Cane. Do you believe she was fully honest in her explanation? Feels a strange thing to argue about at a party."

"Worth following up on."

"And Mr. Arthur. Is he just lonely? Or is there more to him as far as involvement in the case is concerned?"

"I'm leaning away from the latter, but worth tracking. Now, if I can rustle up a chair." He reached over to grab a free one that had migrated to a neighboring desk. "Let's continue spading the facts about our victim and her neighbors, update the board, plan our attack for tomorrow. It's gonna be a late one. We can order pizza."

"Yes!" said Nelson loudly, causing people around the room to glance his way. Morven smiled softly and Marlowe picked up his olive-wood bowl, taking a deep breath.

Marlowe had been awake only five minutes the next morning, was still in bed listening to the rain pounding his roof like a million tiny fists, when a call came in at 6:35 a.m. Tim Finch had been found dead in the alley between the Dixons and the Haydocks.

8

The city switched weather like some people changed clothes: often and unpredictably. Early June had unexpectedly brought solely clear skies and sunshine for multiple days in a row. Usually, this point in summer alternated between morning's misty marine layer, clear blue brunchtime skies, then an afternoon and evening trio of sunshine, spot of clouds, sprinkle or more of rain. The last few phases repeated, occasionally hourly, as the day unfolded. It could make for clothing confusion, never knowing exactly what to wear if you were leaving the house for a full day out. The days were never boring and the lack of excessive temperature in either direction made it ideal for lounging on the deck or poolside with friends, provided you were prepared to bounce inside if rain did drop by.

This Tuesday morning's sharp drop in temperature and persistent drizzle marked the time period locals called Juneuary, as the month's winterizing for a day or two was an annual event. The exact moment the chilly change happened wasn't predictable, or half the population might buy tickets for flights pointed directly to landing at locales boasting typically summer climes. Many attempted guessing, keeping the airport humming, but often ended up returning right when Juneuary hit. Bad luck for them. On the other side of the meteorological coin, the dramatic mercury drop and wet bite slipped off like a puffy coat after a few days, when the sunshine cycle resumed.

The knowledge that Juneuary wouldn't last long didn't make Marlowe's trek north out of downtown in crawling traffic better. The city dubiously boasted over 150 days of rain a year, yet even sprinkles in summertime caused roadway havoc. A bright brilliantly blue day wouldn't have made for a shinier morning. Another unexplained death in the same neighborhood. Tim Finch. A crusty, unfriendly man, but one who certainly seemed healthy and hearty. Heck, his aggressive defiance showed a certain zest for life. A cranky zest, definitely. Marlowe didn't believe this was going to be a death from natural causes.

Adding to it, they still hadn't made enough headway on Lucy Dixon's murder. Marlowe, Morven, and Nelson had worked into the previous night's yawning hours, supported by countless others in different departments. And while leads, good leads, were found to follow up on, adding another case to work on was about to stretch the team even thinner. Rainy, another murder, bad traffic. It certainly was a Tuesday.

They'd left Nelson in the office coordinating background checks and to take the lead on setting up more interviews, deeper questions with the neighbors, hopefully getting some into the office today. That was priority one on the Dixon homicide. Morven accompanied him to the latest crime scene, and he was very glad for a second set of keen eyes and another viewpoint. She'd also brought coffee. Marlowe never felt awake before at least one cup, and rain made the caffeine jolt more necessary.

"Thanks again for the coffee," he said as she drove up 15th Avenue.

"I felt it was a requirement," she replied. "Especially on a Juneuary day like this. Go through Tim Finch's details again while we drive?"

"Happy to. Tim Finch, seventy-six years old. Retired. Lived two houses north of the Dixons, the Howards between them. Not part of the neighborhood squad, as Joyce Howard would say. Obsessed with lawn maintenance. In trouble with Lucy Dixon due to a tendency to spy on the neighbors, as well as being a general pest and perhaps more."

"Pedophile?"

"Not sure the level. Creep, they call him. Potentially trying to extort money."

"But no formal blackmail accusations."

"No. Cautioned for harassing behavior. Not a nice man. He did ask you and I roundaboutly if we'd pay for information, remember, and asked Mr. Arthur for money to not report him to the police."

"For what?"

"Not scooping."

"A serious matter." She smiled.

"Mr. Arthur swears he carries bags. I believe him."

"We don't know much about Finch's death yet?"

"Nope. Haven't heard much. Appears from early reports to be suspicious. Found in the alley between the Dixons and Haydocks, where the party Lucy Dixon was last seen at was."

"I can picture it on the map Mr. Arthur supplied."

"That's it. Found in the alley by an early morning jogger."

"One on our neighbors list?"

"No. Passing by. Noticed shoes, realized they were attached to legs. Called it in."

"The placement in the alley is interesting. Theories yet?"

"Mulling. Willing to listen if you have thoughts."

Morven's enthusiasm crackled as she talked, the windshield wiper beat and smattering of rain providing background. "I believe the two deaths will be connected in some manner. It's too close, and while he's not in the social group, he does reside on the block and *has* been connected with Lucy Dixon and some of the others. The percent of people murdered on the same block within a week of each other has to be nearly nonexistent, and to be unconnected a numerical impossibility."

Marlowe nodded, making a keep it coming motion with his hand before grabbing his coffee and taking a hefty sip.

"With that, I can posit three potential theories. First. One of the group is a serial killer of an odd type. Triggered by an action or actions happening in the neighborhood, driven to murdering, well, neighbors."

"Interesting. For and against?"

"For: serial killers are unpredictable. This second murder seems that. Against: the victims differ in nearly all categories outside of proximity. I feel this theory is least likely. But the scene may tell us more if it was murder and was committed in the same manner, or contains otherwise shared similarities. Two. Revenge. In this scenario, Tim Finch is Lucy Dixon's murderer. His murderer learned this and took the law into their own hands."

"Interesting, again. For and against?"

"For: Tim Finch had a run-in with the first victim and was known to exhibit stalker tendencies. If the perpetrator knew, this could lead to confrontation and potentially our second crime. Against: Tim Finch, from what we know so far, wasn't violent. Also, reading interview transcripts, our other suspects didn't suspect him of Lucy's murder. They could be lying. The third scenario: blackmail gone wrong. Tim Finch we know wasn't opposed to attempting blackmail and spent a lot of time watching the neighborhood. If he saw Lucy Dixon's murder, it wouldn't be out of character for him to try taking advantage by blackmailing her murderer. Who could then have killed him instead of giving in to blackmail."

"Third strike, right down the middle. Interesting. Play it out."

"For: Fits Tim Finch's character to attempt blackmail if aware of information on the first murder. He appears the type of person who would try it and, while trying, potentially push a person who'd committed one murder into committing a second instead of leaving a loose end. Against: We still don't know the motive for murder one, making it harder to draw a line of facts that point to the person who committed murder one killing a second time. There may not be a connection, far-fetched as that feels."

"Solid theories. Well thought out, and while driving in this downpour. Impressive. We'll test those theories, and any new ones, against what we learn." He gazed longingly at Lynley's Café as they drove by, its windows steamed over, cozy soft light filtering through. He consoled himself with a silent, *maybe later*, as they turned west.

They parked about half a block away from the alley due to a handful of police cruisers plus an ambulance and a white van being in front. It was still raining. Morven had added a police-issue slicker over her sienna-shaded suit and a peaked police cap that kept the wet out of her eyes. Marlowe donned a dark-blue baseball cap with a golden "S" on it, while wearing his normal sandy-colored sport coat. No way around it; dampness had seeped in by the time they approached the police tape cordon stretched across the alley's opening into the yards on either side. Officer Troy's large form stood like a guardian at the gates of some mystic opening to the underworld where alley met sidewalk, ensuring no one who wasn't supposed to crossed the tape. A group of ten or fifteen onlookers huddled under umbrellas and tall trees across the street in the Community Center's park. Marlowe glanced their way as he walked by, expecting to see Mr. Arthur, but didn't notice him or Ainsley in the gawker group. And then they were in front of Officer Troy.

"Detective Marlowe, Detective Morven, welcome back." His voice rumbled, accented by raindrops hitting the three hat brims.

"Officer Troy, here we are again," Marlowe replied. "Were you first on?"

"Second. Officers Fisher and Braithwaite were first after receiving the alert."

"Anything of interest from them?"

"Not much. Fish said, 'You better come and take a look at this. You're not going to believe it.' After last Saturday, I could only reply, 'On the contrary, Fish. I rather think I will.' I'd like to think this northerly patch of city is a peaceable one, but these last few days have changed my tune."

"It has been strange. Peaceable would be better."

"That it would. But then we might be out of a job. They called me in to shoo off passers-by. I double-checked the body was indeed dead; it was. The ambulance, plus a few more of us, descended and we began with the procedure. White suits showed up, and the doc."

"You recognize the victim?"

"Yes. Tim Finch. Local pain in my ass, if you'll excuse me speaking ill. Lots of unneeded calls. Not an amiable human. But not deserving of . . . Well, you'll see. He wasn't a favorite, but it's a crime, and we are police officers. Even Tim Finch deserves better. And, detectives?"

"Yes?" they replied in tandem.

"Solve this quickly, please. No more murders here. Especially in this rain."

He held up the tape as they ducked under, walking down the alley, stopping to put on plastic boots and gloves. There were people in full white hazmat outfits and bright lights illuminated various spots. A person gestured them along a marked path that already been swept for evidence. A small tent was perched nearer the west side of the alley about twenty feet in, soon after backyard fences for the Haydocks on the east side of the alley and the Dixons on the west started. The Haydocks' fence was taller, brown wood slats rising directly out of the street. Though if Marlowe's memory served, the backyard itself was raised up two feet higher than the alley. The Dixons' fence gleamed bright white, opposing the cloudy, rain-soaked morning—painted wood slats with a reinforcing short wall of white concrete bricks on the alley side. Approaching the tent and body, a short man wearing one of the white bodysuits came around the front of the tent, spotlights giving him a strangely elongated shadow.

"Doctor Peterson," Detective Morven said. Marlowe raised one hand in lieu of a spoken greeting or handshake.

The doctor's oval face and glasses, which he took off to polish as they talked, were dotted with rain. His head was hooded, one strand of silvering hair escaped and plastered to his forehead, curled like a question mark. He pulled down the facemask he'd been wearing over his nose and mouth. "Detectives. Lovely morning for it. I don't suppose either of you brought a cappuccino?"

"Unfortunately not."

"Ah well. Dream on, dream on, of foamy coffee that's hot. And of bloody deeds and death, this wet morning." As they talked, periodic bursts illuminated the inside of the tent wall; a photographer taking pictures of the body within.

"Sure, Doc." Marlowe flicked rain off his sleeve in a losing battle. "What do we know?"

"I'd say there are more things in heaven and earth, Horatio, though at this stage there aren't that many things I'd go on record with or swear to in court, earthly or heavenly."

"But . . ."

"Victim, as you've been told I'm sure, is Tim Finch. Mid-seventies, male, approximately six feet in height, 180 pounds."

"And . . ."

"You want crime details, a forensic foundation set on blood?"

"It is raining."

"I believe from my initial review that he was killed by a blunt instrument via a blow to the back right section of skull. You'll see this soon, but to provide a preview, an eight-and-a-half by three-quarter-inch white brick was found near the body. Picked up by the CSI team. To my eye, blood and hair remained on it. The brick might match those along this fence, which itself appears to have one brick missing. Hard to see with the tent up, but procedures have been followed. The brick appears to match the traumatic head wound on the victim. I'm not saying this as truth, but first observations."

"Fair enough. Thanks."

Morven had been quiet, but spoke up now. "Any idea on time of death?"

"As you know, every person may be a master of their time, Detective. And as you'd guess, it is too soon to give an accurate time of death. However, and again, do not ask me to testify yet, the street underneath the body was drier than the street alongside the body. Our June rain, unwelcome as it may be, introduced itself to us beginning at one this morning. I would say, then, death occurred after that. If that's helpful?"

"Very," she replied.

"When can the body be transported to its next resting place? To get the final answers to these many questions, alacrity would help. The sooner the better, so to speak."

"As soon as CSI signs off. We'll put an ASAP in."

"Do you need to view in situ?"

"We should. When photos are done."

The doctor ducked into the tent, said something to the person inside, grabbed a black bag and began to walk off.

"One more question?" Marlowe asked.

"'O, call back yesterday!' What is it?"

"What was he wearing?"

"Not exactly my bailiwick, Detective, but jeans, T-shirt, sneakers, jean jacket. Wallet in back pocket. No phone that I saw recovered, but one of these fine people in white may have found one. Keys in front pocket. No hat. With that, I'm off, but expect a full report. Later." He started down the alley.

"Doc," Marlowe yelled. Doctor Peterson stopped, tilting his head. "One last thing. Lynley's Café on 15th. Couple of blocks. Coffee is worthy."

The pathologist gave an exaggerated bow, swinging arms and bag, and said as water flowed off his sleeves, "I am in your debt, as they say, forever."

Marlowe turned to Morven. "That was helpful . . . ish. Surprised you got him on time of death. That usually sends pathologists at the scene around the gully."

"The rain probably helped. He wanted to get out. Timing could point to any of our three scenarios. I lean toward blackmail. Late night payoff more likely than emotionally driven revenge killing, and wandering into an alley late at night to be picked off by opportunistic local serial killer feels a remote possibility, not following the Tim Finch MO of watching what happens from within his own home domain."

"Fair points."

The photographer inside the tent, a woman wearing one of the androgynous full white suits, exited carrying a massive camera in one hand and a bag in the other. She shifted the bag strap over her shoulder.

"Done?" Marlowe asked.

"Yep. Your viewing, if you want."

"Thanks. Shall we duck in?"

Morven's reply was sturdy but soft, "Sure. Can we both fit?"

"Should be able to make it." He crouched down, opening the tent flap allowing both to fit partially in. Tim Finch's body was face down, one hand splayed above the head, one at an unnatural angle to the side. A deep red crease parted his white hair on the back right side, with the hair plastered around his head. The tent had stopped the ground around him from getting soaked, but it was partially puddling. Part of the brick fence was viewable next to him, bright white bricks a grim contrast to the body's sickly pallor and dreary alley surface. Small numbers used to mark various things for CSI dotted the scene.

Morven's phone began to ring, and she slipped out of the tent over to the other side of the alley, answering it. "Detective Morven here. Hello, Nelson."

Marlowe walked over, both crouching near the Haydocks' fence in an attempt to shield a little from the rain. He couldn't hear the exact words from Nelson, but could tell he was talking rapidly. The CSI team bustled around them, a swarm of white taking samples and photos, making measurements, and more. The rain came down, tailing off from steady to scattered.

Morven finished the call and slipped her phone back in her pocket.

"Sergeant Nelson, I presume?" Marlowe slapped his cap gently against the fence, knocking off droplets.

"At full speed. I asked Nelson to call and set up some formal interviews at the station. I requested the Howards and at least Neville Cassell, if not both Cassells."

"Maybe the affair wasn't as over for him as he said?"

"That was my thought," Morven agreed.

"Good thought. Worth following up. Time to light some fires, including a high-ranking one—our august council member. Her story about her disagreement with Lucy Dixon doesn't ring true. I'm going to call her office, see about a follow-up. This alley's crowd is too thick for that particular call, and I tend to feel like a dog in the road when the scientists are humming. I'm going to amble over across the street. Could you track down the lead investigator here, see about anything specific they can tell us?"

"Can do," Morven said, already eyeing the CSI team for a likely lead. "I'll check in with Officer Troy again too. He's got a good scope of the neighborhood. And he'll know which officer has checked in with Toby Dixon, and Rory, as well as the Haydocks. See if they have anything to report from those preliminaries. Plus, I'll get his notes, or whichever officer's, about the jogger. If door-to-door farther afield hasn't happened, we'll need to round up officers for that too."

"Sounds like a strategy. Go team," Marlowe said, smacking his wet cap again against the fence to knock off some of the water, running a hand over his now-wet bald head. Even his mustache seeped drops. Walking cautiously down the alley, he gave one more view to the tent where Tim Finch's remains were before ducking under police tape with a quick salute in Officer Troy's direction. He stopped to remove protective booties and gloves, tossing them into a trash can, then trotted across 77th Avenue toward the Community Center.

The crowd of gawkers, onlookers and reporters perched under umbrellas near the wide trunks of a handful of sky-stretching Douglas Fir and Western Red Cedar trees on the playground's edge, hoping to get respite from the rain without sacrificing a view of the alley's action. *That crowd's thinned since we first pulled up. Crowd control is one rainy-day benefit*, Marlowe thought, angling away from the gathered group to grab privacy for his call.

Time to speed up their investigations. The first round of interviews had set up a solid foundation. Now that they had a few more facts, time to start increasing pressure on the neighborhood folks. Two murders in less than a week? No one was off limits to follow-ups under less convivial circumstances. Including Suri Cane. Giving a look to ensure he wasn't trailed by random crime scene stalkers or roving reporters hoping for a scoop, he stepped onto the big greensward between the Community Center's brick building and playground, glancing toward where Lucy's body had been found as he walked. That scene had been cleared. No police tape remained, and he couldn't see anything indicating murder had happened outside of a few flowers strewn along the sidewalk, soaked with rain.

Pulling out his phone, he called the City Council office number he'd been given, which was picked up before the first ring died down. "Hello, City Council." The voice was far too chipper for a rainy morning in June.

"Yes, this is Detective Marlowe, City Police. I need to talk to Council Member Cane, please."

"One moment, Detective. Council Member Cane is currently unavailable. Could I patch you to her assistant, Fran Collier?"

"That would be dandy."

"Thank you. One moment please."

He watched the crowd watch the police and CSI, listening to five minutes of the "Summer" movement in Vivaldi's *Four Seasons*, wondering if the choice was a deliberate way to get constituents to hang up, before a less chipper, but still fairly chipper, voice came on the line. One with a hint of what he thought might be an Irish accent.

"Council Member Cane's office, Fran Collier speaking."

"Hello. This is Detective Marlowe, City Police. I need to talk with Council Member Cane."

"Is it an urgent matter, Detective? Is it her family?"

"Not her family, but fairly urgent."

"Her schedule is sadly very full, Detective. Can I be of assistance?"

"No, it's the council member I need to speak to. Today. At the station."

"Is it possible to tell me more? Her calendar today isn't grand. She's up to ninety, busy, I mean. Is this a city council matter?"

"A follow-up to a conversation she and I had recently about an incident in her neighborhood. Fairly urgent."

"Let me see. If I move this, then shorten this." He pictured her in front of a monitor as she talked. His water-logged mustached drooped.

"Then we should have time opening here, and she could move here. How about three-thirty, Detective?"

"Grand. I'll meet her at the police station front desk. Thank you."

"Nice one, Detective. Thank you."

The rain-splattered phone slipped into his pocket after he tried and failed to wipe it off with the inside of his sports coat. It was too wet. The Community Center, the lawn he was on, the basketball court, the playground and playfields, the sidewalks, the cove where Lucy's body had been found, the alley where Tim Finch's body had been found, the houses and yards surrounding him . . . wet. If someone wanted to make a TV show about these murders, they'd have the perfect day for it with the city's damp reputation on full display. He switched his view, gazing in the direction where one body was found without focusing, then in the direction where a second body was found, then back, then back again. What was going on in this neighborhood, this village within the city?

The lick on his hand snapped him out of murderous deliberation, causing him to jump back and swing his right arm, nearly knocking over John Arthur, who'd walked up without him noticing and causing Ainsley to begin jumping up and down as if on a doggy pogo stick, letting loose with high-pitched barks.

"Sorry, Detective, we—" John started.

"My fault, Mr. Arthur, didn't see you," Marlowe cut in.

Ainsley barked so much, two wet crows perched on the nearby Center basketball hoop took off for a quieter perch.

"Ainsley, quiet. And John, please. It's too wet for formalities." He bent down, scratching the dog behind her ears, and proffered a treat from one coat pocket, causing her to sit and stop barking, though her tail flicked water off the grass onto their legs.

Marlowe wasn't sure what to make of John showing up at another crime scene, but he wasn't completely surprised either. "Tuesday walk route?"

"We took the normal Tuesday morning walk earlier. This counts as an extra walk for Ains. Not that she loves the rain. I was drawn to the sirens and scene, which is gruesome to admit."

"Natural occurrence, even on wet days."

"I also felt, upon hearing about it, like I should stop by. Pay respects. Or get it out of my system. After talking to you about him yesterday, I almost feel as if I'm responsible. Though I know that sentiment's silly."

"You know who the victim is?"

"Not 100 percent know, to be honest. Heard from Jimmy that he'd heard on their community chat group from nearly all the neighbors that they guessed. Also stood near the crowd, where much gossip is being shared. It's Tim Finch, I take it?"

Marlowe wasn't sure how to reply. He shouldn't confirm the victim's name yet, but John Arthur already knew it seemed, as did other neighbors. The man had put out some interesting, well, strange, but maybe helpful theories. And could be a suspect. He decided it was a solid choice to affirm it.

"We haven't released the name, but yes. Between us."

"Not surprising. Sad, still. But not surprising."

"Why?" Marlowe asked, nervous as to what British TV show he'd be in for now.

"He seemed the type. Generally an unfriendly person. Probably a blackmailer. Nearly every British mystery show has had a character who knows too much, blackmails or tries to otherwise coerce the killer, and then ends up killed. I feel awful reducing it to that, and know that most of the shows aren't direct reflections of real life, but you can learn a lot from them."

"A man is dead, we know that."

"Two people dead. It's that conundrum we talked about. I can't stop thinking about the crimes, how and why they happened, and then feel despair at the fact I'm thinking about them."

They both stood in the rain, Ainsley's tail flicking drops from grass the only sound.

"'Perhaps now he will finally find peace.'" John sighed. Noticing

Marlowe's questioning look, he said, "Sorry. Another quote from the *Father Brown* episode I mentioned. He's got a good heart, the Father. Not sure I could live up to him. But I do hope whatever happens next, someone as pettily angry as Tim Finch was, I hope he's less angry."

"I hope for no more murders in your neighborhood."

"That too, Detective."

"Your British mystery solving friends usually stop at two?"

"Depends on the show. *Midsomer Murders*, usually three. *Father Brown*, usually one. *Unforgotten*, one, but a cold case. *Agatha Raisin*, three. *Shakespeare and Hathaway*, one, or none. I could go on, but let's say an average of two."

"Any have to deal with rain?" Drips were cascading off Marlowe's cap, one plopping onto Ainsley's floppy right ear, causing her to move and execute a tremendous headshake that then spread more drops. You couldn't escape the rain.

"Some. The UK is known for wet weather, too. It doesn't rain as much as shows depicting us, this city I mean. Maybe the show *Vera* rains as much. Takes place on the Northumberland coast. Drearily pretty."

"Vera?"

"Detective in the Northumberland and City Police. Played by the brilliant Brenda Blethyn. A few demons in her past, as they have. Prickly personality at times, as they also have. Drives a battered 1990s Land Rover Defender—a Jeep-ish, seaweed-green truck. Clothes rumpled as if she just woke up. Wears a trench hat—a rain hat—continually. You might like her, she's a bit like you."

"That a compliment?"

"She is incredibly astute at noticing facts other people miss, pulling random threads together, and supports her team, if gruffly. Great show. 'I'm watching you, pet.'"

"What?"

"She calls people 'pet.' Wish I could get away with it. She also says 'now we're getting somewhere' a lot as the show careens to a conclusion. Let's hope you have cause to use that one soon."

"Yep. Speaking of, time for me to mosey. And Ainsley is damp." She'd gone over to Marlowe again, leaning on his leg as he petted her.

"Onward. Busy day, I'm sure. Lots of suspects, clues, facts, interviews, reinterviews. Time for an interview montage?"

Even in the rain, it was easy to see Marlowe's thick eyebrows raise under his hat brim.

"You know, interview montage? When the police or FBI or Irish Garde bring in multiple suspects or people of interest at once. The main characters—the DCI, the DS, the DCs, the detectives—can't interview each one at the same time, so they separate, each interviewing a separate suspect. But then for the show, they cut the interviews together, going back and forth. Dramatic effect, I suppose. Or for the viewer to see how the suspects stack up, how they might contradict each other. We see it happening nearly at the same time, though of course the detectives don't. Interview montage."

"John?"

"Yes, Detective?"

"TV. Real life. Different."

"Just thinking out loud."

Marlowe gave a wave, starting to walk off.

"*Dib, Dib, Dib,*" John said.

"What?" said Marlowe, confused once more.

"One last Father Brown. Originally from the British Boy Scouts, I believe. Shorthand for do your best."

"We will, John, don't worry."

9

At the office, Nelson's activity level bounced from high to nearly knocking over colleagues. He'd started by diving into more reports and backgrounds on the neighborhood suspects, broken up by doing calf stretches while studying the board and squeezing a stress ball while checking with forensics. Then he'd talked to Morven, rerouted into attempting to set up interviews. He'd first got on the phone to Joyce Howard. She'd said that Sarah wouldn't be able to make an interview without getting a sub for her Molecular Cell Biology classes, but that she herself could be at the station at ten. But that was the only time. It seemed almost as if she wanted to do the interview without Sarah.

Her pointedness about time had left him in a bit of a dilemma. He knew Marlowe and Morven wouldn't be back by ten. And knew they'd probably want to take the lead on any interview. However, Morven had said that being a good detective means taking initiative, and Marlowe had told him that often one had to blaze their own trail. Both sides of his internal argument pinged around his head like lead ping-pong balls in the moment's pause before he told Joyce that ten would be perfect. *I'll take the interview myself*, he thought. *I'm ready. Sometimes it's better to ask forgiveness than permission.* He'd attempted setting up an interview with Neville Cassell as well, but the man put him off at first. Nelson convinced him the sooner he talked to them at the station, the sooner it'd be over, leaving it with the interview set up for three thirty.

From there, he'd spent more time on research, hit the canteen for a bagel with salmon cream cheese and a peppermint tea, skipping the atrocious coffee with no need to buy one for Marlowe, and arranged his papers and Interview Plan of Action (calling it his I-POA). His phone rang on his fourth round of rereading his I-POA, and when jumping to grab it, he knocked his tea over, soaking his notes. The front desk was calling to say a Joyce Howard was here for him. He quickly wiped his hands off before heading down, forgetting any notes except a single sheet of paper detailing the odd deposits in Lucy Dixon's personal accounts. It wasn't until opening the door to the station's entry room that he felt a dampness permeating his slacks. Tea. Still warm.

Joyce Howard rose off one of the benches along the walls to greet him, wearing a loose-fitting, khaki-colored trench coat with wide collar and cuffs over a knitwear crewneck dress (which, he thought randomly, was the color of slightly roasted corn husks) and tall, shimmering black boots. Everyone else in from the morning's downpour appeared drowned, ratlike, but she could have walked off a catwalk, hair luxuriously layered around shoulders and not a mascara smudge evident. Nelson appreciated sartorial splendor like only a few other police officers and, as he was working with the detectives, had worn today instead of his uniform a slim-fit, single-breasted navy suit that he *really* shouldn't have spent so much on. Feeling a drip along the back of his leg, he went toward her.

"Mrs. Howard, I am Sergeant Nelson, working with Detectives Marlowe and Morven. Thank you so much for coming down. Sorry you had to make the trip in this rain. Juneuary has hit us like a linebacker."

She smiled breezily. "I'm actually okay with the rain. Wash away the bad feelings. And happy to come down. Hopefully helpful. Sorry Sarah couldn't make it. She's pretty stressed at the U at the moment."

"Come this way, please. We'll go to a room just down this hall." Nelson opened the door, and she passed by, trailing a whiff of floral yet woodsy perfume, for a moment transporting him into a shaded springtime grove. He shook his head. *Keep your brain in the game, Nelson*, he thought, walking with her down the hall. *It's go time.*

"Right in here, Mrs. Howard." He opened the door to one of the station's nondescript interview rooms, one he had remembered to set up earlier with out-of-sight recording devices. "Before we start, would you like any coffee, water, or tea?"

"I believe I'm fine. Though something about this room . . . Does it smell like peppermint tea?"

"Lots of the officers in this station like tea."

"I would have never imagined police officers and tea. This is my first time to a police station. Exciting, I'm sure. You only live once, you know?"

"Um, yeah." The way she talked and her slightly ironic look, all of her, made him lightheaded. And his slacks had slightly stuck to the chair.

"What can I help you with, Sergeant Nelson?"

"First, thank you again for coming down. We need to clarify a few facts and felt it would be best to do it here."

With a brief laugh sounding like some exotic bird, she asked, "I don't need a lawyer, do I?"

"You are well within your rights to have a lawyer present at all times in the station during questioning."

"I was kidding. Just a chat?"

"Correct." Nelson tightened his toes within his Derbies, one of which contained a puddle of tea and soaked sock. He was going to keep focused no matter what. "We are recording this conversation, to be clear. Is that okay with you?"

"Breezy, Detective. Fine and dandy."

"Can we begin by going over again what you did after the party last Friday?"

"Easy enough. I went home, had a nightcap with Sarah after tucking Betty into bed, then we went to bed ourselves. Brushed my teeth first. Can't skip hygiene, Sergeant." Her smile radiated.

"You didn't go back out at all? Back to the party?"

"Nope."

"Did it appear to be winding up as you were leaving?"

"It felt . . . slowing. With Jimmy you never know, as he'll stay up and chat, drink in hand."

"Did Lucy usually stay late?"

"Some nights. She liked a party, liked a drink, liked to talk." The last words contained less of her normal suavity.

"Where were you and Sarah last night?" The quick change of topic question was an old strategy, he knew, but Nelson hoped it might throw her off.

"Yikes, that was an abrupt change," she replied, smiling her knowing smile. "Though I thought we'd talk about last night. Another crime in the neighborhood. Hard to swallow. We were home. Normal night. Dinner, Netflix, studying for Bets. I had a glass of rosé. Bed. Then this morning, all those sirens."

"Talk to any other people last night? In person or on the phone? Anyone not in the family?"

"No, not last night."

"Did you know anything—"

She interrupted him gently. "About the death of Mr. Finch? We heard who it was already. And had nothing to do with it."

"How did you hear?"

"Neighborhood text chain. No lie, I can't remember who mentioned it first. Cassells? Haydocks? Bear with." She pulled her phone out of her pocket, clicked on it. "No, it was the Canes."

"You didn't like him much, Tim Finch? The creep, I believe you called him to the detectives?"

"Very impressive memory, Sergeant. No, we didn't like him. He was creepy. But not so much that we would attack him. We're shook by it. By both crimes."

She seemed so cool for someone being questioned by police. Not a hair out of place, her coat magically dry and draped artistically across shoulders, black boots stretched out under the table. Whereas he felt like a damp paper towel from the waist down, one shoe full of tea, feet tucked under his chair like a short school kid so he didn't accidentally kick hers. He had even forgotten to unbutton his jacket and couldn't remember any of his planned I-POA strategies. But as he placed his hand back on the table, he felt that single sheet of paper he'd brought, currently face down. It seemed worth a try. Maybe she was the one funneling Lucy the two $5,000 deposits. And then he remembered reading in Morven's notes that John Arthur had overheard them arguing, using the word money.

"Can we go back to Mrs. Dixon?"

"Whatever is helpful to you." She smiled.

"You said you were friends with her, but not close friends."

"Not best friends, or BFFs as Betty would say, but you know, friendly."

"Ever have a problem with her, an argument or altercation, or was there any reason you went through a non-friendly period?"

"We were friendly. Simpatico, really."

"Would it surprise you if I said I had a witness who has reported to us that they saw you and Mrs. Dixon arguing in an aggressive manner on your front porch in the recent past?"

She sat silently, moved slightly in her chair, then said, "Who?"

"Is this true?"

"No. Well, yes. Not violently. I don't remember that." She took off her coat, shrugging it onto the back of her chair, looking uncomfortable. Her dress color is amazing, Nelson briefly mused. Wonder where she got it? "You did have an altercation with Mrs. Dixon?"

"I wouldn't use the word altercation. Disagreement is closer to the mark."

"What was the disagreement about?"

"I barely recall. Nothing much. I think some flowers she picked up at the shop that she'd ordered. Big bouquet. Flames of Love. Oranges and reds exploding in colors—lilies, gerbera daisies, salvia, one or two roses, baby's breath. She didn't believe it was worth the money, thought the description given was more expressive than the final flower arrangement."

"The disagreement was solely about flowers?"

"Yes. It was. People can be very attached to a picture they make in their mind, and then when the natural world doesn't match, they get angry."

Nelson turned the paper over so it appeared he was reading from it, saying, "Are you sure it wasn't about money?"

Joyce's face dropped, shocked.

Keeping his eye on the paper, Nelson continued. "In the last two months, Mrs. Dixon made two deposits in her personal account for $5,000. Exactly. In cash. Did you give her that money?"

She hadn't looked up, and didn't say anything as he continued.

"Mrs. Howard? Are you sure your disagreement with Mrs. Dixon wasn't about this money?"

Joyce stretched her sleeves' cuffs around her fingers and didn't reply.

"Did you give her the $10,000?"

"No. Yes."

"Why? That's a lot of money."

"Donation. She called it a donation, at least."

"To?"

"The Lucy Dixon fund, I'm guessing."

"Why would you donate to her? I mean, why give her that much money?"

She rubbed her eyes, her temples, not replying. Nelson sat and waited. Finally, she met his eyes, the coolness drained out of her. "Okay. No use in hiding it. You'll find out anyway, eventually. I was charged with embezzlement. Long ago. Over twenty years. I was just eighteen, working in a chain of flower shops in Chicago. Somehow, my stupidity combined with my stupidity around an unscrupulous older man, the owner, made it so I was in charge of finances for a short period of time. I ended up, mistakenly I swear, leaving with just under $1,000 of the chain's money. The owner left with more, much more, but I was charged. Pleaded out, escaped jail time, just a fine."

"Embezzlement is a serious crime, but how does that lead to you paying off Lucy Dixon?"

"She found out somehow—through legal contacts, I don't know—about the embezzlement charge. We were up late one night, end of the night after drinking heavily, talking about things we've done we regretted. She was good getting people to talk about secret stuff, making it feel admirable, cool somehow. I admitted to once lying on an application. No details, and regretted saying it instantly. But red wine and whiskey and flattery are a potent combination."

Nelson nodded, saying nothing. After a long moment, she continued.

"I didn't worry about it. But Lucy was resourceful, I'll give her that. She must have dug into my history somehow, or made a good guess. She found out about the embezzlement charge, and that I'd never admitted it on the loan application for the flower shop. She came in one afternoon like sunshine and light. Butter wouldn't have melted in her mouth. Then she brought both up, smiling. Wondered if Sarah knew, she said. Wondered if the bank knew. Wondered if I'd like to donate to her favorite charity. She didn't have to name herself, her smile said it. I gave in, gave her the first $5,000, which she said would be it."

"Then she asked for another payment?"

"Yes. I should have known. That was the porch disagreement. I gave in, gave it to her. The shop's doing fine, but that's a lot of money."

"It is. Then she asked a third time?"

"Not yet."

"But you expected it?"

"Yeah. I did."

Nelson couldn't help pushing it further, thinking if he could solve the crime right now how impressed Morven and Marlowe would be. He'd get promoted to detective, probably instantly. "So you decided you had to put a stop to it. Went back to the Haydocks to meet her, or made plans to meet her at the Community Center. She was a blackmailer, so you thought: end it now. Then you killed her."

"What!" She stood up, backing from the table. "What? No. I did not kill Lucy Dixon. No."

"Mrs. Howard, I'm sorry, please sit." He motioned apologetically and she sat, pulling the chair back to the table.

She took a breath. "I would have had to do something, but murder wouldn't be it. I made a mistake, trusted the wrong person, long ago. But I'm not a murderer. Lucy was awful to me. Maybe she was just awful period and we all ignored it. But she didn't deserve to be killed. I would have told Sarah. Will tell her everything, today. I didn't kill Lucy. That's all I have to say, Sergeant. Unless you are charging me?"

He didn't think he had enough to Miranda her, and knew he shouldn't take it any further. And for some reason, he wasn't sold that she was the murderer. Lucy Dixon's blackmail had been harrowing, but enough for Joyce to murder her? He'd need to bounce it off Marlowe and Morven.

"No charges at the moment, Mrs. Howard. I can walk you out. Please reach out if you remember anything more, or if you've forgotten anything. I'm sure I or one of the detectives will be in touch."

Back at his desk, after a stop in the bathroom to wring out his right sock, Nelson began logging interview notes. He didn't have a second suit at the office, and wasn't going to create a stir or fashion car wreck by putting on a pair of police-issued sweatpants from the gym with his luckily unsoaked suit coat and shirt, which meant he'd deal with the remaining dampness and peppermint aroma that wafted about him like a fragrant cloud. He *did* keep backup socks in his backpack and made a quick change. *That dryness is a treat*, he thought, slipping his shoeless feet under the desk.

Just in time, as he heard Morven talking to Marlowe. They'd hung up wet coats and hats on a rack on the way in, but Marlowe's shoes were squeaking slightly in time with Morven's sentences.

"John Arthur at another scene. Curious."

Marlowe pulled out the chair at his desk, sitting down. Morven stood. "Sergeant Nelson, how're things at the ranch?" Marlowe asked.

"A little in the win-some, lose-some category sir. I'm entering notes about my interview with Joyce Howard, which concluded not long ago."

"You interviewed Joyce Howard? Do tell."

"Wait," Morven interrupted, perched on the edge of her desk, Nelson in a chair between the detectives. "What's the herbal smell? Peppermint?"

"Yeah," Nelson replied nonchalantly. "Someone, maybe Hathaway, you know how he is, spilled tea earlier. Peppermint. I had to clean it up. Still smells, doesn't it?"

Her narrowed eyes didn't imply belief, but she said, "It does. A lot."

"Did you know," Nelson asked, "the tea market in the US is growing by 5 percent per year? Catching up with coffee."

"Coffee is better," Marlowe declared. "Now, can we continue along the interview trail? How did you end up interviewing Joyce Howard?"

"Right." Nelson jumped up, forgetting he only wore socks, nearly slipped, caught himself on the desk, and continued as if nothing had happened. "She wanted to come in specifically at ten. I knew you were going to be out, so I"—he glanced at Morven—"took the initiative and interviewed her myself."

"Sounds like you did at that," Marlowe drawled. "And it went how?"

"The recording will tell the full tale of the tape, but to give you the highlight: Lucy Dixon was blackmailing Joyce Howard. I took a chance when remembering John Arthur had heard them arguing about money. Turns out, Joyce has a fairly well-hidden embezzlement charge from when she was eighteen and didn't mention it on her flower shop loan app. Lucy found out, getting the 10K from her in blackmail payments."

"Murder confession?" Morven asked.

"No. She swears she didn't commit the crime, though she was in a corner."

Marlowe leaned back. "Believe she's shooting straight on that?"

Nelson considered. "I think I do, sir. She is a cool character, but I believed her, especially around the fact that Sarah doesn't know about the embezzlement or the blackmail so would have no reason to give her an alibi. In my opinion, we should keep her in the frame as a suspect, but not a prime suspect. It does expand our knowledge of Lucy Dixon, who isn't as nice or as liked as expected."

"Sound reasoning. Get those notes in."

"Nice work, Sergeant," Morven said as Nelson sat back down and turned to her desk, where he'd set up a laptop.

"How was the SOC?" he asked her.

"Interesting," she said. "I'll write it up, but death occurred after 1:00 a.m., making time of death approximately between one and five. Death was caused by a blunt instrument, mostly likely a brick found at the scene, which was the alley between 20th and 21st. Body was near the Dixons' back wall, which is partially made of bricks."

"Wow," Nelson replied. "You got TOD at the scene?"

"That was Morven's doing," Marlowe said, nodding. "Doc wagoned it and the blunt instrument in non-committals, but helpful."

Nelson stood up. "So, it happened here." He pointed at the map of the neighborhood on the crime board. "Perhaps putting Toby Dixon in the frame. He found out Tim Finch killed his wife and took revenge? Or killed his wife, and Tim Finch found out, and he had to kill him too. Or the Haydocks? James Haydock taking revenge on the man who killed his neighbor, who ruined this lovely neighborhood group? Far-fetched? Neville Cassell, who is coming in for an interview at three thirty by the way, killed the man who killed his lover? Council Member Cane cleaning up the streets?" His breath finally ran out.

"Easy, Nelson," Morven replied. "I did talk to Officer Troy, and other officers on the scene who did the door-knocking, specifically relating to the Dixons and Haydocks. Toby Dixon said he had been home all the previous night, hadn't left his house. To quote the officer, 'He smelled as if he'd pickled himself in IPA after rolling in a stagnant field of hops.' And he admitted to being hungover. Rory backed up his story. Could the hangover be a ruse? The Haydocks said they'd had an early night, stayed in, and hadn't heard anything until morning sirens. Alibied each other, but could be covering."

"Same with Joyce Howard," Nelson said. "Home last night. She did know about it being Tim Finch. Said all the neighbors do."

"Fast acting, that bunch." Marlowe's booted feet stretched up on the desk as he reached for the olive-wood bowl.

For a moment, they were quiet. Marlowe breathing in his bowl. Morven pointing at Nelson's stockinged feet giving him a questioning glance. Him trying to ignore her stare by pointedly gazing at the board full of pictures of Lucy Dixon and the neighbors. Then Marlowe spoke up.

"We need to keep dibbing."

"Dibbing?" Morven questioned.

"Digging. Digging. Not dibbing. That reminds me, I was telling Morven how I chewed more fat with John Arthur at the Community Center this morning."

"He was at another scene? In the rain? Morbid curiosity seeker, or suspect revisiting the scene of their crime?"

"Not sure on Mr. Arthur. Mystery obsessive, murderer, or lonely? Anything out of the ordinary on him?"

"Not yet," Morven said. "We need to keep digging. And log today's notes from the scene and from your interview, Nelson. Paperwork waits for no person."

"More interviews coming over today's horizon as well." Marlowe picked up an empty coffee mug while talking. "Perhaps we should invite Mr. Arthur for another interview? Council Member Cane and Neville Cassell are both at three thirty. Make it a trio. But first."

"Yes?"

"Coffee. Nelson, you may want tea? Can you grab it for us? If, that is, you can find shoes."

All three, Morven and Nelson sharing a desk, Marlowe solo at his own, intently focused on screens and notepads. They had dug back into various reports and research and data entry around the two murders, when someone nearby loudly cleared their throat.

"What the . . ." Startled, Marlowe nearly spilled what remained of his coffee, catching it with one hand, steadying it with the other. "Oh, Doc, didn't hear you arrive."

"My wary walking, I suppose."

"Um, sure, that works. What's the latest? We don't often see you up here."

"I felt it was my duty to save Detective Morven and Sergeant Nelson from further stress upon their distal interphalangeal joints."

"Thank you, Doctor," Morven replied. "Which joints are those?"

He grinned. "Your final finger joints. Meaning, I'm saving you from making more calls to my office by stopping here amongst you to drop off the Lucy Dixon nearly final notes. And to give the briefest of Tim Finch updates. I had been partaking of the canteen's cakes and ale and felt stopping here would save time." He held out a manila folder.

"Always welcome, Doctor," Marlowe said, slightly standing to grab the folder. "Highlights?"

"Lucy Dixon, to begin our brief afternoon association here at your desks, detectives. And Sergeant." He made a brief bow, swinging out his arms and white lab coat when rising, like a deranged dove on stage.

Morven and Marlowe, used to the pathologist's eccentric ways, didn't flinch, but Nelson, newer to working with the short, dramatic doctor, shifted backward in his chair, eyes opening wide.

"As surmised in the early hours of our investigation, she died from asphyxia due to external neck pressure caused by—the CSI team and I are in accord upon this currently, but reserve the right of altering if more evidence arises from the depths—the shoelace found at the scene, whose particular form and texture matches marks on her neck. Her murderer would have stood behind her, probably above either from being taller or as she was kneeling or on the ground, and had a hold of the lace on each end, applying pressure that caused her eventual death. Not a pretty picture." He looked around like a conjurer.

He took a breath, then said in an actorly whisper, "Death will come when it will come." Changing to his regular voice, he continued. "Which in Lucy Dixon's case, is estimated to have happened between 1:00 a.m. and 3:00 a.m. on the night in question. She had eaten well, if that's of interest. Pork in sausage form, steak of some kind, flank I'd hazard, peppers, onions, zucchini, cheese, and for dessert, blackberry and apple pie."

"Detailed," Marlowe snuck in.

"It's the details that the devil is within, they say. She ate well. And drank like Falstaff, meaning no disrespect to either her or the Shakespearean character. Drank that night, to render this specifically. She didn't show a history of overly excessive imbibing, though moderate drinking was in evidence. However, the night in question, she consumed in revelry. Wine, whiskey and—not song, as you might expect—but gin and some herbal liqueur or digestif. Unkind spirits, here. She would have been heavily intoxicated at estimated time of death."

"Enough to make it hard for her to struggle against even a small assailant?"

"I would concur with your statement. In addition, it would have made her susceptible, uninhibited. I would imagine easily duped, vulnerable."

"Understood. More on Lucy Dixon?"

"Nothing to call out. Read the full report and if questions arise like dawn light on a winter's day, do reach out. On to Tim Finch, the second of our 77th Avenue NW victims. Out, out brief candles. I must, as you may have guessed, even up here within the heavens, caution by admitting that these details I do unveil could change as we continue on the forensic path."

All nodded, somewhat spellbound.

"Blow to the back of the head, blunt object, death, as the detectives know, probably between 1:00 and 5:00 a.m. On my initial non-alley overview, the brick recovered at the scene with what appears to be blood on it could well be the murder weapon. It matches the wound. CSI is doing DNA checks, act accordingly. The blow it appears came from an angle implying the assailant was above the victim."

"Someone taller?"

"I'd shudder to assume, Detective Marlowe. I do repent, and yet I do despair that you'd have me make that fact. Above. Not taller."

"Understood. Instantaneous death?"

"The full report, Detective, the full report. But so as not to offend, and if you don't hold me too it, I would guess not. The alley showed signs of shuffling, which may have been him and may not. The knees of his jeans had small tears, as if he'd crawled. He could have done them anytime, another time. Take with the grain of salt and do not call me again today."

"Thanks, Doc, thanks."

He walked off, muttering to himself as the three officers waved.

"Always the doc, the doc," said Marlowe. "Let's get the time of death for both victims on the board. What do we now know?"

Both Morven and Nelson began to talk at once, before the former stopped, saying, "Please, you first," exaggeratedly.

Nelson gave a short bow. "Sorry, Detective, and thanks. Thanks both of you, for letting me help out. What I believe is that every neighbor at the party is back in the frame as a suspect given that Lucy Dixon was heavily inebriated and therefore easy to handle. There seem to have been multiple suspects carrying possible motives, and with more background, more could surface."

"Tim Finch?" Morven replied. "He was older but not a small man, so the angle has to be a consideration."

"Agreed," Marlowe said. "Could be getting him to a kneeling position using money as bait, as we know he wasn't opposed to attempts at blackmail, doesn't seem impossible. We are moving forward but need to put our licks in before more time passes."

"Or before another murder."

"I certainly hope not. Let's make these interviews count. Nelson, you want to duo with Morven on the Cassell interview?"

"Definitely, sir."

"Good. Council Member Cane for me at the same time. John Arthur after." He was silent for a moment, then said softly to himself, "interview montage."

"What was that?" Morven asked.

"Nothing. Interview montage. Influence of conversations with suspect Arthur. British TV mysteries on the brain."

"Suspect Arthur?"

"Everyone is a suspect until the case is solved."

"Agreed. Sergeant Nelson, we don't have much time before our interview, but as we are both conversant with the facts of the case and with Neville Cassell's history with the first victim, shouldn't be a problem. I believe we should push him more on his interactions with Lucy after she broke it off. He seems nervous to me, and I don't feel he's told us everything. He's been in more contact with her than he's letting on."

Nelson's hand went up.

"Yes?" Morven's skepticism was mostly hidden.

"Can I come up with an I-POA?"

Marlowe's feet went on the desk and he momentarily closed his eyes, thumbing his suspenders as Morven responded.

"I-POA? I'm not sure I recall that one, Nelson. New addition to the training handbook or the academy?"

"It's one of my own strategic acronyms. Interview plan of action. I-POA. Our game plan, or our strategy you might say for the upcoming interview. You know what they say, 'Proper prior planning prevents poor performance!'"

"I believe I received that in a fortune cookie once." She smiled and grabbed her notebook.

10

Just as Marlowe, Morven, and Nelson were about to head to the front of the station to meet their various interviewees—notebooks and notes in the latter two's hands, a big mug brimming with coffee that said *Davison's Deli: Support Your Local Butcher* in the former's—Marlowe's desk phone rang.

"This is Marlowe," he said into the black, old-fashioned office phone.

"Got it. Fine. That'll do. We'll be down momentarily."

"Interesting." He set the phone down.

"What's up? New evidence to blow this case wide open?" Nelson asked.

"No." Marlowe shook his head. "Both Cassells have arrived. You didn't know?"

"I just asked him, and he didn't mention her. But maybe they've come to confess. Maybe they were both in on it."

"Not so jumpy, Nelson." Morven made calming motions. "Talking to both is a bonus, but doesn't point to guilt automatically."

Marlowe scratched his mustache. "Wondering if cutting them is best."

The startled looks on their faces at his remark caused a smile to ripple across his thoughtful face.

"Cut as with cows, when you separate the herd out." They nodded slowly. "Separating the husband and wife into two separate interviews. I've got the council member. Morven, you could take Florence."

"Makes sense. I'll need to quickly book a room." She leaned back over to her computer, clicked a few times. "Done."

"Neat. Nelson, you up for Neville solo?"

"I think I am. I'm conversant with the case and have studied your earlier interviews with them and others. I can do it."

"Swell. Let's head down."

"Let's get this interview party started." Nelson, notebook clasped tightly under his arm, had a half skip in his step as they started walking.

Walking into the waiting area, they saw the Cassells sitting together talking softly, not noticing their arrival until Marlowe cleared his throat, sounding somewhat like a Mastiff with a cold. Both Neville and Florence backed up on their seats with the noise.

"Didn't mean to startle. Mr. Cassell, Mrs. Cassell, thank you for coming down."

"Want to help if we can." They stood as Neville spoke. He wore a caramel wool sports coat with flannel patch pockets on either side, over a white button-down shirt and faded jeans. She wore slightly muddy jeans, big hiking boots, and a green jacket with the City Parks logo on it. Both reached out hands to the detective, who shook first Neville's and then Florence's awkwardly. *Her palm*, he thought, *feels like a human Beech hand would feel*. Then he rolled his eyes inwardly at himself.

"We're glad you're here. You remember Detective Morven." They nodded. "And this is Sergeant Nelson, helping us with the case."

"It is a pleasure to meet you, Sergeant, and to see you again, Detective." Neville's nods went on sharply as Florence spoke. "We are here, though I did have to come straight from visiting with a family of bigleaf maples in Vicarage Park, bringing a bit of it with me." Seeing the confused looks, she added, "Via the mud on my boots. Will this take long?"

"It shouldn't," Marlowe replied. "If you, Mr. Cassell, could go with Sergeant Nelson, and you, Mrs. Cassell, with Detective Morven, we can get started."

"Wait, wait, I say." Neville's agitation, combined with his military-straight posture, made him appear an offspring of Ulysses S. Grant and the cartoon rooster Foghorn Leghorn. "Why aren't we going together? We did volunteer to come in and help you in your inquiries. We would rather be interviewed together."

"I appreciate your position, but it will speed things up this way."

Florence put her hand gently on Neville's arm, replying, "I am sure it will be fine, Detective. We are capable on our own, naturally. Unless this situation is growing so fast you believe we need a lawyer?"

Nelson and Morven had been standing back a half-step, but he stepped forward to get in a standard speech he'd memorized. "It is certainly your right to have an attorney present at any interview or during any step of the process, Mrs. Cassell."

She stared at Marlowe. "But do we need one?"

"We are not charging either of you with anything currently, if that helps."

"I'm sure we will be fine. We have nothing to hide, right, Neville?"

"Right, nothing." His handsome face grimaced.

"Great. Mr. Cassell, Mrs. Cassell, if you come this way with me and Sergeant Nelson, we'll go through this door." Morven opened the door, and they walked down the hall as it shut behind them, leaving Marlowe in the waiting room checking his watch. He wondered how late she'd be.

Reading a poster on the wall that said, *Wary. Watchful. Wide Awake.* under a picture of a vigilant looking officer, someone had crossed out the *Wide Awake* and scrawled *Wanker* under it in black marker alongside a line sketch of a man with a Victorian-type top hat. *Very strange*, Marlowe thought. *Is the whole city going British?* Walking up to the desk to alert the officer that maybe a new, non-swearing reference poster was needed, he heard Suri Cane's voice. Turning, he saw her finish walking through the front door, talking on her cell phone.

"Yes, Fran. No. No. Yes, I am at the police station. I see Detective Marlowe." She moved the phone a fraction away from her mouth. "Detective Marlowe, one second please." He held his hands up in acquiescence as she kept talking. "Fran, quiet. This won't take long. But to be safe, push my next meeting, with . . . Right, with him. Push it back fifteen minutes." She ended the call, slipping the phone into her shiny black leather clutch, her dress identical to the one he'd seen earlier, except a darker shade of blue.

"Detective," she gushed, "how nice to see you again. And to be here in the station where so many men and women officers work so hard to ensure the safety of our city and its citizens. It is truly an honor. Though one I can't spend nearly enough time observing as I would like."

"Understood, Council Member Cane. We appreciate you moseying down to talk."

"Moseying? I wish I had the time. But I am always helpful in regard to our men and women in blue. And in brown," she added, smiling at Marlowe's tumbledown jacket. "I wish I had more time, but my time isn't my own as I, like you, serve the people."

"Let's head this way and get started." He motioned her toward the door Morven and Nelson had gone through.

"Excellent. Into the hallways where the hard work gets done by the city's hard-working officers."

Traipsing through the door, he wondered if he was going to be the audience for a stump speech the whole time.

As Nelson and Neville walked into an interview room, he took the man through the preambles, offering coffee, tea, or water (each curtly declined), mentioning the recording (which was ignored), and then they sat down across from each other. Neville sat board-straight, hands at his side, brown eyes wandering the room instead of making eye contact.

"Thank you again, Mr. Cassell, for coming in today to help us with our inquiries. As you know, we are now investigating two incidents in your neighborhood. With that, I'd like to first ask you to detail your movements last night."

"Last night? Last night I went for a bike ride directly after work, from 18:00 hours until 18:45, riding west until 8th avenue, then north. Do you need the full route?"

"That won't be necessary. The rest of the evening?"

"After I returned, we had dinner—grilled chicken and broccoli—until 20:00, at which time we began reading. I am reading the personal memoirs of Ulysses S. Grant. Florence was reading Whitman, I believe. We had a glass of red wine at 21:30—one glass of wine each—and then retired to bed at 22:30."

Wondering how long this interview might take with such detail, Nelson asked, "And the rest of the evening, did you go out at all?"

"Stayed in bed until rising with the sirens at 06:30. That would be my normal time of reveille."

"Nothing strange occurred last night? Did you hear or see anything out of the ordinary?"

Neville shook his head 'no' gazing at the floor, still sitting as if a sheet of flat iron was pinned under his jacket's back.

All three officers had decided earlier to take it for granted that the identity of the second victim was neighborhood knowledge, leading Nelson to ask, "Did you know Tim Finch?"

"Know him, Tim Finch? Yes, knew him. Not well, mind you. Not well. Not a good neighbor. But I knew who Tim Finch was. Disciplined lawn."

"Ever have problems with him? Unfriendly interactions?"

"Problems?" Now he stared at the ceiling.

Nelson marveled at how he moved his head so many directions not budging his body a millimeter. He knew Neville had never actually been in the military, but decided he must have studied it, watching the man talking without making eye contact.

"Problems. Tim Finch. No. One time he made me stop on my bike to tell me that he knew I was riding on the sidewalks, which is against the law. I never, ever ride on sidewalks unless absolutely needed to, to avert accidents. So I kept riding."

"That was it?" Neville's one brisk nod shifted his chin an inch directly down, then up.

Morven and Florence Cassell ended up in the room where Nelson had interviewed Joyce Howard earlier. Before sitting, Morven mentioned the recording and offered tea, coffee, or water.

Standing, Florence cocked her head to one side, considering. "I think I'll pass on beverages, but thank you." She sniffed. "There is a peppermint fragrance in this room. Do you pipe that in to instill a calming energy when interviewing?"

"No, Mrs. Cassell, the police certainly wouldn't do that," Morven replied seriously, at first not noticing the small smile playing around Florence's mouth, then seeing it. "You're joking. I'm not sure why it smells like peppermint. A spill not cleaned up thoroughly, most likely. Do you mind sitting?"

"Not at all. Detective Morven, correct?"

"Correct."

"Do *you* mind if I remove this jacket? It's slightly sodden still from working outside."

"Please do. Be comfortable. We just have a few questions."

Florence put her jacket on the back of her chair and sat, crossing her well-formed arms in front of her over a simple maroon collared shirt with the City Parks logo.

Morven wondered if she worked out, or if her job involved a lot of large tree shifting. Sitting herself, she said, "We've talked to you briefly before, but as you know, we now have two cases we're investigating. I'm going to start by asking where you were last night."

"In the evening? Home. Neville went for a bike ride, then we ate dinner, read, had a glass of wine, planted ourselves in bed. I woke once with the rain, which always wakes me up. Then in the morning when the police cars broke open the dawn."

"Thank you. We want to establish everyone in the neighborhood's movements. Also, to check if you saw or heard anything strange or out of the ordinary."

"No, nothing at all. Except police sirens."

The rudimentary room Marlowe and Suri Cane were in was much like the other two: walls the color of slightly chewed gum, one mirrored wall, dingy ceiling with medium-strength tube lighting, tile floor, single table with four chairs in the middle. Suri skipped any beverages and glared around the room disdainfully when Marlowe mentioned recording.

"Recording?" Her eyes snapped to his. She sat very prim, her face angling when she answered as if the room might be full of cameras.

"If that's okay?"

"Of course, whatever you do for others. I am of the people, Detective. And between us," she said with a coy nod, "I'm used to being recorded as a council member. We have to be in the public eye, both of us, which is a burden, but one we are willing to hoist for the good of our city and the people within her."

"Sure, right." Marlowe tried to reconcile being in the public eye, unconsciously rubbing his hand across his bald head. "Thank you again for coming down, Council Member Cane. A few follow-up questions. As you know, there has been a second incident in—"

"Appalling, Detective, appalling. I know you are doing all you can, but two major crimes in such a calm neighborhood. I know you know Captain Rebecca Innocent; we've met at the same functions and have just begun to sing in a local choral group together. She is a strong leader for the city. If you need more resources, I'm sure she wouldn't mind if I mentioned it to her."

Captain Innocent was Marlowe's boss's boss, and he mostly wanted to stay out of her view if possible. "That is very kind of you, but I believe we are set for now. To get back to the second incident, can you tell me where you and Mr. Cane were the night before that incident, Monday night. And did you notice anything out of the norm?"

She struck a thinking pose for a moment, raising her hand to her chin, before replying. "My schedule, as you know, can be full. I do try to save family time, because family is so important. Monday nights tend to be ones I spend at home, and this preceding one was no different. I was actually home by six. I made dinner." She winked at him. "Well, between us, I ordered pizza from Poole's Paradise Pizza. The children love it. And I have a fondness for pizza as well, especially when made by a local business like Poole's. Local businesses are the lifeblood of the community. We had dinner and then I assisted the children with their homework before putting them, and myself, to bed. They were in bed by nine, and I was by nine thirty, admittedly with a stack of reports to read. I was up early the next morning, five thirty, making breakfast, checking my calendar and emails, before the dedicated officers arrived in the morning. You know, Detective, I have championed staffing incentives for our police in hopes of increasing numbers, as our current officers are stretched very thinly."

Nelson decided one more Tim Finch question, which would hopefully move them into what he thought was the juicer Lucy territory. "Did you notice Tim Finch having issues with any of the other neighbors?"

Neville began to move his chin to the left, then stopped, gazing at the top of Nelson's left shoulder as if the detective had an angel or devil perched there. "Having issues with other neighbors? Now that you mention it, I heard at the Haydocks that the Howards had issues with him. They thought he was spying on Betty, which is criminal. I believe Lucy jousted with him as well. Not completely clear skies on what about. Not clear. Not a good neighbor, Tim Finch."

"Speaking of Lucy Dixon, I'd like to ask a few follow-up questions about her as well."

Neville's eyes, now watching over Nelson's right shoulder, contracted as if a 200-watt bulb had been turned on. Nelson noticed, his adrenaline kicking in.

"You mentioned to Detectives Morven and Marlowe that you left the party at the Haydocks the night before her murder at ten thirty."

"Correct, 20:30."

"But Mrs. Cassell stayed behind?"

"Stayed behind for a short while. She was home by 21:00."

"You didn't mention, however, when we talked to you, that Lucy Dixon had returned to the party before you left. Why not?"

"Didn't mention?" Neville's eyes closed completely. "Didn't I mention that? I must have thought that it wasn't important. Or forgot. I forgot, that's it. I must have forgot."

"You forgot that the woman you'd been having an affair with, a woman who was subsequently murdered the same night, was at a party you were at?"

"Yes. That's it. I can understand if it appears odd. It was odd to see her there, see her again. You can understand."

"What did you do while your wife remained at the party?"

"Whiskey. I mean I had a whiskey. Watermen's single malt, two ounces." His eyes remained closed as he talked.

"What did you and your wife do when she returned to the house?"

"Do? We did nothing. Nothing at all. We brushed our teeth and went to bed."

"You didn't go out again?"

"Absolutely not we didn't go out again. Racked out. Bed."

Morven felt she should get more specific, keep the interview on track. "Did you know Tim Finch, the victim from last night?"

Florence considered a moment. "Know him? Not really. I knew of him, and had some brief interactions with him."

"Interactions?"

"I saw him in his yard when walking past now and then, said hello. He rarely replied. Once, he made a petition to have a few of the large trees in the park removed, saying they ruined his view and were causing his house to decrease in value. I ended up being the one to say they didn't. He might have known it was me. Hence the lack of replies. Foolish man, really. Sad. Like growing sunflowers and potatoes next to each other."

"Can you explain that last reference? I'm not much of a gardener."

Florence's light laugh was bright in the dull room. "Sunflower seeds can release toxins that inhibit potatoes' growth. They aren't good near neighbors. Tim Finch felt that way to me. He wasn't a good near neighbor and inhibited the surroundings from being one beneficial patch. But, Sergeant, that doesn't mean he should have been uprooted completely."

"What do you mean?"

"Killed. It reminds me, if you don't mind another plant story. One about Mr. Arthur, do you know him?"

Morven nodded her head to indicate Florence should continue. She didn't want the interview turning into a tangential ramble, but knew Mr. Arthur was another suspect on some level. Getting more insight into him couldn't hurt, and it was bringing together a picture of Florence for her.

"He had a nightshade plant in his driveway and kept trying to take it out, as they can be poisonous if used the right way. But the roots, the roots go very, very deep. He asked me how to completely remove it, and I told him not to bother. Trim it back, avoid the berries, all will be well. Tim Finch had lived in his house as long as I can recall. Why bother removing him? Ignore him and trim him back, metaphorically, as needed. But not complete removal."

"I see." Morven didn't quickly move into another question, and Florence filled the momentary silence.

"Sad story, Mr. Arthur. He used to come to our neighborhood gatherings more often, with his wife. He was quite a storyteller, nice to talk to, though he could go on. He once said, quoting some TV show he liked, that 'he himself could talk the hind leg off a donkey.' I liked that. Then she was sadly uprooted in tragic circumstances. I've barely seen him since. Once or twice at the Haydocks, walking his dog. But he started to 'keep himself to himself,' to use another phrase he liked. I always hope he'll find something to get him talking again."

Morven was beginning to feel Florence carried some deep ethical currents which wouldn't keep her from 'uprooting' someone if she felt it was definitely needed. She decided to switch victims.

"Was Mr. Cane home?" Marlowe's laconic nature contrasted awkwardly against Suri's tendency to speechify.

"Monday?" For the first time, she appeared less sure. "Well, now that you ask, he wasn't. Monday is his night to go out with a friend. He was out the entire evening."

"Returning?"

"I was asleep. He told me that it was eleven, that he saw the clock when checking on the children."

"His friend's name?"

"Is that really needed, Detective? Is my husband some kind of suspect? I can assure you, he had nothing to do with —"

Marlowe held his hand up as she increased in volume. "Just to have the details correct. Saves time later for our thinly stretched officers."

"Indeed. Indeed! We want to help, Detective, in any way we can, as each good citizen should." She'd recovered her studied poise. "He was with an old friend of his, Benjamin Matthews."

"Did you know Tim Finch?"

"The victim? Not really, Detective. I like to know all my neighbors, all my constituents, so I can serve them properly. But I never made a connection with Tim Finch, sadly. I'll regret that now, of course."

"Any issues with him?"

"No. I never really talked to him. Neither did Steven or the kids. I know there was friction between him and the Howards, perhaps Lucy Dixon too. Sometimes neighbors have squabbles."

"But you never squabbled?"

"Never. Well, once he did make a point of stopping me when I was walking past his house to say he didn't vote for me. How strange!" She laughed uneasily. At his strangeness or at the fact that someone wouldn't vote for her, Marlowe wasn't sure. "You know, Detective, some of us are dung beetles, some are butterflies, or parrots. I heard that on a television show once and it stuck. Mr. Finch, not to speak ill of the dead, may not have been a butterfly."

He wasn't sure how to reply to that, so switched trails. "About our other incident. We have your movements the night before Lucy Dixon's murder. Can we again talk about the party?"

"I believe we've gone over that, Detective. Is it the best use of time to go over it again?"

Nelson made a sideways move, hoping to get Neville to jump. No reaction. "You said in our earlier interview that your affair with Lucy Dixon had ended."

"I did say that, it's true."

Remembering what Morven had mentioned about believing Neville had been in more recent contact with Lucy, Nelson picked up a piece of paper he'd brought, pretended to read it. It was blank, but he'd felt the paper in his earlier interview provided something concrete to hold on to and made a good prop, and Neville couldn't see it was blank. "Then why would her coming to the party again that same night be such a problem? Were you angry with her? Still in contact with her?"

Neville's face dropped to his hands, back finally bending. He didn't reply for a few minutes, until Nelson prompted, "Mr. Cassell?"

The man's head rose. "No, I wasn't in contact with her. But I had sent texts recently. To her. Trying to get to see her. I'm sure you have them; I've seen shows were the police get a victim's texts. I sent them, but I didn't harm her. I couldn't. But I sent texts, not friendly ones. But as Grant said, 'My failures have been errors in judgment, not of intent.'"

"What does that mean, Mr. Cassell?"

Dazed, he replied, "What does it mean? I shouldn't have sent those texts. I knew better. Know better. I'm not a sad sack, Detective. Not a fuming ex-affair haver. Not even much of a text writer. Not the same as a solid conversation if you ask me. But Lucy loved to text, send pictures, even though I told her not to. Didn't want Florence to know, of course. Once it became obvious even to me that it was over, I did erase all she texted me. I decided to man up, realize it had happened and was over, and let it go. Let it go. Florence didn't have to know, no one would have to know."

"And then?"

"Then the next time we saw Lucy, I was trying to avoid the interactions being awkward, but she, smiling in the way she did, part demon, part cherub, said the word 'affair' three times when talking to me and Florence. Randomly. End of the affair. Affair of the heart. Tide in the affairs of men. Affair! Florence didn't notice, but I did. The next time we saw her, she kept bringing up motels, hotels, assignations. Always smiling. She seemed to enjoy it. I knew Florence would pick up on it eventually."

"You wanted her to stop?"

"You're damn right I wanted her to stop. She ended it, so let it end."

He shoots, Nelson thought as he said, "And so you killed her," in his mind continuing, *he scor—*

"What! No. No, I did not. I did not. I texted her pleading, angrily, because I wanted to meet to ask, to beg her to stop or we'd stop coming to neighborhood events. But then Florence would ask questions, and the others. The others would know too. I couldn't take it. I wanted her to stop, but shouldn't have sent those texts. Easy way out. I was weak, weak.

But I didn't kill her. Instead, I told Florence myself."

"When did you tell her?"

Completely collapsed onto the table, Neville whispered, "The day before the party."

"But you still went to the party? And saw Lucy?"

"Florence insisted. Said we'd stand tall and wouldn't let the bad weather break our branches. Good old Florence."

"You didn't see Lucy again after the party, at all?"

"No, I swear. Give you my word, vow, I didn't." His voice was muffled and weak, and Nelson decided he'd had enough. For now.

"Interesting observation about Mr. Arthur," Morven replied. "We've spoken with him. Can we move on to the earlier incident?"

Florence nodded yes, leaning her head back as if to check the white ceiling tiles for cracks.

"You told us that the night before Lucy Dixon was murdered you saw her at a party at the Haydocks." Another nod. "And that you stayed at the party until approximately eleven?" Nod. "But you didn't tell us that you saw Mrs. Dixon later in the evening, only that she left not that she returned. Why is that?"

Florence sighed. "I should have. I felt like an oak blocking sun from grass in a way, not saying anything. But I didn't want to muddy the water and, as I didn't kill her, felt it didn't matter. That it could stay private."

"In a murder inquiry, nothing's private. We need every fact. Everything can be relevant. Can you tell me what happened when she returned?"

"She was tipsy and alone. Full-on Lucy in bloom. A big 'I'm baaaaaack' when she returned. Neville left instantly. I stayed longer."

"Why did he leave?"

"You know about the affair they had, Neville and Lucy? I can be blunt?"

"Honesty is very helpful, always."

"Agreed. He had just told me and became overwhelmed by the awkwardness. Neville had a somewhat sheltered upbringing. Military family, though he never joined up, moving a lot. Lucy overwhelmed him."

"In what way?"

"She was, let's say aggressively flamboyant. Like a horny peacock with her colorful feathers spread out. He'd never experienced that. But the affair ended, though Lucy wasn't one to not use it to raise emotional hackles. She enjoyed stirring the pot. He knew what was coming, so left when she arrived."

"But you stayed, knowing the same thing. Why?"

"I didn't want her to think she'd won or could have that much effect on us, I suppose. Funny thing? She didn't even talk about it. Saw Neville leave, smiled knowingly, asked for a drink, winked at me, and started talking about Toby being face down, three sheets, blotto."

"You didn't stay long?"

"I wasn't in the mood for her boisterousness. And wanted to check on Neville."

"Your work, is it physically demanding?"

Florence didn't appear thrown off by the line of questioning switch, just considered it for a second before saying, "I never thought about it. But it is, often. Planting trees, moving trees, hiking here and there. It can be. Interesting question, Sergeant. Popping up like a daisy unplanted."

"Did you go out again the night Mrs. Dixon was killed?"

"No."

"Did Neville?"

"No."

"You were angry." Morven took a chance. "She was like a weed taking over your garden. Did you uproot her?"

Florence smiled ruefully, shaking her head. "No. I didn't think of her like a weed. More monocarpic. Do you know that? Flowers that flower and seed only once. She flowered once within Neville's, and my, life. But that was it. I knew it and had no need to uproot her."

"I believe it would be helpful to go through it again, yes. You know how investigations are, Council Member—double checking to ensure we have everything correct," Marlowe said with a note of admiration, possibly faked.

Suri preened. "I do. I pride myself on knowing the details of all city functions. I'm not a leader who is afraid to dig deep. Ask away."

"I thought you would." His mustache twitched. "With that, please tell me again what you and Lucy argued about."

"Proposed intersection islands. Seems silly now, doesn't it?"

"We've heard it was heated. Traffic islands seems unheated. Was that it?"

"Yes, of course."

He didn't reply, just looked at her expressionless, like a tired mustachioed Great Dane, and waited. She looked back for a moment, then began to fidget a little, then a little more.

"Council Member?"

"Well, as long as this part of the recording is between us." Marlowe remained passive. "I'm sure I can trust you, it's solely that I don't *want* to speak ill of Lucy now that she's passed. I'm a good neighbor, but she had a way about her that sometimes got under my skin. She had been dropping hints, or I thought they were hints, in front of everyone that my marriage with Steven wasn't all it should be. That we weren't happily married. But we are. We are. Family is *so* important, Detective. She just kept at it, making jokes about ridiculed public figures and tarnished reputations, all the while with an, well, an evil smile across her face. She could be a not very friendly neighbor. I finally had to ask her to stop. And she laughed. She laughed! At me. A council member. I may have gotten heated, and I regret it now, but I don't regret sticking up for my family, as I wouldn't regret sticking up for my city." She pounded her hand on the desk, the sound like a shot.

Marlowe waited a beat, then said, "Did the argument end there?"

"Yes. We left soon after. Steven told me to ignore her, that she was *that* way. But she could get under your skin like a swarm of fire ants. I was angry with her behavior. I didn't see her again after that, and I do still feel horrible about what happened to her. We must partner together—citizens, police, politicians, all of us—to ensure we have safe streets, safe parks, safe neighborhoods, Detective. Only by working together can we make this city the beautiful place it should be, a place all will enjoy living within."

She'd reined her deeper emotion in, climbing back on the stump. Marlowe let her ramble a bit longer, but knew the interview had hit the end of the trail.

11

Remarkably, the three officers' interviews ended simultaneously, like a photo-finish three-way tie at the end of a tightly contested 100-yard dash. This led to a hallway crowded and awkward as the Cassells and Suri Cane were being escorted out.

"Neville. Florence. You're here too?" Suri hid the initial strangeness of meeting in a police station with loudness. "We have to pull together to support our police officers and neighbors in moments like these, I believe. Glad that we are doing our part, together."

"Together, right," Neville replied, while Florence nodded her head slowly in the affirmative.

"Indeed, we—" Suri began.

"Sorry to interrupt, Council Member Cane," Marlowe interrupted, "but can we move this way? Don't want to clog the halls."

"Certainly. We know how busy the police are." She took the lead, striding forcefully down the hall. "Come this way, Neville, Florence."

The Cassells and officers followed in her wake, rerouting her once when she nearly took a wrong turn in the direction of the holding cells. Bursting through the door into the reception area like water coming out of a geyser, she pulled Neville and Florence behind her.

"I always say it's our neighbors who make the neighborhood, and we,

Steven and I, are so happy to have settled in, even with the tragic recent— Oh, Mr. Arthur." She stopped abruptly as she saw John Arthur, causing a clownlike chain reaction: Nelson bumping into Neville, Morven into Nelson, and Marlowe into Morven. Florence had smoothly sidestepped.

John was talking to the officer seated behind a glass barrier, the spot where visitors checked in upon entering the station. Even seated, the officer's nearly six-foot-five height loomed, boosted by broad shoulders, dark sideburns, and a handlebar mustache nearly rivaling Marlowe's. John turned away from that imposing presence slightly to respond to Suri, grinning. "Council member? Neville? Florence? A meeting of the Neighborhood Watch Alliance?"

"We are doing our civic duty, assisting our fine local police," Suri rolled out. "As it seems you are as well."

John walked over, shaking hands with Neville, Florence, and then Suri. "Hello, hello, hello. And yes, I've come down to talk to Detective Marlowe, who is behind you, I see, with Detective Marlowe and Sergeant Nelson."

Each officer had managed to make it out of the hallway by the time he finished, the full group occupying the center of the room as other visitors curiously watched.

John, Neville, and Suri spoke at once.

"You—"

"I think—"

"Yes, to talk—"

Marlowe raised his hand, worried they were about to become a vocal stampede in the middle of the busy police station. "Excuse me." His volume quieted the others. "Thank you for your help. Detective Morven, Sergeant Nelson, please escort Council Member Cane and the Cassells out and answer any final questions. We will be in touch." He motioned one arm toward the door and, with the other, motioned to John Arthur, for a moment looking like a traffic cop. "Mr. Arthur?"

Marlowe strode back down the hall with John as the group separated. Before they got to the door, John touched his elbow. "Sorry, Detective, one moment." Marlowe's eyebrows raised to a point it felt they might cross his head's top as John trotted back to the front window, saying something to the officer, before trotting back.

"Here now, ready for my close-up. Or interview. Had to say a final word to Officer Coleman. He has 'the dignity of a Bishop, the trap-jawed determination of a board chairman during wage negotiations, and the shoulders of a weightlifter.'"

Opening the door, Marlowe gave him a half-exasperated, half-curious look, as if he'd spoken in a foreign language. It was a look from Marlowe John was getting used to. "Don't say it: British mystery quote."

"Not this time, Detective. American book. *You Can't Live Forever* by Hal Masur, 1959. I do read, too."

"Now I know." Moving down the hall, he continued. "What was that about?"

John gazed around the station hallway as if it were an art piece. "Officer Coleman? Forget my pulp description, he's as nice as they come. We'd been talking about dogs when the neighbors tumbled out like hungry toddlers at snack time. When I checked in, I noticed he was looking at pictures of terriers, which reminded me of Wee Jock, the terrier in the show *Hamish Macbeth*. You know it? Small town off the coast of Scotland. Police constable who walks his own path, played by reliable and relatable Robert Carlyle. *Full Monty* star."

Marlowe both nodded and shook his head as he opened the door to the interview room. Neither stemmed the monologue.

"Officer Coleman and I were chatting about dogs. He didn't know the show but is going to watch for it, and it turns out he and his partner are thinking about adopting a dog. I had to show him some pictures of Ainsley, of which I have a fair amount on my phone, like dog owners do." He took a deep breath. "Then I had to talk about the fantastic dog rescue that rescued her, and who we adopted her from, Forgotten Dogs Rescue, and then everyone rushed through the door, distracting me before I could give him the rescue's information. I wanted to go back and do it before I forgot. Make sense?"

Marlowe nodded again, hoping to dam the outburst by motioning to the seats while shutting the door.

Before Marlowe could speak, John said, "Same room as Council Member Cane's interview, I'm guessing?"

"How?"

"Her perfume, it lingers. And strangely enough, I noticed it once outdoors at the Haydukes. Coconut, almondy, vanilla. Not sure what brand, but I felt worth a guess. That would have been an interesting interview to attend."

"Clever. Christian Dior Hypnotic Poison. Possibly."

"Very Sherlockian nose and perfume knowledge. Impressive, Detective."

"Not really. Wife, ex-wife, used to wear it."

"Makes sense. 'What a lovely thing a nose is.' If you don't mind me changing a quote."

"Wouldn't have known."

"No? Jeremy Brett playing Sherlock Holmes. Classic. Absolute classic. What a lovely thing a rose is. He was –"

Marlowe's hand shot up.

"Apologies, Detective. I can ramble."

"Hadn't noticed. But while hearing about TV shows is, well, is, it's a busy day."

"Sure. Two murders now, so lots of interviews, including the council member, our neighborhood's rising political star. She did it."

"What?" Marlowe's bemused countenance, which he found to be his normal state of being when talking to John Arthur, switched to shock as if he'd been hit by lightning while riding a horse.

"BST. She did it." John's eye's twinkled, his response unusually succinct.

"BST? What do you mean?" Did the man know something?

"BST. Biggest Star Theory. She is the biggest star in the neighborhood cast. She did it."

"Mr. Arthur, John, please. You've lost me. Explain."

"Happy to." He laughed. "It's just a theory, like a scientific theory, like Kepler's Laws of Universal Gravitation or the Big Bang Theory. Only this one is around murder."

"Real or TV?"

"Mostly TV I suppose. It's a theory my wife and I came up with after watching a fair amount of *Midsomer Murders*, *Poirot*, *Marple*, *Father Brown*—all those mystery shows that have guest stars each episode."

"Guest stars?"

"Well, there's the ongoing cast, and then there's—"

"I know what guest stars are, just not how it relates to Suri Cane being a murderer."

"Sorry, not as clear as could be. Here's an example. In the *Father Brown* episode called 'The Owl of Minerva,' Adrian Scarborough is one of the guest stars for that episode. Now, the short-but-striking Mr. Scarborough is a fairly well-known actor in his own right in the UK. He even stars as the lead in a new mystery series, *The Chelsea Detective*, which is more modern than *Father Brown*. In it, he's a slightly quirky police detective solving crimes in the high-rent Chelsea district in London, while living on a houseboat—"

"John!" Marlowe exclaimed.

"Yes?"

"Wandering into the wilderness."

"Check. Anyway, Mr. Scarborough shows up in the *Father Brown* episode, and as we'd—this was when my wife was still alive—seen him many times in a host of shows, mysteries and whatnot, when he popped up in that *Father Brown*, he's immediately recognizable, and we both said, 'He did it!' at the same time, as he was the biggest guest star in that episode. Because it's always the biggest star who did it. Biggest Star Theory. When you watch enough, you start to recognize actors who have been in multiple shows and probably command a bigger payday, and so get the juicier parts. The murdering parts. It's comforting in a way to see an actor you know appear in a new show, even if it means they did it."

Marlowe, sucked in, couldn't stop himself. "Doesn't that get predictable?"

"Yes and no. Part of the theory is a sub-theory that writers and directors understand BST, too, and play against it. Meaning sometimes when a more known actor shows up, and the viewers say 'they did it,' then the star becomes victim number two. Or is innocent. Like when Orlando Bloom—you know him, right? *Pirates of the Caribbean*. Legolas in *The Lord of the Rings*. Hunky movie star, seems a generally nice guy."

"I am familiar with the actor Orlando Bloom, yes."

"He's a guest star in an episode of *Midsomer Murders*, way back in Season Three, called 'Judgement Day.' Originally aired 2000, I believe. We saw it after he was already in LOTR. Back then, it wasn't as easy to see British Mysteries over here as it is now with streaming services like Acorn and BritBox. PBS Masterpiece Mysteries was a godsend if you could catch it, and there were DVDs of many shows if you could find them. We picked up an all-region DVD player just to be able to order DVDs straight from the UK to– "

"John?"

"Yes?"

"Orlando?"

"There's Orlando Bloom, starring as a shady character wonderfully named Peter Drinkwater. You'd think the minute he, star of the big screen, arrives, bam! BST. But then he gets stabbed in the stomach with a pitchfork, and not even that many minutes deep into the episode."

The room was silent for a moment before Marlowe said, "Ugly way to go."

"Hmm?" John was staring at the ceiling.

"Pitchfork to the stomach."

"Very true. I was just thinking."

Warily, Marlowe asked, "About?"

"Suri. She is in a way the biggest star—she's a council member, high-profile, well-known in the city, does a fantastic job by the way, to my thinking. She's a big star in her sphere. But is she the biggest star in the group of neighbors? Or to us as viewers?"

"John?"

"Yes?"

"TV versus reality."

"Indeed! But you can—"

"Learn a lot from TV mysteries. You've told me."

"Rambling again."

"It's all right. Interesting even. A little. But do you have any pertinent information *outside* of BST theory around Mrs. Cane?"

"She argued with Lucy I've heard."

"We are aware."

"She's very protective of her family. Her career. Both intertwined. Hard to see which she is more protective of."

"That's astute. But . . ." Marlowe opened his hands, palms up.

"Not facts."

Marlowe nodded like a bald and bearded sage.

"'Police work is facts, evidence, alibis, not gossip,' as Inspector Hardcastle said to Poirot in 'The Clocks.'"

"Poirot, the Belgian?"

"You have it, Detective. You'll become a connoisseur of fictional British detectives yet."

"British Belgian?"

"Belgian British transplant. British writer writing about a Belgian in Britain."

"Curious. Are you starting to see yourself as a Poirot? A Father Brown? Or another favorite?"

John beamed. "A fastidious ex-police officer turned private detective or a crime-solving priest? No, neither of those. Why?"

"Why are you so interested in the case? Or cases?"

"Finding the first body. Neighborhood interest. I did know the victims, and the suspects you've brought in, those I've seen."

"Fair enough. But . . ." He held his hand out again, this time as if reaching for a large ball. "You seem more involved."

"I do? I do. I'm repeating myself. Wait, am I a suspect?"

"We are—"

"Following all lines of inquiry. Sorry, I knew that was coming. I guess I *should* be a suspect, everyone should until the murders are solved. I found the first body, though why would I have called the police?"

He pushed his chair back, crossing his legs in front of it, putting his arms behind his head while staring at the ceiling. He was wearing, Marlowe saw, blue socks with pictures of cartoon Rottweilers on them pulled halfway up his calves.

"Unless you believe I'm pulling a double-blind of some sort. Calling the police to throw suspicion off myself. Clever. Would I have done it, then gone to get Ainsley to add that big dollop of realism to my duplicity? Villains do often return to the scene of the crime, though I wouldn't think that translated to reality. I am a suspect."

Like stone, not a mustache hair of Marlowe's moved.

"But why," John continued, "would I murder Tim Finch? Outside of him being a fairly insufferable jerk, which does constitute reason enough in many shows. Because he saw me murder Lucy Dixon, of course. You're hypothesizing that murder A obviously ties into murder B, and B is probably Tim Finch trying to score blackmail money, as that seems what he'd do. You are, right?"

Marlowe's immoveable face gave away nothing.

"Sure you are. I showed up at that second scene. With Ainsley again, my doggy alibi, who certainly wouldn't give me up if I'd been out nights. Did I make the big board? You have to have a big board. There's always a big board."

Nothing.

"You can't tell me that. I've been asking a lot of questions, which could be seen as trying to uncover what you've found out. Classic criminal move. But motive? Why would I kill Lucy to start?"

"Why would you?"

"It would have to be something from the past. Deep in the past."

"Why is that?"

"It's always something deep in the past. There are bound to be recent motives that appear plausible. But it's the past. Trust me."

"Always the past . . . on TV?" A smile briefly caused Marlowe's mustache to twitch.

"Exactly. Detective Barnaby, either of them, eventually has that ah-ha moment when he uncovers whatever it is in the past that drove the first murder. This is, I'm sure, no different. But where does that leave me as potential killer?"

"Did you know Lucy in the past?"

"Question-question. A wonderful tactic. Why would I tell you if I did?" He smiled ruefully. "But I didn't. In some ways, I wish I did."

"Why wish that?"

"I hate to admit it, again because it feels a flaw in my character, but mulling over the case, talking to you about it, it's, well, been enjoyable. Fun, even."

"Like a stampede."

Flummoxed, John said, "Stampede?"

"Feels cowboys both hated stampedes—dangerous, hectic, wild stampedes—but after the monotony of the trail, maybe liked them, too."

"'My mind rebels at stagnation.'"

"Quote?" Marlowe'd talked to John enough to guess.

"The incomparable Jeremy Brett as Sherlock Holmes. You might be right on the stampede. I don't want to say my life since my wife died is monotonous, but there is a certain regularity to the days. Thinking the case over is completely different."

"From watching a murder mystery to living it."

"Exactly. You don't know what to expect, how you'll feel or react. It's tragic. I feel for those involved. But can't stop going over what I know in my mind. That's the interest. Talking to you, talking about the British mysteries? If I'm honest, it helps fill some of the silence that seems to have surrounded me since my wife died. We used to watch those shows together. At home, I talk to Ainsley, to myself, now that Marlene is gone. Avoid that silence. But it's not enough. Sometimes, I think I need to fill the space with talk, and talking about TV, the British mysteries we liked, maybe balances out the silence. That silence, it can be frightening. The shows always end solved, unlike life, where everything, the pain, the mystery, the why, is so ongoing. I didn't do it. But I won't be sad if I get to stay on the big board."

"We are—"

"Following all lines of inquiry!"

After the interviews, debriefing with Morven and Nelson, and strategizing for the next day—Marlowe couldn't help himself, instructing both of them to dig even deeper into everyone's past. He wasn't going to ever let them know John had suggested doing just that—Marlowe felt he deserved a drink and found himself strolling down the hill toward Gary's and Settler's Square.

Passing the vacant lot home to ragged and dead grass, broken beer bottles, and a rusty sign from six years ago that said construction was about to begin on a shiny apartment complex called Thassingham Towers, of all names, he nearly ran over a little boy, three or four, in a long jean jacket, dusty hat with the Seafarer's "S," and long red shorts, pulling a little red wagon with a tiny dog, a Chihuahua mix, in the back. Marlowe didn't see an adult nearby and stopped to watch as the boy came to the very end of the block where sidewalk ramped into street. The boy twisted his head intently both ways as if the street was bumper-to-bumper with cars instead of completely empty, saying, "Easy. Dangerous. Can't go too fast. Must watch both ways. Both. Ways." Then slowly, instead of going into the street, he turned the cart around and began walking and pulling back the other way, past Marlowe.

"Everything okay?" Marlowe asked. "No danger?"

"Dangerous," the kid said, pointing his thumb at the dog, "is the only thing dangerous here. Dangerous Dave. Don't get too close."

The Chihuahua, wearing a ruby red collar with sparkly zirconia studding, paws on the front edge of the wagon, cocked its head at Marlowe.

"Won't do it. Nothing amiss?"

"We don't miss nothing, Dangerous and me. All clear. Both ways. And we don't talk to strangers." He crossed his arms and stuck out his chin.

"Very smart. Parents around?"

The kid hitched his thumb in the direction the wagon pointed. Turning, Marlowe saw a harried-faced man in gray sweats and a checked sweater staring the opposite direction, then at them, then walking rapidly toward them.

"Your dad?"

The kid nodded exasperatedly, pulling the wagon down the sidewalk at a glacial pace, before stopping, slanting his head back saying, "Hey. You."

"Yes?"

"Neat mustache."

The next morning, the sky returned clear and bright blue, following the city's idiosyncratic weather patterns. Juneuary turning to June and then who knew what would be happening in an hour, in two. Wind, rain, sun, hail, frogs falling from the sky, Marlowe considered possibilities as he drove solo up 15th Avenue once more back to the crime scenes, thankful that no new murders had happened. Two was more than enough. He'd stayed at Gary's only an hour and a half the night before, sipping a beer. Gary insisted he had a Fuller's London Pride, to help him understand the British constitution and thereby the detectives he'd been hearing so much about, who, he could assure him, liked a well-pulled pint as much as any American gumshoe. He'd had a second one while chatting the British mystery canon with Gary as they watched the Seafarers run up a six to one lead, go down six to seven in the eighth, then pull off miraculous back-to-back homers in the ninth to win eight to seven. He took the win as an omen of good luck, scooting out as the ball cleared the fence on TV, waving off the amiable bartender's invitation for celebratory shots. Then, instead of heading home for an early night of *Gunsmoke* and letting his mind wander, he stopped back at the office, going over case notes for hours, feet up on his desk, before finally finding his way to bed.

Burrowing into the notes, he decided to unleash Morven and Nelson on more background, the forensic reports, and double-checking Steven's alibi via a talk with Ben Matthews. It was more likely a breakthrough would come via these background avenues than what his agenda entailed: a second interview with Toby Dixon, and if possible, the Haydocks. He knew the former should have been done the day before, but the man's grief had been so overwhelming, he'd put it off. Calling earlier to ensure Toby remained corralled at home, and hopefully sober, he'd gotten a guttural response of, "Yeah, I'm home. Solve Lucy's murder yet?"

It wasn't going to be a pretty interview. Marlowe felt fortifying first would be a solid start, so pulled his saddle-brown 1978 AMC Matador into Lynley's parking lot; he was driving his own car to skip going into the station. The car displayed a topographic map of dents but ran smoothly. Nate gave him a floppy wave as he got in line behind a woman in full running attire, headphones, and an umbrella (being prepared, never a bad idea) and a man in jeans and a Seafarers T-shirt whose bald head almost out-shined Marlowe's. Hearing Nate ask everyone to repeat their order at least once, Marlowe wondered if maybe some sort of chalk board might be helpful. Before he got beyond prototyping, an Americano filled one hand and a croissant the other, and he was backing out of the door.

Angle-parking in a Community Center spot across from the Dixons, he mulled British mysteries while munching croissant and taking cautious sips from the coffee, now cooled slightly below scalding. He couldn't help himself. Belgians with mustaches, older women in villages, clever priests drinking pints, ex-pat cops on islands, the legendary Sherlock. Should he have a magnifying glass and deerstalker hat, getting down on hands-and-knees in the alley? Rain probably washed the clues away. Be talking to elderly residents twitching behind curtains with endless glasses of tea? He hadn't noticed one yet. Spend his time scouring UK DVD sights, ordering a stack, and solving the case with binge-watching? He'd gain ten pounds in a week, he decided, munching the last bite or croissant. Might as well go at it the old-fashioned way: door-knocking.

Toby Dixon's appearance could have been the picture next to a dictionary definition of three-day bender. His hair stuck up at odd angles, he wore the same shirt from their earlier interview, his jeans boasted ketchup, oil, and beer stains, and he had skipped shoes and socks.

"Detective," he spit out, "solve Lucy's murder yet?"

"We are working hard on it, Mr. Dixon."

"Not hard enough." He took a swig from the beer bottle in his right hand, an Appropriate Adults IPA.

"Mind answering some questions?"

"Why not. Need a beer?"

"Little early."

"You didn't lose your wife."

Marlowe didn't reply, following him back into the living room and the tenuous couch.

"As you know, Mr. Dixon, we've had another crime committed nearby, in the alley."

"So, Lucy doesn't matter anymore?"

"We are working on both. Can you tell me what you were doing Monday evening and early Tuesday morning?"

Toby held up the bottle. "Mostly this. Helped Rory practice some. Tried to ignore the neighbors. Sympathy's fine, but I can't deal."

"You didn't go out?"

"Nope." He took a long swig.

"Did you see Tim Finch?"

"That creep? Glad he's—" He realized what he was saying, paused, went on. "Well, not glad he's dead. He was a creep. I didn't see him. I avoided him."

"Did you hear anything that night in the alley, see anyone?"

"Nah. Gotta admit, Detective, I probably drank too much. I was face down by nine, out until the sirens woke me. They shouldn't be so loud."

Marlowe heard a *thwap... thwap... thwap* coming from the backyard in the silence between questions.

"Any range wars with Tim in the past?"

"Range wars? That's funny. Howards might have. Like I said, I avoided him."

"Lucy?"

"Lucy liked everyone. Everyone. Wait, she did get after him once. He was a creep, creeping people out, watching her with his telescope, that kind of thing. She made him stop. Wasn't afraid of him. You think these crimes are connected. Could he have killed Lucy?"

"Was it that bad between them?"

"Nah, she just put him in his place. If it had gone farther, I might have had words with him."

"Never did?"

Thwap... thwap... thwap.

"Nope. If he was involved in Lucy's death, I would have . . . but I didn't. Didn't see or hear anything."

"How long has the fence in the alley, white bricks, been there?"

"The fence?" He took another pull of the beer. "Longer than we have. Built out the yard, but never thought to fancy up the alley."

Thwap... thwap... thwap.

"Mind me asking what that noise is?"

"Noise? Oh, that. Ball hitting glove. Rory's in the yard practicing."

"Okay to talk to him?"

"He's hurting, but okay. Short. I'm gonna grab a beer. Follow me through the kitchen."

They went past the dining room into a surprisingly clean kitchen, completely white, with a door that Toby opened for Marlowe, pointing him to the backyard. He went down a set of stairs off a small deck to see Rory, a tall, lanky, teenager whose red hair sprouted from beneath a Seafarer's cap. He had on jeans, sneakers, a long-sleeved plain white T-shirt, a baseball glove on his right hand, and was throwing a baseball into a handmade backstop with a net in the middle, which would send the ball high into the sky when thrown at. The rest of the yard had sturdy built-in benches along one fence wall, wooden (Marlowe guessed handmade) fence-mounted planters bursting with pink rhododendrons and azaleas, a Seafarers metal *Hit It Here* sign, and a line of license plates hanging from the fence: Florida, Oklahoma, Minnesota, Illinois, Washington. Rory kept throwing as Marlowe spoke up.

"See the game last night?"

"Yep."

"Expected the comeback?"

"Yep."

"I was worried in the eighth, myself. Seafarers curse and all." The team's seemingly endless string of spectacularly disappointing seasons endured.

"Not this year. They break it this year."

"Hope so. Mind if I ask you a question or two?"

"No. Okay if I keep throwing? Good practice. Keeps my mind off Mom."

"Sure. I'm Detective Marlowe by the way. First, did you hear or see anything strange the night of the Haydocks' party?"

"No. Didn't stay long. Other kids a little too young. Came home, watched some videos, went to sleep."

"What about Monday?"

"Monday? Oh, the other. . ." Throw, catch. "Watched the game. Tried to do some homework. Here."

"Alone?"

"Dad—Toby—was here too."

"All night?"

"Yeah. Passed out. He's taking it hard."

"You hanging in there?"

"Trying. Gotta keep practicing. Mom'd want that."

"Hear or see anything Monday night, Tuesday morning?"

"Nope. You gonna find out who killed her?"

"I'm going to do everything I can, Rory. I won't stop until I have."

"Thanks. You think the Seafarers make the playoffs?"

"Hope so, Rory. I hope so."

12

Marlowe hadn't gotten much more out of Toby or Rory Dixon. The latter he felt didn't know any more, and no matter how he tried, he couldn't get the idea of Rory as a teenager who'd kill his mother in the Community Center park. Maybe he was missing something, but his gut told him no. It also told him two of the croissants at Lynley's would have been better than one, but he tried to ignore that. You couldn't always go by your gut, or soon you'd need a new belt.

Toby'd finished another beer leaning against a porch post while Marlowe talked with Rory, then opened a fresh one as Marlowe passed back through the house. Toby could drink more than a thirsty horse. He considered asking the man more questions, seeing if beer intake loosened his tongue, but realized Toby passed tipsy into a maudlin drunk stage where he only wanted to list Lucy's virtues, a list never-ending. For Marlowe, none of it seemed fake. Sometimes, his grandfather used to say, a tree is a tree. Marlowe wasn't exactly sure what he meant, but in this case had become convinced that Toby's grief was real, not some elaborate cover-up for spousal murder followed by a second murder to cover the first.

Sometimes a tree is a tree. Especially when sitting on your car parked under the outstretched leaves of a massive bigleaf maple. Did British TV detectives ever spend time mulling cases gazing up at tree branches?

Probably not. They probably gazed at tea steaming in delicate teacups, or big tea mugs, depending on the time period. Reading Shakespeare. Pacing outside of churches hundreds of years old. Eating cookies. Or were they called biscuits?

Shaking his head, he shifted his weight off the car and began to walk across the street. "Time for the Haydocks'," he said out loud, causing the woman jogging by in a bright pink bodysuit and black sneakers to stare for a moment, then smile. He smiled back, but she'd passed him, continuing down the block. *She probably thought I'd already had a Negroni at the Haydocks*, he said, though this time only to himself. Too early, once more. It *is* five o'clock somewhere, probably well into the aperitivo hour in Florence. Ah, well. Turning into the Haydocks' yard, he expected James to be sitting on the porch, but the whole yard was empty.

He knocked, receiving no answer, the noise of knuckle on wood echoing lightly in the nearly enclosed yard. Just as he was raising his hand to give it another try, the door opened slightly, Joanna Haydock peering around the edge of it.

"Hello, Mrs. Haydock. Detective Marlowe."

She gave her a head a tiny shake, as if to toss off a cobweb. "Of course. Detective. Sorry, I was miles away."

"Somewhere nice?"

Her smile started faintly, then got wider, like sunshine in the wee hours of morning. "Only the couch, scrolling pictures from past trips overseas. So, yes, nice. How can I help you?"

"I have a few more questions."

"Sure, come in." She backed up, opening the door wider. "James isn't here, he's back at work. Geraldine is at school. Just me. Not sure I'll be helpful, but happy to try."

She was wearing jeans, brown sandals, and a lime-green, long-sleeve T-shirt. She sat on the white couch on the extended side of the L, in the living room, pulling one leg under her with a slight grimace. Marlowe perched gently on the couch's short side.

"As we investigate now two serious crimes in the neighborhood, everything helps."

Nodding abstractedly, she said, "Sure."

"Thank you. First, what were you, the family, doing Monday night?"

"That's the night Tim Finch died. We were here, the three of us. Still in shock. Watching TV. You probably want to know what we were watching. I've seen a few mysteries, Detective."

He held up his hands as if to say, 'what can you do?'

"We were not watching a British mystery, if you're worried about that. My guess is you've heard about a few of those from John."

"We have talked to Mr. Arthur."

A smile stole across her face again. "He's a good friend. He wasn't always as TV show talkative, you know."

"No, I didn't. What changed?"

"Marlene, his wife, also an old friend, died. Tragedy. So much tragedy. It changed him, as you'd expect. First quieter, then more talkative. To cover the pain, I suppose. Everyone copes differently."

She went silent, the only sound a tree branch scraping the side of the house in the wind. She shook her head once more, started back up. "Anyway. Monday. It was a show Geraldine wanted to watch about vampires. Morbid, but funny, not scary. I can't remember the name. James can, if needed. We ordered pizza from Poole's Paradise. I had a glass of rosé. James had some drinks, gin I believe. We were in bed earlier than normal, like ten, ten thirty. Woke up to sirens." Her voice faded like a song ending.

"Thank you, Mrs. Haydock. We appreciate this is tough. Did any of you hear anything that night from the alley? See anything?"

She answered slowly. "No, we were inside. I—Can I say this? You won't care. It's legal here anyway. I took an edible, and James had a fair amount of gin, leading to deep sleeping. It was needed."

"Understand. Did you know Tim Finch?"

"Not well. Unfriendly, odious person." She paused for a minute, shook her head once more. "I shouldn't say that. *Mortuis nihil nisi bonum.*

You know it?"

"Speak only good of the dead."

"That's it. Read that somewhere, stuck with me. Tim Finch. Dead in our alley. It's distressing. We didn't know him well, but still. So much violence, so close to home. But not sure I said more than a handful of words to Tim Finch." She held out her hand, staring at it.

"No problems with him and you or Mr. Haydock?"

"No. We knew he was a troublesome neighbor for the Howards, and that Lucy Dixon had butted heads with him. But we never talked to him. He gave off an air of misanthropy that wasn't conducive to streetside banter. He'd stare at you. Ugh, I don't want to speak ill."

"I get it. Not nice. Anyone else you know have confrontations with him?"

"Nothing drastic. Unfriendly, annoying, but not so much to lead to violence."

Taking a different tactic, the mention of John Arthur stuck in his mind like gum, Marlowe asked, "Did you know Tim Finch before you moved to this house?"

"No, we didn't have that pleasure."

"What about Lucy Dixon?"

"No, we didn't know Lucy before they moved in."

"How long have you lived here, by the way?"

"It's fifteen, no, sixteen years. A great place to live. Until . . ." she trailed off.

"Recent events."

"Yes."

A high-pitched barking and a scratching noise came from the door to the backyard. Joanna pushed herself off the couch, saying, "The dogs! I nearly forgot they're outside. I should really let them in. Is that all?"

"For now. Thank you for the help."

"I hope it's been helpful. It's all so troubling. Sometimes, I don't understand the world."

Leaving the Haydocks, Marlowe moseyed around their house back to the alley where Tim Finch's body had been found. The police presence was already gone, outside of a small piece of yellow tape stuck in the Haydocks' wooden fence. If you didn't know what had happened, it'd appear like any other alley in this part of the city. Various fences constructed from various materials and garages restraining backs of backyards, garbage cans, a few stray bits of trash decomposing like a fading history, tree branches here and there stretching out over dusty blacktop, oil stains, a tread mark in mud.

Pacing back and forth between the Haydock fence and Dixon fence, avoiding the spot where Tim Finch had lain, Marlowe heard the *thwap, thwap, thwap* from Rory's baseball throwing and catching, and a low conversation coming from the Haydocks' side of the fence. One from TV, he decided. You couldn't get away from neighbors in a neighborhood like this even if you tried, not completely. The houses were too close, no matter the foliage and fences, and if you disliked a next-door neighbor, well, you'd still have to see them through a window as they washed dishes, mowed the yard, or stood on a ladder repainting their shutters. It was part of city living. You learned about them without meaning to.

But here, where a murder was committed, and across the street in the Community Center where another one was committed, he felt the neighbor connection went another level, past the superficial, deeper. Not with Tim Finch, necessarily, though his intrusive ways dug deeper too. The party group, however, seemed somehow more involved. Why? It could have been Lucy Dixon herself, the way she reveled in uncovering facts about people, dug into personal lives, opening people up like oysters to see inside. For personal gain, sure. But also as a facet of her personality, driving her to it.

None of which has helped me blaze the final trail to solving this case, even if true. He sat on the white brick Dixon wall listening to the baseball thwap into

Rory's glove, staring at the gap where one brick, the one that killed Tim Finch, was missing.

What do we know for sure? We know two people were murdered. We know Lucy Dixon, while a lot of fun, rubbed a few of her neighbors the wrong way, pushed them, even blackmailed them. Was any of it enough to brand one of them the murderer? Joyce Howard? Suri Cane? Neville or Florence Cassell? They all had motive, but there's motive and then there's motive, like snakes that'll bite you and snakes whose bite contains enough poison to kill. Depends on the snake. Were any of them the type who would kill when pushed? Were there snakes in the UK?

Marlowe stood up, dusting himself off, and walked toward the car. This case. Somehow John Arthur was figuring into it even when not there, and even as Marlowe mentally put the man into a not-a-suspect pen. For now. If he was the killer, there'd have to be a Lucy interaction yet un-veiled, or some motive deep in his past. And why would John bring up the deep in the past idea if that was the case? Unless it was a double-blind, or triple-blind plan, and John didn't scream super criminal. More lonely person who watches too much TV. *He does have good ideas,* Marlowe admitted to himself.

Laughing again, he got in his car and pulled out, knowing he was going to stop at Mr. Arthur's house. Why not? He needed fresh perspective and wasn't opposed to taking help wherever he could get it. Two murders. They needed solving. If Mr. John Arthur could help, Marlowe wouldn't turn down that help. And if he was wrong about John, and he was involved as more than a bystander, he'd make a mistake and Marlowe would be there to catch him.

He could hear Ainsley barking happily as he neared the door, noticing her brindle tan face peering out at him from under the front window blind pushed up by her nose. Before he knocked, the door opened to reveal John, now holding Ainsley by the collar as her tail whipped back and forth at knockout speed. He was wearing shorts again, this time with tan socks with an octopus print and a green T-shirt boasting a picture of a rottweiler in a Santa hat and wrapped in Christmas lights.

"Detective Marlowe. What a surprise. It's nice to see you. Wait, you're not here to take me in for questioning?"

"Should I be?"

"Nope. Though I do have some thoughts about the case."

Marlowe let that slide. "You know it's summer?"

"Summer?"

Marlowe pointed at the T-shirt as Ainsley jumped up to lick his hand.

"This shirt's too jolly to only wear for the winter holidays. Rottweilers, so silly. We used to have three. But what am I doing, come in." He backed up, saying, "Ainsley, come on, give the detective some room," while dragging her into the living room.

In a moment, Marlowe was again on the blue couch under the massive, framed copy of *La Divina Commedia*, Ainsley perched next to him, attempting to lick his face as he gently held her back with one hand. John took the other couch.

"Detective, what can I help you with? What brings you back to the neighborhood? More interviews? Revisiting the scene of the crime for inspiration?"

The man was uncannily accurate at times. "A little of the third, and the fourth. You watching me?"

"Just a good guesser. More interviews—"

"But no interview montage," Marlowe deadpanned.

"Well," John replied in the same manner, "you can only have one an episode."

"These things I'm learning."

"You can—"

"Learn a lot from TV."

"That's it."

Gazing around the room, he noticed a photo of John he'd missed the first time. One of him and an attractive brunette a few years younger, both wearing large, mirrored sunglasses and smiling at the camera, an unmistakable renaissance dome in the background.

Nodding in the photo's direction, he asked, "Is that Brunelleschi's dome on the Florence duomo?"

"It is indeed. Very keen eye, Detective. I didn't know you knew Florence."

"A little. And that's your wife?"

"Marlene, yes. We loved Italy, visited twenty-some times."

"I'm jealous. Just twice for me." He looked again at the picture, paused, and said, "Mind me asking how she died?"

"No. I don't love talking about it, but understand the question. It was a car accident. She was a nanny for years, after running some nature-focused child education programs for the city, before she got tired of the bureaucracy and, well, idiots. You understand. Anyway, she decided to focus on smaller groups of kids. She had been a nanny for the same family for ages, great people, great kids. One of them, though, had a tendency to walk without looking where he was walking. One day he walked into a busy street, right in front of a truck. She ran and shoved him out of the way, but was hit herself."

A silence dropped, the only noise Ainsley shifting from sitting to lying down with her head on Marlowe's leg. He began petting her, almost unconsciously.

"Sorry to hear it, John."

"Thanks. Hard to believe, and I still expect her to be walking into any room I'm in, every time. Though maybe that's cliché."

"Clichés are often clichés for a reason. A dog really is a man's best friend." He waved his hand at the sleeping Ainsley.

"As your grandfather used to say?"

"Probably he did, at that."

"I was somewhat surprised you or Detective Morven or Sergeant Nelson hadn't asked me before. I was starting to think it was a *London Kills* kind of situation."

Marlowe's eye roll was so substantial, it was surprising it didn't cause the dog to move. "*London Kills?*"

"Police procedural. Good stuff, shot very realistically, documentary cinematography nearly. Starring the rugged-but-stylish Hugo Speer as DI, detective inspector, David Bradford. First episode opens with him coming back to work after extended leave to help with a murder, annoying the always entertaining and always a smidge pissed off Sharon Smalls as DS Vivienne Cole, who thinks she's going to lead the murder investigation team. Tension."

"But?"

"How's it tie in? This is the kicker. DI Bradford's wife has vanished, and secretly, or not so much, the team of detectives think he murdered her."

"Did he?"

"You know I can't spoiler that way."

"John?"

"Yes?"

"We never thought that you might have killed your wife."

"That's a relief. Now, how's the not-TV cases? Two murders. Bringing it up, I know I shouldn't, but I *have* been thinking about them, a lot. I'm sure you have your lines of inquiry and have faith in your police team, but it's hard not to think about."

"Understandable."

"I suppose getting me up-to-date on the interviews and what you've learned is completely out of the question?" John's voice contained a hopefully not too pushy note.

Marlowe watched him for a long moment. He knew it was indeed out of the question. But the man did have good ideas. He petted the dog.

"Not being shot down outright. I'll take it, Detective. What if I ask you some questions, then you decide what to tell me?"

Marlowe gave a solemn nod, then grinned, saying, "As long as you endeavor to keep it between you, me, and Ainsley."

"Endeavor. He would keep it quiet." He saw Marlowe give him another 'what are you talking about' glance, and quickly continued, "Endeavor Morse? Inspector Morse? No?"

"No. Maybe only this case."

"Stay focused. To start, let me say, like the honorable Hercule, 'it is the psychology I seek.' We'll begin at the Cassels, last seen at the station. Neville was having an affair with Lucy. My guess is, knowing both, she ended it and then rubbed it in a bit, gently, but caustically, too, if that combo is possible. Neville freaked out, as he hadn't told Florence, so begged Lucy to stop. She, knowing Lucy, would find it fun. Warm?"

Marlowe pointed up at the *Divine Comedy* print, to the "Inferno" pillar.

"Very warm. Is it enough to drive the restrained, wound-up Neville to murder? I don't see it. Florence? Maybe. But maybe not, for what's really only an indiscretion. Nothing rooted, as Florence herself might say. Moving on. The Howards. We know Joyce and Lucy were seen arguing. I saw them. Not a crime of passion here, as Lucy appeared hetero. Revenge? I'd say not. Another guess: Lucy found something out about Joyce's past. Money related perhaps. Joyce is cool, but seems layered, like earth strata. There are layers not seen. Lucy would dig them out. She was an archeologist of personal secrets. And then turned to blackmail. That seems a path played out in many shows. That's the best explanation."

"You wouldn't think blackmail would be unexpected from Lucy?"

"'On the contrary, Detective Marlowe, I usually find the most likely people behaving exactly as I would have expected.'"

"Poirot?"

"Marple."

"Figures."

"Lucy dug, and when you dig deep, you find secrets. Eventually, you want to let it be known, and blackmail is one way to control that interaction. Blackmail is enough for murder. Where's that Joyce/Lucy hypothesis fall?"

Marlowe pointed up again at the Inferno.

"Moving on, the Canes. I can't imagine the councilor endangering her career, but what if that was it? Her career in danger. Lucy, observing, digging again, unearthed a fact she thought might do just that. Or endanger her family. Suri is a possessive mother bear. How sharp are her claws is the question? And Steven? He wasn't at her recent interview at the station I noticed, and was never seen arguing with Lucy. What about my council member theory?"

Another upward point.

"Then we have Toby Dixon. Jealousy? Wife having at least one affair, perhaps more. But he loved her, worshipped her in a way. I don't see it. Tim Finch, victim number two. Also a murderer? Toby finds out, kills him. Curious, but Tim Finch was petty, small, a wannabe bully. Murderer? I don't see it. I see him seeing Lucy's murder occur, then trying to blackmail off of it. Then finding out too late blackmailers often are the second or third victim. You feeling that way?"

Marlowe started to point up, stopped, and said, "I'm curious in the same way. Yep."

"'Curiosity becomes something of a habit with policemen.'"

"Marple?"

"Morse. Endeavor Morse."

"He's back. Moving on?"

"Onward. Were any of them, and we haven't talked about Sarah Howard or the Haydocks, but if I know my police detectives, everyone remains a suspect until the credits roll, any of those mentioned so far pushed by circumstances into murder? My little gray cells are not Poirotian. As much as I've thought the scenarios through, I haven't had the pieces click. That ah-ha moment hasn't ah-ha'd. Plus, the questions from earlier remain: the shoelace, the dragging, the lack of a struggle, the clothes, the Center, the alley. They have to be important." He smacked his knee, causing Ainsley to bounce up and off the couch like a coiled spring.

"Do they?" Marlowe thoughtfully asked.

"Yes. The early facts always end up being important. But—"

"That's TV."

"I knew you were going to say that. There's something we're— Something *I'm* missing. I don't want to speak for you. Something obvious."

"Maybe it's a fact we don't know yet," Marlowe said consolingly.

"I hope we don't have to wait for another murder to figure them out, that we're in a two and not a three."

Marlowe held up one hand with two fingers raised, and one with three. "Two murder show vs. three murder show. Two is awful, but three? Not sure the neighborhood could take it."

Ainsley trotted over to a window, then back to Marlowe, then to John, then to the other room, then back. John all-of-a-sudden noticed her pacing.

"Ainsley, sorry. Need to go to the backyard?" She bounded to the vicinity of the door leading outside. "Guess that's a yes. Detective, want to wander to the yard?"

"Sure, I have a few more minutes."

They walked through the room with one wall full of bottles—spirits, liqueurs, smaller bottles, bigger, hundreds of them—then through a small kitchen with light wood cabinets, a five-burner gas stove, and a stainless-steel fridge, before heading into the backyard.

"What's with the bottles?" Marlowe couldn't hold back being slightly impressed.

Sheepishly, John said, "Embarrassing. I used to write about cocktails, bars, distilleries, that kind of thing. You end up with samples and shelves that'd make a corner bar blush."

Down the small stairs from the kitchen doorway into the yard, John led the way to the huge deck and chairs. At the bottom of the stairs, Marlowe turned back toward the other part of the yard, the lean stretch running alongside the house. A sidewalk paralleled the fence, between them an overgrown area, weedy, packed with terracotta shards, plant pots in need of plants, a rusty metal black bison statue, concrete circles in which beads had been artistically stuck, shells, scalloped pieces of blue and yellow pottery, a tattered footstool with peeling white paint, a green iron frog, and more he couldn't make out beneath overgrown grass and cobwebs.

John noticed him. "I need to deal with that. Marlene made it like a collage. I haven't really done anything with it. It's going to take some energy I'm not sure I have currently. Maybe overgrown is okay?"

"It's how I'd picture Mrs. Havisham's garden."

"What the Dickens?"

"Always a fan, since we read *Great Expectations* in high school. All police officers should read Dickens. Good insight into humans."

"Agreed. He liked a mystery too."

"Fair enough. Wait, there's not a show where he's a fictional British detective?"

"Not yet. Not a bad idea." They sat in two of the deck chairs. Ainsley, who'd spent her first moment perched over some grass, joined them, her two front paws on the arm of Marlowe's chair.

"What happened to the day?" Marlowe gazed up. Bright blue and cloudless when he'd arrived, he could now only see one shrinking blue section, shaped like a horse's head, surrounded by ominous clouds the color of lead.

"When it doesn't rain here . . ."

"You know it will soon."

"City living. Back to the case?"

"Maybe not. Outside and all. But solid theorizing. Glad for the help."

They talked for a few minutes about the city, the weather, the Seafarers' chances, then Marlowe got up to go.

"Duty calls. Hey, license plates." He'd noticed the mobile made of them when turning back to the house. Kansas, Texas, Kentucky, Washington, Kansas again.

"My wife loved to keep those. There are a few in the Havisham garden too."

"Interesting. That a thing? Dixons had them in their backyard as well."

"Never considered it more than a Marlene thing. Where have they lived, or licensed?"

"Let me see . . . Washington, naturally. Florida, Oklahoma . . . Minnesota and Illinois."

Ainsley scooted around right as they approached the stairs, bounding past and nearly sending Marlowe into the railing.

"Sorry, Detective, sorry. She's a whirlwind."

"No bruising, no foul. Wish I had her energy."

"Me too."

At the front door, Ainsley bounded over and up onto the couch facing out the window. Marlowe, nearly out the door, said, "John? If you have more ideas, don't be a stranger."

John brightened. "You will be the first to know. I will sit and think about the past, the present, and voilà, all will become clear like the rabbit appearing out of the magician's hat. Or nothing will become clear, like the mud on the magician's shoes."

"Poirot? Marple? Brown? Endeavor?"

"Just Arthur, Detective. Just me."

Marlowe navigated his car back downtown along 15th Avenue, past Pearl's seafood take out, four car repair garages, Hastings massive grocery store, dreary faceless chain and invitingly quirky individual cafes, Muddy Paws pet store, and numerous apartment buildings of assorted shapes and sizes named after navigation or maritime terms—the Beacon Bldg, Flotsam and Jetsam Towers, Nautical Flats, Pilots All-Penthouses—trying to tap into the city's port history. Maneuvering around surprisingly busy midday traffic, he drove into a less built-out stretch of road highlighted by a local community pea patch alongside a golf course – the city in microcosm – hitting the stoplight adjacent the 9th hole when the iron sky opened, as if a shovel-full of water flipped over. The rain was back. He could barely see with the windshield wipers on high, making it even more difficult to drive while sipping a second coffee and eating a second croissant.

Traffic crawled. He considered calling Morven to check in, but it'd be bad form as an officer to slide into a fender bender, worse if caught on the phone. He was just anxious. The cases. People had died, they needed to solve their murders. Pictures of the suspects and victims flashed in front of his eyes as if perched on the wipers. Dixons, Howards, Haydocks, Canes, Cassells, Tim Finch, John Arthur. He knew the break would come. Heck, might have come through work Morven and Nelson were doing while he was interviewing and talking to John. A white Tesla pulled into his lane without a blinker, causing him to stomp on the horn and brake simultaneously. He'd be a victim if he didn't focus. Putting coffee in the cup holder and finishing the last crispy croissant corner, he turned up the radio and peered into the downpour. "Blue Eyes Crying in the Rain." That figures. Well, if Saint Willie can't watch over the wet drive downtown, nobody can.

Navigating the omnipresent road construction on downtown's edge, today closing five blocks of Second Avenue, while the rain came down in soaking sheets, emptying sidewalks of all but a few hardy folks huddling under an umbrella in line at Chuck's Chowder, Marlowe had nearly reached the station when, as if a metrological switch flipped, the sky went from fearsome gunmetal gray back to nearly blinding clear blue the color of spring's first irises. He hadn't even time to switch off the wipers, scraping the now-dry window loudly as the car crawled alongside the soaring white stone courthouse. Its doors were flung wide, a mass of people in three-piece suits flooding out like fish in a just-opened sluice. The city's weather: part magic, part psychotic. Every building passed, at a pace that'd make a snail blush due to drivers dealing with the snap transition from rain to blue sky, was the same—doors open, people streaming out into the sun, glazed smiles, barely aware of their surroundings outside of the lack of precipitation.

After nearly clipping an errant bike messenger with banana-yellow vest and matching bag flung over shoulder, headphones on, green cap flipped backward, looping around a glass delivery truck stopped mid-street, and scoring the last lonely parking spot on the fifth floor of the station's lot's farthest southern corner, Marlowe sat in the car for a moment. Radio off. Coffee done. Croissant now crumbs he'd try to remember to shake off his suit coat and shirt when he got up. The concrete wall in front of him was tagged in fat black letters: *Have a Nice Day, Fuzz*. That was as confusing as the weather. Friendly enough. But fuzz? Friendly? Not? Sunny, rainy, sunny? Feeling he'd traveled farther than the sevenish miles on the odometer, Marlowe opened the door, slowly making his way to the station stairwell.

Walking, he thought of John and of the many TV shows the man brought up. *Maybe I should spend the rest of the day binging British mysteries? Morven, Nelson, and I could get popcorn and milkshakes, set up a wall of TVs, let the accents, green fields, pubs, rolling hills, London alleys, and Poirot's mustaches soak into our brains.* Couldn't hurt. Stepping into the station, he brushed crumbs off his worn brown coat, shirt, and slacks. Better a crumb pile in the hall then a messy shirt in front of the team. And now, time to get to work. Commercial break is over. Back to the show.

13

Morven and Nelson arrived at the station within five minutes of each other. Morven, first in, quickly got her computer up and running, divesting herself of jacket and hat before Nelson showed, so that by the time he did, she was already entrenched with an ultra-focused face, and it seemed she'd been there hours.

He walked briskly up while buttoning his impeccable baby-blue suit coat over a white shirt that appeared to have been freshly ironed in the elevator, tie a nearly imperceptible shade darker than the suit. He had decided another day with the detectives, another day to dress up. Morven gave him a slow glance.

"Decided on banker's hours with Detective Marlowe out?" she asked, twinkling.

"What? Wait? What are 'banker's hours'? Good or bad? I'm right on time. Aren't I?" Nelson flustered his reply.

"Banks at one point in history were open only for a few hours a day. Banker's hours, meaning not working a full day in relation to others."

Nelson stammered, "I'll work a full day, and I already worked out, which is a type of work, as we police officers need to stay in tip." He stopped talking as she started laughing.

"Kidding, Sergeant Nelson. I'm only minutes ahead of you myself.

No coffee in attendance even. Shall we caffeine up before diving back into the background cross-checks?"

"Very funny, Detective Morven. At least Detective Marlowe isn't here. Coffee sounds good. I'll take two sugars."

"I'm not fetching it for you, Nelson." She threw a pad of Post-it notes at him. "Come on, let's see if the canteen coffee has made it to sludge consistency."

"Race you?" Nelson asked, angling toward the door.

She stood slowly. "It's far too early for running, Sergeant," she said, walking past him, shaking her head.

Coffee in hand, computers on, Morven sat upright at her desk, Nelson's laptop perched on one corner. "This morning's plan of action is more background cross-checking and alibi checking on Steven Cane. Along with collating any forensics info landing on our desks."

"Landing like an unexpected bird," Nelson distractedly replied, eyes stuck to his screen. "Did you know the average person would have to eat nearly 300 pounds of food a day to maintain their weight if they had the metabolism of a hummingbird?"

"Nature documentary last night?"

"Nah. I have an ex-girlfriend who's a trivia buff. I'm not much for holding on to a head full of numbers, but that fact stuck with me." He missed Morven's grin. "I dream about it, being able to eat that much and not gain weight. Plates of creamy fettucine alfredo. Mountains of gooey apple fritters. Chocolate peanut butter milkshakes by the bucketful." He drifted off in a reverie of carbs and calories.

"Nelson? Nelson?" He snapped around as she raised her voice with the second mention of his name. "We can get breakfast soon. Let's map out how to approach Mr. Cane and Mr. Matthews."

"Right. The interviews. What are you thinking?"

"Usually, we would bring them in, but for an alibi check like this, we often keep it casual if possible, and we can follow the same approach here. Let's call the alibi first, Ben Matthews, set up a quick meeting somewhere outside of the station. Java Jersey is nearby. If he doesn't agree, we can suggest we'll stop by his place of work, which usually causes interview subjects to rapidly pull an about-face and agree to meeting anywhere at any time as long as it's not their office or place people they know might see them with the police. No one wants to be seen with us. I have his contact numbers. Want to call or want me to?"

"I can do it." Nelson jumped for more experience at all facets of detective work, and was out of his chair peering over Morven's shoulder at her screen in a second.

"Easy," she replied. "I have to pull up the numbers." A few clicks later he had them, and Nelson was back at Marlowe's desk, phone at the ready.

"Hello, I'm trying to reach Ben Matthews. This is Sergeant Jamie Nelson of the City Police Department. Thank you." He was silent for a minute before speaking again. "Hello, Mr. Matthews? Sergeant Nelson, here. That's right, City Police. We were hoping to talk to you today. Nothing serious. Yes, it is in relation to that, just routine questions. You don't have time to meet today? We could just come by your office for a quick chat. No? How about Java Jersey café on 3rd avenue? Is ten good for you? Perfect. We will see you then."

Turning to Morven, he said, "Nice advice on the office stop by insinuation. He was resistant until that strategy went into play. Now, he's avid to meet."

"Fantastic. Well played. Solid work these past few days in general, Sergeant."

He beamed. "Thank you, Detective."

"We can both go to the interview. But there's one thing you forgot to ask me."

"What?"

"If the café has bagels. I'm guessing you're starving after that hummingbird talk."

Arriving at the café ten minutes ahead of time, they scoped out tables. Like a duo of lawyers, both were in suits, Morven in a tailored chocolate-brown with flap pockets and a peak lapel over cream shirt. Nelson went up to the counter as Morven angled for a table. He returned with two cappuccinos precariously balanced in one hand, a plate with two bagels and cream cheese in the other.

"Very thoughtful of you Nelson, thanks," she said.

"What do you mean? This is all for me." He put everything in front of one chair, before pushing a coffee and bagel toward her. "I'm kidding, one of each is for you. Quick question?"

Morven nodded, blowing steam off her coffee, little warm clouds vanishing in the air.

"Was there a reason on the choice of seats?"

She'd picked a small wooden table in a far corner, as far from other seating as possible, placing two rattan chairs for them so that they faced the doorway, with the third chair opposite, facing a floor-to-ceiling window out onto busy 3rd Avenue. "Here, we're out of range for other customers listening and, hopefully this doesn't sound devious, but he'll be looking right into the sun."

"What's with the island theme in this café?" he asked, taking a bite of bagel with one hand and with the other pointing in a wave at the décor consisting of a series of beach pictures, fishing nets affixed to the wall, framed art made from shells, and one photo of a deep-red antique Triumph Roadster.

She took her own bite, replying after briefly chewing. "I've had other interviews here as it's close, makes acceptable coffee, and isn't overcrowded most hours. The owner is from Jersey."

"New Jersey?"

"Nope. The Isle of Jersey. The largest of the channel islands in the channel between England and France. Jersey has dual heritage from both countries, though it's part of Britain."

"Did you have to research that?"

"Once, I waited a long, long, long time here for a suspect who never showed. Ended up talking to the owner. Friendly. Seafarers and Ospreys fan. We got to talking when I realized I wouldn't be meeting anyone. That's an interview I should have showed up at the suspect's office for. But today's just a quick alibi check, so I don't think we'll have a runner. Actually . . ." She took a last bite of bagel and a sip of cappuccino. "If I don't miss my guess, which is informed by his LinkedIn photo, so not completely a guess, he's walking in right now."

Finishing her sentence, Morven got up and approached a fit, mid-forties white male walking in. He had sandy blond hair and a slightly darker mustache, wearing a golden Harrington jacket over a collared, beige button-down and brown slacks, no tie. Handsome in a Redford style, outside of barely noticeable bags under his eyes. If you took away the casual office attire, he wouldn't have been out of place on a fashionable California beach at the end of the long, fun day.

"Mr. Ben Matthews?" Morven stretched out a hand, which Ben shook abstractly, gazing around the café. "I'm Detective Morven. Could you come this way?" She navigated the other tables toward Nelson. "Would you like anything before we sit?"

"No, thank you. I'm fine," Ben replied, voice barely audible.

"This is Sergeant Nelson, and like I said, I'm Detective Morven. Thank you for meeting us. We only have a few routine questions, double-checking some facts around a current case, and felt meeting casually would be best."

"Thank you for not coming to the office." He gave them both extended views. "Though you wouldn't seem out of place in an office setting."

"Where do you work, Mr. Matthews?" Morven had her notebook out, and while she already knew the answer, felt warming him up would be smart.

"A company called Honey Bee. Silly name, I know. We help design apps, mostly loyalty driven apps for other companies—supermarkets, boutique clothing chains, that kind of thing. Our offices are only a few blocks away."

"And what do you do?"

"Marketing manager. One of two. Basically, I help design and strategize marketing our services to new clients."

"How long have you been there?"

"Five years. Well, four years and nine months."

"Is that where you met Mr. Cane by chance?"

Ben smiled for the first time since arriving, instantly making him appear five years younger and less tired, as if he'd just had a sip of coffee himself. "Steven? No, not there, though he did do some freelance PR for us. We've known each other for more years than I'm comfortable mentioning, as I don't want to spread around how old I really am. Since college, Detective. Years back."

"Where did you go to college?"

"University of Florida for my hazy undergraduate degree, where I first laid eyes on Steven. Then the University of Denver for an MBA under the eyes of the Rockies."

"And you've remained friends since Florida?"

"Friends, yes. Close friends." Ben smiled again. "We did lose touch outside of the occasional catch-up email or letter. Though hopefully still young, at heart if nothing else, I still write letters." Looking at Nelson, he said, "You might not remember letters. I kid. I lived in Denver for ten years after graduate school. Then I moved myself and my wardrobe out here. You could say Steven sold me on the beauties and benefits of the city. It was an easy sell."

"Got it." Morven paused, feeling if she did, Nelson might speak up. After a moment, and a small nudge under the table, he did.

Nelson leaned in conspiratorially. "Can you let us know where you were Monday and Monday night?"

"Monday?" Nelson and Morven both nodded. "Monday. I was at work. All day. Home by six, puttered around the apartment. I live up on the hill, and you probably already know my address, as you seem the type to do your background research." He'd leaned in a little himself, and gave Morven a sideways glance. "Then I met Steven at six forty-five. We had dinner at my place. I made fettucine alfredo with chicken, if that's intriguing?"

Neither said anything, and he went on. "Then we went over to the Whimsey Lounge at eight forty-five; I can recall checking the clock when he called to say goodnight to the kids. We had some cocktails and bubbly, left at midnight. He came back to mine for a nightcap, leaving at around one."

"Wait." Morven held her hand up, leaning over to Nelson, whispering. They both stood as Steven Cane approached the table.

He put his hand gently on Ben's shoulder, causing him to slightly jump and turn, bumping the table and sending Nelson's coffee cup spinning closer to the table's edge and a ceramic-shattering crash. But before it hit, Morven, her tableware safely in the middle of the table, grabbed it.

The three men didn't say a word, awestruck, but she recovered quickly, putting the cup back on the table. "Crisis averted." It was as if she'd unblocked a drain, as the three began talking simultaneously.

"Apologies for—" said Steven.

"Steven, what are you—" said Ben.

"Awesome snag, Detective—" said Nelson, reserved police posture overwhelmed.

Morven held up her hands firmly, one toward Nelson, one toward the other two, a gesture pointing to spending past hours on traffic detail. "Everyone, stop. Mr. Cane, I'm Detective Morven. Please sit."

Grabbing a chair from a nearby table, he pulled it close to Ben.

Morven lowered her hands. "Thank you. Mr. Cane, this is unexpected."

"Apologies, detectives. I happened to be walking by, saw Ben through the glass, and felt I should stop. I didn't realize he was conversing with the police."

Nelson recovered enough to reply, "That's quite a coincidence, you walking by at this exact moment."

"Oh, it's not," Ben said. Steven was about to speak, but Ben put his hand on his arm, stopping him. "It's okay, Steve. Better to be honest when we can. Officers, I called him when you called me. He knew we were meeting."

"Why?"

"When the police call, one gets nervous I suppose. And when I'm nervous, I tend to call Steve. Old friends." A smile lit up his face. "But everything I told you was true about Monday. The bartender I'm sure remembers us."

"Why did you need to know anyway?" Steven's normal calmness didn't hide a minute tremor in his voice.

"As you're aware," Morven said, "we are now investigating two serious crimes in your neighborhood. We need to know the details around the movements of a number of people for our inquiries."

"That makes sense."

Taking another route, Nelson asked, "Mr. Matthews, did you know the Canes' neighbor Lucy Dixon? Or Tim Finch?"

"I've heard of them both. Tragedies. I'd never met them, however. Steve regales me on occasion on our Monday nights with tall tales of the neighborhood, or sweet home suburbia as I call it."

"Do you meet every Monday?"

"Yes, nearly so. The week gets so busy with Suri's council work, and the weekends too. She desires one evening to spend some alone time, or with the kids only. Mondays are it. And in addition to that, Ben and I are old friends, so having a steady date, so to speak, to catch up is a comfort. We've been doing it for years."

Ben's hand had remained comfortably on Steven's arm the whole time, but now he raised it, rubbing his eyes before saying, "It'd be nice to see each other more often, but the Monday nights are what we have, currently."

"Mr. Cane." Morven's voice was pitched low. "Do any of the neighbors, Lucy Dixon for example, know about your Mondays?"

"Intriguing question. If I were a lawyer, I'd wonder at the relevance. No, I don't believe any of the neighbors have met Ben. Lucy specifically? She did hint a certain direction to me and Suri. Never directly.

That wasn't Lucy's way. Hints."

"You never said anything to me," Ben said.

"I didn't want to be a bother. It was not a big deal, and not related to her death, officers, I swear. If she would have asked directly, I would have said Ben is an old friend, as would Suri. We are not liars. But I did not want it to be a distraction to your investigation. That is it."

Back at the station, Marlowe, Morven, and Nelson continued various case tasks; entering interview notes and suspect histories; rounding up forensic details; sniffing, in Marlowe's case, the olive-wood bowl, feet up on the desk, mulling over the morning's events and how each part of the puzzle was fitting together. His eyebrows moved up and down as he mulled, like a set of bushy overactive caterpillars perched on his forehead.

"The problem is," he said angrily aloud to himself, though loud enough that the other two heard every word whether listening or not, "that the pieces don't seem part of the same puzzle. Or that there are extra pieces that don't fit, like trying to put six horses in a barn with five stalls. My brain has fizzled. Coffee. Java. Joe. Kickstart the little gray cells, as John said, following, I believe, the Poirot path."

Seeing Morven and Nelson staring at him curiously, he cocked his head in their direction. "Oh, you two. Still here, our own home away from home on the range?" They nodded slowly. "No, I haven't gone round the bend. Do need coffee. You?"

Both nodded again, more rapidly. The station coffee was muck, but better than nothing. Marlowe got up, kicking out one leg and then the other. "I'll grab some brown gargle then. Stretch the stovepipes."

After Marlowe ambled off, Morven whispered, "Increased cowboy slang plus increased coffee means he's either frustrated or ready for a breakthrough. FYI."

"Okay." Nelson stretched the "ay" out an extra beat.

"Detective Morven," Nelson said, still whispering, "I gotta tell you again, that cup catch at the café was amazing. Like snagging a home run away at the fence, or a hail Mary in the end zone. A-may-zing."

"Thanks, Nelson, once again. Maybe we let it slide now. It was only a cup."

"A-may-zing. That is all."

Marlowe arrived back a minute later grasping the handles of three mugs in one hand, and a fourth in the other. He set two on Morven's desk, where Nelson was sitting, too, and then sat back at his own desk, a mug in each hand.

"Thirsty, Marlowe?" Morven asked. "Or is someone else coming down?"

"It's a two-cup moment. Maybe three. Four. More."

Taking a hefty sip from one mug, then the other, he leaned back, closed eyes. Morven smelled her coffee, grimaced as if she'd been assigned to sift through the mounds at a garbage heap in hopes of finding a single kitchen knife, then took a tentative sip. She managed not to spit it out, but shook her head. It was truly awful coffee.

Marlowe liked it, sipping from one mug then the other one for a few minutes, until draining every drop. Pulling his feet off the desk, his front chair legs hit the ground hard.

"Okey-dokey, it's either flooding myself with more coffee, or time for a team conference. The former might keep me up later than the moon, so let's try the latter. You in?"

Morven turned from her computer. "After that speech, who wouldn't be. Where'd you like to begin?"

"Fair question, Morven. Forensics. Latest on Dixon scene?"

"It could be the most DNA-heavy scene in history. That shady corridor, we'll call it for the purposes of this crime conference, is overwhelmed with DNA. DNA stew. The scientists have managed to match DNA found there with sample DNA from all three Dixons, the Howards, the Haydocks, the Cassells, Steven Cane and the Cane kids. Even Tim Finch. The latter could be called surprising, but as for the rest, it's where the kids play, and the parents too."

"Not helpful, but part of the picture. What about the shoelace? Lucy's clothes?"

"Nothing." Morven crossed her hands as if wiping a counter. "Nothing but Lucy Dixon's."

"Hmmm. Finch scene?"

"Somewhat the same situation. We don't have a full report, but it's an alley, so contaminated by lots of DNA. One note: the brick we surmised as the murder weapon did have Toby Dixon's DNA on it. But nothing else, outside of Tim Finch's."

"It is his fence. But could be fences here don't make good neighbors." He knocked fingers on the table. "Let's run down suspects. Wait. This time, with an eye on the past. Mr. Arthur. He believes the past is the key. Maybe he's right. Start with Steven and Suri. Ben too. Recent first."

"Great. Nelson, grab the ball and run with it whenever. The Canes. Neither liked Lucy. Both were in Florida at University when Lucy lived in the state. Could there be a connection that far back? If so, it's related to Ben, I believe. He and Steven are obviously in an intimate relationship going back years."

"Obviously?" Marlowe's eyebrows raised.

"To me, their body language didn't signal just friends."

"Fair point."

"They seem to have a regular relationship sanctioned by Suri, though one she wants to keep secret. Lucy found out, or knew from the past. That knowledge was threatening."

"We know," Nelson spoke up, hesitating at first, "Lucy wasn't opposed to using her knowledge for gain, right? The Canes are their own alibis, with Ben for Monday. Murder to protect a political career?"

"It has happened." Marlowe rubbed his mustache. "No solid evidence. But possible. Howards?"

"Joyce was being blackmailed we know, thanks to Nelson's interview; that's a motive, a strong motive." Morven moved to the board, pointing at the Howards. "For her and Sarah. They're also their own alibis. Didn't like Tim Finch, either."

"No one liked Mr. Finch." Nelson moved next to her, pointing at the second victim. "Also, Joyce and Lucy were in Illinois at the same time. Could there be some history we don't know about?"

"Perhaps," Marlowe said. "Possible. Cassells?"

Nelson pointed at the Cassells. "She dumped him, so maybe revenge? That could be a strong motive. I read that one in five homicides are an IPH."

"IPH?"

"Intimate partner homicide," he said, staring at his shoes.

"Indeed, Nelson. More for the Cassells?" Marlowe took a deep breath of the bowl.

Morven answered. "Motive, more in the present. For him, obsession and anger over her stopping the relationship or threatening to tell his wife. For her, jealousy? I don't see that as much as protection of Neville. She'd go to great lengths to protect a tree, so why not murder to protect her husband? In the past, not as direct. However, we did find that there was a short window when Lucy lived in Oklahoma that corresponded with Neville Cassell working there. Maybe more in the past?"

"Interesting. Next?"

"The husband. Toby Dixon. Found out Lucy was having an affair with Neville, or someone else. Or found out about her separate bank account. Multiple motives."

"True. Drunkenness could be an act. Or a cover. Gave us the box of receipts to dodge. Makes sense. Married her here?"

"Yes, eleven years ago. You've talked to him most. And that brick with his DNA. It's his fence, but sets him up as a suspect. Kills Lucy in a drunken rage. Finch sees him, lets him know, and so he kills Finch too."

"Not sure I'm as sold on Toby. But your points are valid as a vulture, as my grandfather would say. And there is anger. What about the Haydocks?"

"Party throwers," Nelson replied. "In the center of it. Reading your notes, it seemed maybe they liked Lucy more than most? Could that be a ruse to throw us off the track. Lucy was involved in various ways with *all* the neighborhood, so is there something with the Haydocks we've missed? I know we don't have the motive, but there is a past, let's call it, coincidence. Cross-checking, they lived in Minnesota at the same time as Lucy."

"Interesting, these coincidences in residence. No one stays in one place anymore. Any details from those time periods that show Lucy in conflict or proximity of specific others?"

Shaking her head, Morven said, "Nothing specific yet, but we're digging."

"Hard work." Marlowe mulled. "We'll cross the gully."

"Detective Marlowe?" Nelson deliberately stared toward the ceiling. He knew his boss liked John. "What about Mr. Arthur?"

"Any coincidental past?"

"No, but . . ."

"But?"

"This British TV mystery obsession. Could it have bubbled over into real life? Wife dies, strain or grief or loneliness pushed him into a vigilante direction, and he decides Lucy should die due to her unsavory behavior. Figures he can get away with it cause he's spent so much time watching crime shows. Sees himself as one of the characters, but one going from detective to judge, jury, and executioner. A guy twisted by TV crime?"

"To me, a stretch, Sergeant. But we won't discount him."

Quiet descended onto their corner of the room, before Marlowe spoke again. "We need more coffee." He stood up, a mug in each hand. "Or I need. Then let's go through them again." He started walking off, paused, turned back. "Mr. Arthur did say something that keeps nagging, worrying at me like a rock stuck in the tread of your shoe, scratching as you walk."

"What's that?" Morven asked.

"He wondered if this was a two-murder or three-murder show."

The next morning was starkly clear and sunny enough to make the previous day's rain fade from memory like a stain from a well-washed shirt. The only physical rain presence left was under large bushes and thick trees, where the ground still smooshed if walked upon. In John Arthur's backyard, the scraggly patch of lawn, deck, and sidewalks were dry, only the shadiest corners of what Marlowe called Mrs. Havisham's garden maintaining moisture.

A delightful start to a summer's day, John decided, standing on the deck waiting for Ainsley to come scampering from the side yard with a bright red ball in her mouth. *So delightful that my mind can't stop thinking about murders*, he thought. As if laughing at him, a crow perched on the wire above the back fence, cawed stridently, cawed again, then flew off cackling in the wind.

Ainsley bounded up, springing off the sidewalk like she also might fly off, before landing on the deck and running past John, pirouetting, running back by, stopping to gaze up at him in that peculiar way dogs have that lets you know you aren't paying enough attention to them, the most important thing. He'd been staring fixedly at the two deck chairs. Not focusing, just staring.

"Apologies," he said out loud, bending to face the dog. "Sorry, Ains, my bad. I should be chasing you, grabbing that red ball, or both. I'm shirking my dog owner duties, I know." He placed one hand on either side of her head. "But now I'm on it." With the last word, he rapidly grabbed the ball out of her mouth, tossed it up in the air twice as she bounced and bounced and bounced around him, tossed it once off the deck right next to her, but not quite close enough for her to snatch it, before flinging it rapidly underhanded down the side yard.

Ainsley launched herself like a four-legged furry rocket off the deck, loping after the ball, feet barely touching the ground, then grabbing it, sprinting back toward John. This time, he grabbed it as she ran by him on the deck, his hands moving surprisingly fast, and instantly swerved to toss it, sending her launching off the deck once more. They went on like this for a pure ten minutes, until Ainsley's tongue hung out as she panted around the toy. John filled up a dish with fresh water, and she finally dropped the ball to lap up a quarter of the water in the dish before flopping down on the deck, happily exhausted, brindled sides breathing in-and-out, eyes beginning to droop.

"Tired now? It is wildly sunny. What a day. Hard to believe we've had two murders not blocks away. And no murderer, yet." He was so used to being only around the dog that he didn't always even notice anymore when he carried on one-sided conversations with her. Close neighbors probably thought he'd gone around the bend, but it didn't bother him. Maybe he had. He wasn't going to stop conversing with the dog. The silence would be too much. Sitting next to her, scratching behind her ears as she dipped her head, eyes drooping, he said, "Dogs are good conversationalists anyway. Good listeners. With lots to tell, in their way. What did Poirot say about the dog in 'Dumb Witness?' 'But you and I, we know, one does not have to speak in order to tell.' You could tell me who did it, I'm positive. By smells alone. But you're napping. So, it feels I should be able to solve it."

Standing and walking toward the house, Ainsley's head bounced up as if a rabbit had run across the lawn. "You can stay. Relax. I'm just going to get some water for myself. It's warming up."

Returning, John sat back down, highball glass in hand. "Turns out, not too early for a gin fizz with extra lemon slice. Might grease the mental wheels." He scratched her behind floppy ears, and she quickly closed her eyes as he kept talking after a large sip.

"I should be able to solve it. I know the suspects. The clues, to a point. I should be able to sit here and charge my little gray cells with gin, or use my years of watching villagers out of the window, or utilize psychology, or be a psychic. What did Hathaway say? 'You don't need to be a psychic to be a good private investigator.' But I'm not a PI. Just a person who watches mysteries." He leaned back until lying flat on the deck next to the dog, legs hanging off the edge like a toppled scarecrow.

Watching a cloud shaped like nothing definable cross the sky, John sighed. "Your human mother didn't make the connection of the show *Shakespeare and Hathaway*, the Hathaway part referring to Anne Hathaway, Shakespeare's wife, until like the second season. Funny thing is, it didn't click with me instantly, either, though I never told her. Some secrets, eh, Ains? Sometimes it's the obvious things you miss at first. Hathaway in the show is a husky ex-cop wearing yesterday's suit, Shakespeare a bubbly ex-hairstylist. 'Shakespeare' is inescapable, but 'Hathaway,' well, silly to miss it. Obviously, the reference to Anne. Sometimes the obvious—"

He sat up, swiveling his head around the yard. Then he stood, pacing as Ainsley, back awake, watched him, her head going back and forth as if intently focused on a tennis match played by cats. He spoke to himself, or to her, pausing between words as if on a fuzzy long-distance call as he paced.

"I can't believe . . . It should be . . . What's the worst thing you ever did? What if . . . Wait, that makes some sense. I'm an idiot. That should have been a red flag. But . . . it fits. It fits. Psychology if you want. Clues if you want. The past and the present if you want. I was right in a way all along. Or, Marlene was. Sometimes the obvious."

Ainsley, on her feet, was watching him when suddenly she went racing at the house, jumping up the stairs, stopping to give John a backward glance when realizing the back door was shut.

"What? You want to go in? Is someone at the door?" The dog heard every delivery driver, visitor, mailperson before they even knocked and considered it a personal affront if she didn't get to give them at least one of her high-pitched barks before they walked off. He followed her up, opened the back door and, walking inside, heard a hard knock.

"Correct again, Ains. Dead on it." He paused between steps. "Bad choice of phrase."

Shooing her onto the couch, blocking the door from her, he grabbed the handle.

"Oh," he said, opening the door, "it's you. A surprise and not a surprise."

14

Waking up that morning, the numbers two and three were stuck in Marlowe's mind like stray calves in a mud wallow. He'd gotten home at a decent hour, forgoing Gary's in hopes of a solid night's sleep, which he felt was necessary to jumpstart thoughts around the case. But after tossing and turning as if sleeping on the hardest rocks in the Rockies, he'd given in, gotten up and watched a few episodes of *Gunsmoke* half-heartedly, considering various case angles. Finally turning off the TV and rolling back into the bedroom and bed, details of episodes watched flitted out of the window like so many elusive black and white bats. There was a circus in town in one—a strongman and a fortune teller who Marlowe thought, falling asleep, might be helpful with the case.

Rolling out of bed, raising the blind and letting the early sunshine in, it hit him—if this was a three-murder show (*case*, he reminded himself, *case*), who was the obvious third victim? Who seemed hellbent on going over various permutations of the case, who showed up at the second crime scene bright and early, who talked to Marlowe in plain view of every neighborhood house multiple times, who was well-known to be obsessed with mysteries, who might seem to a killer as a person knowing too much about the murders, and thereby be someone who'd be safer out of the way? Mr. John Arthur. Why hadn't he considered that sooner?

Rapidly getting himself together—teeth brushed, washed up, dressed, cold coffee from the cold pot in a mug—he called Morven.

"Morven, you up?" It had taken three rings. She'd probably stayed up deep into the night too.

"Detective Marlowe. Yes, I'm awake. I'm at Luther's London gym, actually. Couldn't sleep, so came in for an early workout."

"How long before you could be ready to saddle up and meet me northerly?"

"Nearly immediately, only need to quickly shower. My work clothes are with me at the gym. I have a locker here, so I keep an extra suit in the locker."

As usual, he was in awe of her preparedness. "Can you call Sergeant Nelson, too, pick him up? All hands."

"No problem. Turns out we go to the same gym. A lot of police go here. I saw him on the way in this morning, going to an aerobics class. Called 'Here Comes the Sunshine Sweats' if you can believe it."

"Appreciate it. Get him, get ready, meet me in front of John Arthur's. You remember the address?"

"Definitely. Wait, it's not?"

"Nothing definite. A feeling."

"Will hit the cruise lights and sirens and be there in no time. You'll be amazed."

"Always amazed. Drive safe. Not sure it's not a fool's errand, but something is sticking in my craw."

"You don't want that, Marlowe. It's bad for your digestion."

"Morven?"

"Yes?"

"It might be too early for jokes. See you and Nelson before long. And thanks."

Driving up 15th Avenue, back once more toward the crime scenes and the suspects' houses, Marlowe couldn't decide if the trip was foolishness personified, imagination taking over, or years of instinct stepping in via a deeper sub-conscious level, like an underground river that bubbles up into a small pond. Sometimes you had to loosen the bridle and follow the horse, as his grandfather was fond of saying.

To balance out his potential foolishness, he slowed down, stopping for a quick to-go cappuccino at Lynley's. *There's always time for coffee is another old saying, mine, and I'll think better if I get one.* After the normal friendly slight shouting match with the proprietor, tucking back into the Matador, gulp of hot coffee downed, he was on 77th NW slowly motoring past the Community Center where Lucy Dixon's murder began his relationship with this neighborhood and the people in it. Right at the western edge of the Center's playground, he saw Joyce and Sarah Howard in what appeared to be a serious conversation, arms raised, half in, half out of the morning sunshine and shade, their daughter languidly circling on a merry-go-round behind them. He hesitated, started to pull over, then continued, turning on to 23rd.

As he did, he noticed James Haydock turning the corner in the opposite direction. Wearing a deep midnight-blue hoodie, matching watch cap, dark blue jeans, and sunglasses, his bearded face turned downward, hands stuffed in his jacket pockets, Marlowe nearly didn't recognize him. Again, he started to pull over, changed his mind, and continued down the street, passing the neat and messy, brick and wood, big and little houses on either side. Each different, but somehow alike too.

Marlowe pulled up in front of John's cottage, the yard flush with blooming dandelions, at the same time as Morven and Nelson arrived in a nondescript blue sedan, obviously a police loaner. He took another quarter-cup-sized gulp of coffee, grabbed his trademark sports coat and sluffed into it, then met them at the short steps that led into the Arthur lawn.

"Good morning, both."

"Good morning, Detective," their voices chimed in unison, as if they'd practiced it in the car.

"Thank for the rush. I had a thought, that as Mr. Arthur was theorizing about the case, might be worthwhile to talk to him. Learn more." He stared at a dandelion. "And maybe warn him. Don't want him talking too much to the wrong person."

"You think he's in danger?"

"Don't know, Morven."

"Curious. An ounce of prevention is worth a pound of cure, they say. Here's a funny thing."

"What's that?"

"Nelson and I saw the Cassells riding east on 80th on the way here. One block away. Nearly stopped."

"Curious indeed. Let's go see if he's awake. Strange, I don't hear Ainsley. The dog, that is."

Marlowe trotted up the stairs to the front door, Morven and Nelson following. His first knock only delivered echoes.

"Maybe he's walking the dog?" Nelson offered up.

Then they heard a bark from the backyard, and Marlowe, glancing over his shoulder at the other two, gave a second, harder knock. Two seconds later, the door opened simultaneously with the closest window blind raising half a foot, showing Ainsley's nose.

"Oh," John said, opening the door, "it's you. A surprise and not a surprise." He had only noticed Marlowe to begin with. "And Detective Morven and Sergeant Nelson. The full investigative team. The murder team. Hopefully not here to put the cuffs on me?"

"Not today, John. Just fancied a talk."

While John held Ainsley's collar, she'd still managed to pull up to the door, stretching her muzzle as far as possible so she could lick Marlowe's hand.

"Not something I'd expected to ever say, but always happy to talk to the police. And your ears must have been burning, because I'd decided to call you. Not the full trio, but glad to see everyone. Want to come in? If not, Ainsley might pull my arm out of the socket."

"Sure."

Inch-by-inch, John slowly dragged Ainsley back into the living room, loudly saying over her excited barking, "You all remember, she is a very friendly dog. But knows little in the way of respecting personal boundaries. She will clean your hands happily. Marlowe, walk in through the bottle room there and into the back yard? It's so nice out."

"Sounds a plan. I know the way. Morven, Nelson, through here." He directed them as if they were cars at a busy intersection through the room full of bottles, which caused Nelson's eyes to widen as he stared, pointing them through the kitchen. "That door leads to the backyard. Go on out."

John, still holding Ainsley, brought up the rear. As Marlowe reached the door, he hesitated, turning around. "John, I should have asked. Why were you going to call?"

"I solved the murders. Thought I should tell you."

Marlowe simultaneously pulled his left ear, an unconscious gesture only resorted to in moments of extreme surprise, and raised his eyebrows to heights yet unseen by John, stopping midway through the door.

John smiled, saying, "No questions yet. Let's get settled with the others in the yard. I believe there are enough chairs."

Ainsley sprinted off the back porch once John let her go, sniffing each of the others in turn, licking Marlowe's hand, taking a long head scratch from Morven, smelling Nelson's shoes and backing away, then coming back to Marlowe for another pet and hand licking, then jumping off the desk to smell the patch of grass, then back to Marlowe, Morven, and Nelson's shoes, this time stopping at the latter long enough for him to also pet her. Finally, satisfied apparently, she turned rapidly in a circle, lying down at the end, eyes closed, right as John reached the deck. He motioned the others to the various chairs spread around the massive cherry tree stump the deck was built around.

"I believe John has something to tell us." Marlowe's eyebrows raised.

"Everyone comfortable?" Nods. "Not too hot? Beautiful day, but can get hot back here." More nods. "Anyone need a drink? Water? Coffee?"

Marlowe barely believed his own voice, turning down coffee. "We're fine, John. You gonna sit?"

"Would it be all right if I stood? I thought I might. If you have the time, will you allow me what's probably going to seem a very long leash?" Ainsley's eyes opened for a moment, then closed. "And allow me to seem quite silly? If so, I thought I might do a detective monologue. I'm no detective, not like you, but this may be my only chance."

"Forgive us for not knowing, but what the heck is a detective monologue?" Marlowe's eyes twinkled as he spoke, while Morven and Nelson appeared more confused than bemused.

"How could you know? Not positive that phrase is used outside of this house. I've heard it called a summation gathering too. That ring a bell? Closed circle of suspects?"

Catching three blank looks, he laughed.

"It's when at the end of a murder mystery, or I suppose any mystery show or movie, the detective gathers the suspects together in a room, or a boat salon, a hotel bar, or on a backyard deck. And then summarizes the case, going through why each is or isn't guilty, before finally landing on the actual guilty party. Perhaps Poirot was the first to really define the form, I may be wrong about that, but loads of private and police detectives do it. Poirot, of course, but the chain of detective inspectors in *Death and Paradise* too. They even made a joke of it when they changed lead detective. *McDonald & Dodds* has done it, and others like –"

Marlowe raised his hand up in a gesture John was now familiar with. "John, what's that to do with us? Are we your suspects?"

John raised his head skyward, laughing louder, causing Ainsley to jump, give him a cockeyed glance, then lie back down. "Apologies to each. I thought if you'd allow it, I could do a little detective monologuing with each of you *standing in* for a suspect? You could play the parts, and I can lay out my reasoning. Then you can tear it apart if you want." He turned from Marlowe to Morven and Nelson, sitting closer together. "I forgot I only told Detective Marlowe, but I think I solved the murders."

Marlowe wished he had a camera at hand for the other officers' faces. Deer in headlights didn't come close to it. Nelson's mouth hung open as if it might never close again. Marlowe spoke up. "Strange way to go about it, John. But if Detective Morven and Sergeant Nelson are okay with it"—the other two didn't say a word, Morven slowly nodding, Nelson slowly shutting his still open mouth—"it's your house. You have the stage."

"Thank you. I'll probably fumble it, but I've dreamed of detective monologues. Probably every habitual mystery watcher has. Actually, though the detective speechifies, monologue isn't entirely accurate, as there will be questioning and answers and denials from the suspects. With that, let's start by assigning each of you a suspect to represent, since the real ones aren't here. There are, I realize, more suspects than people to play them, so we may have to double up. Or Ainsley can be one. Or this statue of St. Francis, or the cherry tree stump. We will find enough. To begin, Detective Marlowe, you be the Canes, Detective Morven the Cassells, and Sergeant Nelson the Howards. We'll go by family or couple. If you really want to get in character, feel free to use different voices. Marlowe, you could do one for Steven and one for Suri, as an example."

"John?" Marlowe gently interrupted.

"Too fast?"

"Opposite. I believe we get it."

Morven was half bemused, half wondering if this was a waste of time. "Yes, we are just going to refute or answer questions John brings as he's accusing us. Us, meaning for me, the Cassells. An interesting way to reconstruct the case, as we will be playing suspects we've been questioning." Nelson recovered enough to nod.

"Exactly it, Detective Morven. You put it much better than I did." John paced slightly as he talked.

"Sergeant Nelson, you good?" Marlowe asked.

"Yes, sir. It's different. I don't remember reading about this in the manuals. But yes."

"John, monologue away."

"Excellent," he began and stopped pacing, placing his hands together in front of him as if about to pray. "To begin, let us agree that this was a crime most passionate." His voice slipped slightly into a French accent halfway through the sentence before he noticed, paused, and went on in a normal voice.

"Or crimes. Though it was Lucy Dixon's murder that drove Tim Finch's. And hers was a crime done in anger, immediate passionate anger. One unplanned, taking advantage of a moment in the middle of the night to strangle her from behind, dragging her a short way in the process. Could it have been a random stranger?" He deliberately looked at each officer before pacing again. "I do not believe so. Too much to chance. No, this murder was done by someone known to the victim, someone the victim would feel comfortable around, would feel, as Lucy usually did, in control around. Lucy liked to be *in control*, allowing her to control the narrative. Until that fateful night, she lost control."

Marlowe, knowing John was enjoying it, tried to hide his grin at the theatricality. Nelson stared ahead, while Morven began to appreciate the exercise, even if over-the-top.

"We can agree, someone she knew killed Lucy Dixon. And it had to be a person from the neighborhood. Who else would know the ins-and-outs of the Center? Who else would not have to worry if their DNA was found; they all spent time there. No, in our three-legged, crime-solving stool of means, motive, and opportunity, the legs point to one of the neighborhood crew committing the murder after attending a party with the victim.

"But who, my friends, *who* had a motive so great as to lead them to strangle a nearly naked Lucy Dixon. Who had such anger? She was not, outside of a superficial jolliness and generally fun nature, a nice person. That could be said. She liked control too much." He turned and pointed at Marlowe. "Even you, the newest members of the neighborhood group, the Canes, she wanted to have some control over."

John cupped his hands and said in a stage whisper to Marlowe, "Don't forget, you're both Canes.

"This led to an argument witnessed by many between Suri and Lucy the night of the murder. I say that Lucy had discovered some buried fact, from the past or from the present, that you, Suri, believed presented a threat to your burgeoning political career."

"It was nothing," Marlowe said. "Suri would say she is not a murderer. Lucy was insinuating—"

"Insinuating what?" John broke in. "Perhaps about you, Mr. Cane?"

Marlowe rolled his eye fractionally, then, humoring John, looked away, looked back, "About me? Steven? I have nothing to hide."

"Except," Nelson couldn't hold back, "your long-term intimate relations with Ben Matthews."

"Ah-ha," said John. "A threat to your rising career and family. Lucy was dangerous."

"But," Marlowe replied, "we were home together asleep during her murder. And Steven was alibied for Tim's murder. I couldn't, wouldn't, strangle her."

"And you didn't." John clapped his hands. "No, you would do much to protect your career, but murder? It is *much* worse for politics than divorce. And how would you have gotten Lucy to that park? Removing her clothes so neatly? You were angry, frightened even, but not to the point of murder, of strangling a woman larger than you. This crime would take a level of strength, physical strength, as well as a mental fortitude. Who then, might have that strength as well as the motive?"

He walked in a slow circle, expanding it, before turning rapidly to view Morven. "The Cassells, perhaps?"

She was perched up in her chair, as Marlowe, now off the imaginary stage, stretched his legs out.

"Neville and Florence. The neighbors who have lived here longest. Intimately knowledgeable about the park. And in Neville's case, intimately knowledgeable about Lucy Dixon?"

Morven spoke up, her voice toned down a notch. "That's too far, Arthur. Neville, I mean I, wouldn't stand for talking that way in front of others."

John's eyes lit up. "You see, my friend, the anger is there. Years of bike riding and exercise have made you strong enough to strangle her. And who better to convince Lucy to disrobe in the park for a final past-midnight outdoor tryst? Where your passion for her combined with your feeling of abandonment at her stopping your affair and her threatening to tell your wife drove you to killing her."

"We'd finished already." Morven had begun to appreciate the exercise, thinking like the suspects. "Finished. I was angry at first. At myself. And at her. She had a way of getting into your head, like an invading army. But no honorable man would kill a woman. I'd already told my wife, so that's not a motive." Morven paused for a moment to imply the character change, before continuing. "Neville couldn't kill anyone. I, Florence, have been married to him for fifteen years, two trees growing next to one another. He's no killer."

John's awe at her performance made his reply a moment slow. "Ah, who knows who is a killer. But here, I agree with you. The psychology is all wrong, as Poirot might say. For the military bluster and straight-backed nature, Neville doesn't run the hot rage. He would let Lucy control him before killing her. But you, madam, you might, I think, kill to protect him. You left the Haydocks right before Lucy. Waiting, you could have talked her into the park and, shall we say, pull her up by the roots."

"I could kill, if necessary." Morven nodded. "I've unearthed many a sick plant. But I knew Lucy and Neville were over, and her gossiping and controlling ways, to use your words, they were like a season, here, then done. She was essentially shallow, and I had no need to uproot her. My motive wasn't strong enough, even if I did potentially have opportunity and perhaps the means."

"Very official of you, Florence. It turns out, I agree. For one, you live directly across from the Haydocks, and if James watched her walk off, he would most likely have noticed you. You would go far to protect Neville, but understood Lucy's essence—her desire to control, but also her ability to be moving forward. Which is very important. She could have an affair, end it, joke about it, forget about it. She could commit an act others might find distasteful, abhorrent even, and move past it. Which leads us to the Howards."

He stopped right in front of Nelson. John whispered at him. "No need to do the voices, Sergeant, if that's bothering you," before going on in his stage voice. "The Howards. Motive? Indeed, as Lucy was blackmailing Joyce."

"How did you know?" Nelson managed a voice remarkably like Joyce Howard's. So much so, both Marlowe and Morven leaned closer, as if to try and see if he'd pulled out a hand-held recorder from his interview with her.

"Elementary, my dear Nel— I mean Joyce. Lucy obviously had a hold over you, and the signs point to blackmail, something from your past that was threatening your future, and your family's future. Blackmail is a strong motive. Many murders have revolved around it. The number of shows underlining this fact must grow into the hundreds. But I digress." He held up one finger, mimicking the exclamation point in his voice.

"You have a motive, but could you murder Lucy alone? Perhaps. But why not with the help of your wife? Two strong women, it would be a matter most easy. Lucy is walking home, having had much to drink. You two are waiting on your porch. You call to her, convince her to traipse through the park. Simple enough, you both are very personable. She had always been trying to get the group to streak through the park. Then when she isn't looking, you, or both of you, commit murder."

"But we aren't murderers." Nelson's voice cracked. "I'd paid Lucy blackmail." He began talking to his left hand. "Sarah I hadn't told about the blackmail, so she wouldn't have been involved. And she would have known if I had left the house that night. It would be too risky." He put his left hand down, raising his right and talking to it in a slightly altered voice. "Joyce, you should have told me. That witch. But she isn't lying. Neither of us left the house that night. Or the night Tim Finch was killed. We wouldn't put Betty at risk by a murder in the park. The motive may have been strong, but not that strong."

"To have gone together and killed her as a team, leaving your daughter at home? No. And while spouses lie for each other as a matter of course, nothing"—he gave a sideways glance to Marlowe—"correct me if I'm wrong, shows that Joyce left the house without Sarah that night or that two committed the murder. It seems against *character* for them to operate apart, as they often seem extensions of each other. But it is good you brought up Tim Finch. His murder we must also solve." He'd begun walking in increasing circles as he talked. "We take for granted that Tim Finch saw Lucy's murder and was himself blackmailing the killer, or wanting to. Joyce, you were already paying a blackmailer. Would you not try the same strategy before killing him? But he was killed immediately. So, who?"

John had reached the edge of the deck and teetered on it for a moment, nearly causing Marlowe to jump up, until the older man recovered his balance.

John turned away from them for a moment, then turned back, his hands again pressed together as he gave a slight bow. "Who, we might ask, is often responsible for the death of a spouse?"

Nelson's hand shot up, up, up.

"Sergeant Nelson, I believe that was rhetorical," Marlowe drawled. Nelson's hand went back down.

"That's right, the other spouse. In this case, Toby Dixon. We don't have a Toby Dixon assigned. Ainsley?" Her head popped up. "You be Toby. Marlowe, weigh in for the speaking parts."

Now talking toward the general area of the dog, he said, "We only have your word that you passed out when Lucy returned to the party. It could have been a well-detailed charade. A drunken act. You could have faked passing out and waited up, then taken her to the park. And you could easily have killed Tim Finch in your own alley."

Marlowe leaned down nearer the dog and gave her a scratch over her left ear, saying, "My motive?"

"Motives, more like it. Not one, but two. Jealousy at her affair with Neville Cassell, plus others in the past we may not know about. Financial gain, as most likely she did not leave a will and had an insurance policy. You would be the beneficiary of her dying." He cupped his hand facing Morven, whispering as if to hide it from Ainsley/Toby. "Do we know about a will/insurance?"

Whispering back, Morven replied, "Will gives equally to Toby and trust for Rory. No life insurance."

"Then financial gain is not quite as big of a motive. But jealousy is. You play the fool, the drunk, and then you wait until the time is right to strike. The jealous husband, so simple. However?" He looked dramatically down at Ainsley, now asleep. "I do not believe it. Why? Because no one drinks that much beer for a joke? No. But because it is all wrong. You adored Lucy. You were the one person who thought she could do no wrong. Was it an act? Sadly, it wasn't. You adopted her son, became invested in him, and her. Love can lead to hate, but I don't believe adoration can lead to murder.

"Which leads us, funny enough, back to the beginning. And then . . ." John's eyes opened wide, accompanied by a pause. "Back even further. Back, back, back. It was always my belief there would be some occurrence in the past that caused Lucy's murder, because it is so very often an occurrence in the past in fifty percent, no sixty-five percent, maybe more, of the shows I've watched. Why not here? But it is the beginning *and* past we must go to. And the beginning here?" This time the pause even more dramatic, the eyes even wider, like owl's eyes, arms out in a wide semicircle. "The Haydocks' party."

Marlowe slipped off his suit coat, resting his chin on his hand, vaguely looking like a walrus in the Thinker pose. Morven had leaned back into her chair, legs stretched out in front of her, feet crossed. Nelson actually perched on the edge of his seat, as if the best student in a lecture hall. John smiled as he took it in.

"It was the party where the suspects and victim last saw each other. But what actually happened? What do we know? We know, we think, the Canes left, Toby and Rory left, the Howards left, Neville left, Lucy left but then came back, then Florence left. Lucy stayed for a bit before leaving again, walking homeward. We know basically what happened at the party. We have corroboration on all of the details. Except one."

Nelson gasped. "Which one?"

"That Lucy left the party and headed home. We have only James's word on that. Even Joanna had gone to bed, leaving James hosting, as so often happened when they had a party for the neighbors. After she left for bed, we have, sadly, only his word for what happened next."

"Are you saying you believe James is the murderer?" Morven asked. Marlowe kept his thoughtful pose.

"I wish I wasn't, *mon amis*. Oops, I'm no Poirot. I'm not a police officer or detective. I'm just a person who has watched perhaps too many British mysteries. A person who could be wrong. But I do not believe I am. It's what fits."

"How so?" Marlowe asked.

"Jimmy has the best means, opportunity, and motive. First, the party. Everyone left, leaving only him and Lucy. He can consume copious amounts of cocktails and feel it less. She was already drunk and came back, drinking even more heavily, becoming more susceptible. Jimmy could have easily talked her over to the darkest corner of the Center to either begin her desired streaking or promising more. Her affair with Neville was over, why not Jimmy? As a doctor, he has rubber gloves at home, easy to grab. He plays coy, she's drunk, she takes off her clothes in anticipation, he strikes. He said to me that they drank a fair amount, talked a lot, then he walked her to the sidewalk and offered to walk her home. She said she was fine, and he watched her walk down the block. That was a lie, but 'there's a germ of truth in every lie.' They did drink a lot, talk a lot, and he walked her to the sidewalk. But then talked her over to the Center.

"Then he goes home, feeling nobody would ever know. But the always watching, always spying Tim Finch sees them enter the park together, decides to play the blackmail game and ends up losing. That murder is also easy, *too* easy to take seriously at first. They make plans to meet in the alley. Jimmy never even has to leave his yard. He removes a brick earlier when no one is around. When Tim is waiting, reaches over the fence with the brick. Bang! Murder number two, this time with no witnesses."

After a moment, Marlowe stood up, stretching his arm skyward, suspenders strained but not breaking. "John, it makes sense. But motive?"

"In the past, my friend. I'll admit, I didn't see it and let my friendship with Jimmy take him out of the frame. It wasn't until you mentioned the license plates the Dixons use as decoration, like us, in their yard. Minnesota was one. Jimmy and Joanna lived there. It was where two of the defining moments of their lives happened. Geraldine was born, and Joanna was injured in a hit-and-run accident—she still limps. What's the worst thing you ever did? The worst thing Lucy ever did was drive the car that hit Joanna!"

"Is this fact?"

"I believe if you run down the cars Lucy owned when living there, track down times they were taken for repair and compare it with the dates Joanna was in the hospital, you'll find they match." He cupped his hand again, whispering to Morven, "Looking this up is possible, right?"

Morven's nod rapidly affirmed.

"Okay," Marlowe said, "but is that enough motive?"

"Enough motive? An injury, perhaps. But a murder? Definitely."

"Murder?"

"You see, Joanna was pregnant when that accident occurred."

"Two different pairs of baby shoes on the shelf," Marlowe said, half to himself, half to John.

"Two pairs. Only one pair actually used. Only one pair now left with the same type of shoelace I'd be willing to bet."

"Because he took the one from the second pair and used it to strangle Lucy Dixon"

"Dragging her after strangling her, like Joanna was dragged when hit."

"Makes sense, John. Hard to prove. Lucy isn't alive to admit to the hit-and-run. The dates you mentioned, if a match, are good. Shoelace might get something. Might. But hard to prove."

"He'll confess with that."

"Why?"

"Because he changed his drink."

"What?" Marlowe was going to say it, but Nelson actually got the word out first.

"The day after Lucy's murder, he and Joanna stopped by. We had a drink, and I would have expected him to have whiskey. His favorite, and the kind of strong drink usually desired after tragedy. But he turned it down for gin."

Marlowe whispered, mostly to himself. "A night where so much happened, it caused him to change his drink."

John gave him a sideways questioning look, which Marlowe nodded off, so John continued. "He's not a murderer. I mean, he *did* commit a murder. Two. So factually, a murderer. But not premeditated. One was spur of the moment, in unanticipated anger, rage even. The red mist descending. The other was reaction, fending off a blackmailer. Rage again. But the *idea* of murdering, I believe goes against his underlying nature. Or what he believes it is. Who knowns what anyone will do when pushed hard enough? Maybe everyone's a murderer in certain situations. But for Jimmy, now, he's had time. Bring the facts together, he'll admit it. He's my friend, I know him."

"No one knows anyone, not that well," Marlowe replied. "But we'll try."

Ainsley stood up, stretched to what seemed twice her length, one back leg in the air, before loping off down the side yard, grabbing the red plastic ball, running back and standing with it in front of John.

"Must be playtime. Monologue over." He reached down, grabbed the ball, tossed it.

"John," Marlowe said. "Nice work."

"Yes, nice work, Mr. Arthur." Morven stood up, followed by Nelson. "You really thought that through. I believe it makes solid sense. We can track down the dates and see if CSI has more on the shoelace, then bring him in for an interview. Or more than one."

Nelson said, awe in his voice, "I just want to say: wow! What a reveal. The way you said it, it makes perfect sense and seems so simple."

"Thanks Detective, Sergeant. 'Every problem is absurdly simple when it is explained to you, bah bum bump,' to quote Jeremy Brett as Sherlock Holmes. One of the finest Sherlocks. Couldn't have done it without talking with you three of course. Which reminds me. In my going on, forgot to ask: why'd you all stop by?"

"Honestly, John, we were worried about you," Marlowe replied. "Thought maybe you'd gone on a TV binge. Felt you could use some human company."

15

It had been a hectic day-and-a-half for Marlowe and the team since leaving John's house, packed like a sardine tin—as Marlowe said to the amusement of Morven and Nelson before leaving for the night—with background research, phone calls, more phone calls, and finally a multi-hour, many-cups-of-coffee interview at the station with James Haydock and his lawyer. Morven and Marlowe, though both their calm demeanors belied the fact, were a bit flabbergasted, but the interview ended much as John had guessed; they laid out the facts and uncovered history, and after leading up to it, the crime scene scenarios, and James confessed apologetically fairly quickly. There were different kinds of confession: showy, confused, railing at society, blame-throwing, frustrated, coy. And sometimes, like here, apparently genuinely apologetic.

Once he decided to confess, James walked them through the evening Lucy Dixon died. When she came back to his house once the Cassells left, they'd drunk more, switching to high-proof whiskey, and Joanna soon went to bed. He swore she didn't know about either murder. He and Lucy stayed out, sipping whiskey, and soon she slipped into a state far beyond tipsy. She'd gotten, he said, "a little familiar, hand slipping on to my thigh," but he'd managed to not let it go too far. Then Lucy went into a slightly slurred rendition of her, "what's the worst thing you've done" routine. He took it in stride, admitting to once backing a moving van into a past neighbor's truck, demolishing a mirror, and never reporting it. The story set Lucy off on a ramble, which led to her admitting that once she'd hit a person.

The revelation raised James's hackles, especially when she continued, saying she drove off and never said anything to anyone, getting the car fixed by telling the repair shop she'd bumped hard into a deer, which, she laughed, wasn't out of the question when they lived in Minnesota. He pushed her on dates, she was drunk enough to admit the general timing, and it clicked: this was the person who had hit Joanna, injuring her for life and causing the death of his unborn child. He instantly saw red, in the same moment realizing revenge would be easy. Pouring another whiskey, he moved closer to her, redirected the conversation flirtatiously, dropping in the second-worst thing he'd done: streak around a golf course.

The word streak set Lucy off. She insisted they streak around the Center and then "see where it led them." Putting up token resistance, he quickly agreed. On the way out of the house, he plopped her with a final drink on the porch, ran inside, grabbing plastic gloves, using them to take the shoelace out of the baby shoes that should have belonged to his child, putting it in his pocket. Leading her to the recessed sidewalk-and-garden area, he'd shifted off his shirt and shoes as she stripped almost completely, then he cuddled up behind her, slipping gloves on. In her drunken haze, she didn't realize until it was far too late. He'd dragged her away while staying on the sidewalk, as she'd dragged Joanna. He didn't throw up until he returned home and tried to have another whiskey.

In the second murderous situation, James had received a note from Tim Finch saying he'd been seen Jimmy with Lucy, hinting at how 10K would blur his memory. James instantly burned the note. He also replaced the shoe lace with a newer one later. Ambling about the neighborhood, James caught Tim outside, instructing him in passing to meet in the alley, late. He'd planned to pay the man off, but right before the meet was going to happen, that loose brick caught his eye. When

Tim Finch entered the alley, James peeked over the fence. The idea of the man making money off his pain and rage incensed him. Seeing a chance, he threw the brick over, hitting Tim in the back of the head, killing him without leaving the yard. Two murders. Marlowe was glad they'd got them solved, with a full confession.

Glad enough that he insisted clocking off at a reasonable hour, handing James along into the next pair of police hands. There was more work to do, loads, there always was. The next morning wasn't going to wait on them. It wasn't going to care if they knocked off at a reasonable hour, either. Which is how he found himself heading down the hill to Gary's in what could still be called the happy hour timeframe, evening awash like a renaissance painting with early summer sunshine. It had rained in the morning, and for an hour been so windy branch avoidance became a rush hour mantra, but now, sun reigned ascendant. He'd invited Morven and Nelson, offering to buy the first round, but they'd declined. Morven was going to a kickboxing class at Luther's London gym instead, and when Nelson heard that, he'd begged to come along, saying he'd always wanted to try kickboxing. Hopefully, Nelson wouldn't come in black-and-blue.

Walking past the construction pile, deciding to stop calling it a "site" until building commenced, he passed a group of mid-week revelers racing haphazardly through the Square wearing neon running clothes with numbers pinned to their backs, smelling strongly of beer and whiskey. Two men in porkpie hats and rumpled brown suits had propped up a card table on the edge of a rare downtown patch of grass, the table covered with a chessboard and pieces, the game (from his quick glance) halfway through with no clear winner in sight, other men standing on either side. A woman in black tights and a green Seafarers' T-shirt walked two ninety-pound Rottweilers, both wearing matching green Seafarers collars, one of which managed to stretch around and lick his hand. Another night in the city. Not bad at all.

Gary's was packed. Opening the door, he couldn't see an empty table, for a moment nearly backing out, unsure if dealing with crowds was the prescription for relaxing after the day he'd lived. Peeking around the door to bar's corner, the last stool, my stool, he thought territorially, was actually free. Wedging his bulk around a table of office workers drinking gin-and-tonics and between a few stools and the front wall, he shucked off his coat using a move like a shimmying manatee and placed it over the stool. As he sat, he realized John Arthur, blue baseball cap on, was on the stool next to his bent over reading a copy of *The Mysterious Affair at Styles*. A beer sat in front of him.

"John," Marlowe said, somehow unsurprised.

"Detective Marlowe. Gary said this was your habitual corner. I thought I might find you here, and here you are."

"Not *too* surprising."

"I'd heard through the neighborhood grapevine that you'd called in Jimmy, so I wasn't a 100 percent sure you'd make it down this way. Duty calls, and you have to answer."

"That's it. But even duty takes a few evenings off." He searched for Gary, saw him at the bar's other end, caught his eye, received a towel shake and a 'be there when I get there' smile. The crowd was noisy as a pack of gulls over a spilt salmon sandwich, but the corner cocooned somewhat, making conversation not as tough as expected.

"You've been here before?" he asked.

"Not as much as I'd like. Gary seems a charmer."

The named man showed as if by magic at the last word, saying, "I believe I've been mentioned?" Without waiting for a response, he continued, "Chock-a-block in here, gents, but I'm yours for a moment. What'll it be? Negroni? Gin-and-tonic?"

"Something celebratory. But not silly?" John suggested.

"That fits the case, I'm guessing. I've just the idea. Sbagliato. Negroni with the gin replaced by prosecco. Means wrong in Italian. Which might be the opposite of the outcome, one hopes, but I like it. A drinking oxymoron in a roundabout manner. Sbagliato, like the great Negroni itself, having a bit of a moment. Tasty. Bubbly. Dandy?"

"Perfect idea for me. Marlowe?"

"I'll go with the majority. Bubbly it is."

Turning to make their drinks, Gary said over his shoulder, "Marlowe, did I already tell you the history of the Negroni?"

"I believe you have."

"Best thing, as it's too mad in here for stories."

Soon drinks were before them, Gary taken off into the crowd, stopping here to pick up empties, there to wipe a table, there to take an order.

Savoring a sip and setting his glass down, John smiled. "I suppose you can't tell me where the case is at? I'll admit to being curious."

Marlowe took his second sip, rolled eyes, laughed. "Be kinda strange if you weren't curious. Like a horse not wanting to chew grass after a long ride."

"Grandfather saying?"

"Yep." He took another sip. "Not bad, this Sbagliato. Wrong. I feel it's okay to say that your surmising was the opposite: right."

"I'm not surprised. Sad, but not surprised. And the confession?"

Another sip. "Let's just say you weren't this drink about that either. Not wrong. I guess hours of TV soaking into your brain paid off."

"I'm taking that as a compliment. And glad to have pitched in, in a minor way. Though unhappy I was right, too. I suppose 'one must face things as they are,' as Miss Marple said. Even when it's old friends." He sipped his drink. "Funny that I was right about the case days before, but wrong too."

"What do you mean?"

"BST."

"The big star idea. Thought that was the council member."

"Biggest Star Theory was the right idea, but *she* was the wrong star. She might have been a rising star in local politics, but the character in this case that I knew best, the biggest star to me as the viewer, in a way, was of course Jimmy. I should have picked it up from the start."

"John?"

"Yes, Detective?"

"TV versus real life. And you can just call me Marlowe."

"But you're such a detective. You've got a memorable jacket!"

Marlowe's eyebrows raised one step higher, then he laughed along with him. "I guess it is, at that. Okay, Detective. But which one?"

John's confusion was for once evident as his rare silence.

"Once you wondered if I was a Detective Tom Barnaby or a Detective John Barnaby. Believe those are the names? Now you know me better, which one?"

John considered. "I'd say you're neither. Neither has a mustache, for one. And your jacket is singular. Maybe Detective Marlowe Barnaby? The newest cousin to take over *Midsomer*?"

"Marlowe Barnaby. Not bad. But John?"

"Yes?" He stopped, his almost-empty glass halfway to his mouth.

"I do have a first name."

Before John could say anything, Gary appeared with a flourish of bar towels, pointing at their empty glasses. "Drinks must have been brilliant. Another round?" They nodded, and as he began construction, he said, "Nearly slipped my mind. I have a surprise for you, good Detective. A little barmy tonight, so I'll close caption. Keep your eyes on the telly." He pointed to the TV, handed them fresh drinks, then rushed the other way, bending over and fiddling with something.

"Cheers, by the way," John said, raising his glass. "Here's to a case solved."

"Cheers John."

John took a deep sip. "Wonder what Gary's got up his sleeve? And I wonder what the next case will be?"

"The next case?"

Before Marlowe answered, they heard Gary clap his hands, looking their way. The bar's hustle and bustle quieted, all eyes for a minute on the screen, which went black before white lettering appeared: *Midsomer Murders*. Even as the crowd noise rose, the theremin-driven opening, so familiar to John, could be heard.

They both sipped their drinks and began to watch.

AUTHOR'S NOTE

The names, characters, and situations represented in this novel are, of course, wholly invented. Except those names and characters from cited television shows, movies, and books, and Ainsley the dog, who is definitely based on a real dog. She's sitting next to me as I type, as she often sits while I'm watching British and other mysteries.

I'd like to give a huge thank you to Ainsley for her invaluable assistance, as well as an even bigger thank you to my wife Natalie, who gave me the okay to let others read this book, written for her as a birthday present. Also, big thanks to Jon and Nik, for all their help and assistance in getting the book done, and to Elizabeth White, mystery book editor extraordinaire. And a final thanks to you for reading it. If you enjoyed it, and I hope you did, please give a read to *Ballgame*, the second book in the series.

Printed in Dunstable, United Kingdom